Everything Forbidden

Also by Jess Michaels

Fiction

PARLOR GAMES
(with Leda Swann and Julia Templeton)

Coming Soon

SOMETHING RECKLESS

Don't miss the next book by your favorite author.
Sign up now for AuthorTracker by visiting
www.AuthorTracker.com.

Everything Forbidden

JESS MICHAELS

AVON

An Imprint of HarperCollinsPublishers

HarperCollins books may be purchased for educational, business, or sales promotional use. For information please write: Special Markets Department, HarperCollins Publishers, 10 East 53rd Street, New York, NY 10022.

FIRST EDITION

Interior text designed by Diahann Sturge

ISBN: 978-0-06-128394-9
ISBN 10: 0-06-128394-0

Library of Congress Cataloging-in-Publication Data
Michaels, Jess.
    Everything forbidden / Jess Michaels. — 1st ed.
        p. cm.
    ISBN 978-0-06-128394-9
    I. Title.
PS3613.I34435E94   2007
813'.6—dc22   2007034826

07 08 09 10 11   OV/RRD   10 9 8 7 6 5 4 3 2 1

For Miriam. Hope you like your "naughty neighbor" story. Thanks for all your help in making it a reality.

And for Michael, who knows me so well. Your chocolate and sushi breaks are always perfectly timed.

Prologue

"Oslo?"

Miranda Albright ducked under a branch, batting twigs out of her face as she attempted to calm herself. Frustration bubbled inside of her, threatening to overflow and wipe away her last thread of control. The urge to throw herself down in the middle of the woods and have a childish tantrum was nearly overwhelming.

"Oslo!" she hissed out a second time, this one through clenched teeth.

No dog miraculously appeared.

"Dratted animal," she muttered as she stepped over a fallen log and moved further into the tangled branches of the trees.

She had been following her mother's dog since he broke free

of his lead what seemed like hours ago. At the rate his short, little legs could carry him, they could well be in the next county by now.

Or in the very least, their neighbor's property.

Just as the thought crossed her mind, she heard a low, masculine chuckle echo from nearby. Instantly, she stiffened at the sound and peered around to determine its source. It came again, this time huskier.

It actually *was* her neighbor, she realized with a start. She'd heard the Earl of Rothschild laugh before and this was definitely him. Naughty, like he had a secret he'd never share with her. It was a teasing laugh, a taunting laugh.

Quietly, she moved toward the sound. All she could hope was that her mother's blasted Pomeranian hadn't interrupted the man during his afternoon entertainments. She had only met him a few times, mostly at country gatherings with her parents, but he'd never struck her as a man of much patience. Just by the way he held himself, the way he looked at others, it was clear he was accustomed to getting what he wanted, when he wanted it.

Certainly, Rothschild had never appeared to be the kind of man who would appreciate the devil disguised in fluffy orange fur racing across his picnic blanket. She was certain she'd get an earful from him and his companions if her worst imaginings turned out to be true.

Prepared for a stern berating, she stepped into an area where the trees thinned and peered in the direction his voice had come from. What she saw froze her in her spot, jaw slack.

She had assumed she would find the Earl with a group of

friends, fishing in the pond, perhaps, or sharing luncheon. Any kind of normal diversion would have been expected with the fine summer weather.

Instead, what she saw was a very different kind of entertainment. One that widows and married women whispered about in secret—but wouldn't yet share with her, telling her that her time would come soon enough. An activity her mother vowed she would speak to Miranda about only when she was preparing for her wedding night.

But this was not Miranda's wedding night. And yet she couldn't look away. There, right in the open air for everyone to see, was the handsome Earl of Rothschild, and he was with a woman.

There were so many things in the scene before her to shock her, Miranda wasn't sure where to begin. For one thing, Rothschild was shirtless. Oh, she'd seen men without shirts before, despite her mother's attempts to shield her. Sometimes the field workers went without and Miranda would catch brief glimpses from her father's carriage as they rode along to town. The sight had always given her a forbidden thrill. A feeling multiplied by what she was secretly witnessing at present.

Those workmen, who often appeared soft, even from a distance, didn't look anything like the Earl. Muscles tapered down his lean body, moving beneath the surface as he shifted his position on the picnic blanket that had been laid out beside the lake. His skin was tanned, as though he often went without the decent protection of a shirt. And a few tousled locks of dark hair fell across his forehead like a disheveled, tempting devil.

When the woman beneath him moaned, Miranda started.

She'd been so focused on the man, she hadn't really looked at his paramour. Did she know her? There was nothing immediately familiar about her, not that Miranda could have recognized her with her head lolled over to the side, facing away from the brush where Miranda was concealed. And at present, her face didn't concern Miranda as much as her state of undress that went beyond even Rothschild's.

The lady's gown was in a pile beside the Earl's shirt and jacket. She was wearing only a sheer chemise, which was hiked up around her stomach, leaving her utterly bare from the waist down except for a pair of lacy white stockings and satin high-heeled slippers. The slippers were impossible to overlook as they were thrown over the Earl's tanned, defined shoulders.

He was kneeling between her legs and he was . . .

Miranda tilted her head, squinting to see better despite the fact that she knew she shouldn't.

Dear God, he was *licking* her . . . *there*. There in that place her mother told her to ignore, but she secretly didn't. In the place that was tingling madly as she watched Rothschild pleasure the moaning, squirming woman. The unknown lady's hips lifted and her back arched with every stroke of his tongue. Her cries grew louder with each intimate kiss.

Miranda shifted. She should turn away. She should *run* away! This was no place for her. These were no sights for her. But she couldn't make herself stop watching. Stop waiting for what she would see next. She couldn't stop the growing ache deep within her body, one she had felt before, but never so sharp and needy. She shut her eyes briefly, but the moans continued to echo and they elicited a brief image.

One of Miranda being pleasured by the Earl instead of this faceless woman.

Her eyes flew open, widened at the shocking thought. What in the world was she thinking? She covered her mouth to keep her startled gasp from revealing her spying, but she still didn't look away from the scene being played out before her.

Now Rothschild got to his feet and Miranda got a clearer view of his partner. She was definitely a stranger, not a village woman or a member of a neighborhood family. The woman sat up a little, leaning back on her elbows with a grin as she watched Rothschild shuck out of his trousers and give them a casual kick to the side.

Miranda stared. While she may have seen a man's chest before, this was something entirely different. Muscular legs met an equally muscular backside, and both were just as tanned as his back and arms. Dear God, that meant he went outside naked on a regular basis.

And then there was the thrust of muscle between his legs. Miranda had heard the servants call it a cock when they didn't know she was within earshot. It was as hard as any other part of him, curling up toward his belly at full attention.

The woman below him licked her lips as she stared just as blatantly as Miranda did. The stranger smiled, a wicked, knowing expression that made Miranda feel very young and naïve. And jealous. There was such a confidence in the other woman's every move. A sure sensuality that Miranda recognized, but wasn't yet able to master, thanks to her mother's constant criticisms and intrusions.

"Come down here," the woman ordered, opening her legs a little further.

"Oh, very pretty," Rothschild drawled as he looked at her blatant offering with a wicked grin.

He dropped to his knees between the woman's splayed thighs. His mouth came down hard on hers, his arms pinned hers above her head. And then, he thrust his hips forward and his cock disappeared into her body.

Miranda had heard whispers about sex from servants and married friends. Varying accounts described it as anything from heavenly to horrible. But judging from the lusty moans from the woman on the picnic blanket, Miranda was beginning to think *heavenly* was a closer description. If it made that woman feel anything like just watching them made Miranda feel, it *had* to be heavenly.

Miranda shifted a little, longing to touch herself, longing to ease the tension building like an inferno between her thighs. She knew her own hands could bring her pleasure. She'd done so in the past, reveling in the exquisite release.

Would that be what it felt like if a man like the Earl spread her wide like he was doing to that woman, and drove into her with those short, circular swivels of his muscular hips?

Would Miranda moan and cry out like that if it was she Rothschild was taking instead? If it was *she* who he claimed so blatantly?

She squeezed her eyes shut again as hot blood rushed to her cheeks. How she wanted to know the answers to those wicked, unspoken questions. How much she wanted to experience that type of passion.

A nudge on her hand made Miranda yelp in surprise. She looked down to see that Oslo had found his way back to her and was sitting at her side, little tail wagging wildly and head cocked with a quizzical bent as he waited for her.

She cast a quick glance toward the couple as she snatched up the dog and held him to her chest so he wouldn't escape a second time. With her luck, Oslo would bolt into the clearing and reveal her humiliating intrusion.

Rothschild didn't seem to have heard her cry, but the woman beneath him clenched her hands around his muscular upper arms.

She moaned, a broken, wanton sound, before she said, "Did you hear that?"

Immediately Miranda crouched down lower, peering through the high grass and praying she wouldn't have to endure the ultimate disgrace of being caught. No doubt the wicked Earl would assume she had been spying on him for quite some time. Worse, that she was aroused by what she saw. She would never live that down. *Never*. How could she face him afterward?

Worse, what if he marched her home and told her parents what she had been doing? She couldn't bear their reactions. Her mother, especially, would make her life hellish if she knew.

Miranda held her breath as Rothschild lifted his head. His breath came in pants.

"What?"

"A cry," the woman insisted.

Rothschild slowly circled his hips and the woman cursed, a word Miranda hadn't heard before, but didn't need to be familiar with to know it was *not* ladylike. Why did that vulgar phrase make her thighs even wetter? It was like everything forbidden was also undeniably arousing.

"It's probably those absurd peacocks Brendan brought with him last week," he panted, driving his hips forward again with a groan. "Ignore it."

"Hmmm, pea*cocks*, eh?" The woman giggled as she wrapped her arms around his neck and pulled him down for a deep kiss.

Miranda waited until the two of them were utterly engrossed in their coupling before she gathered Oslo closer and began to crawl out of their line of sight. Even when she knew they couldn't see her and dared to stand up, she continued to hear the woman's moans of encouragement and Rothschild's grunts of pleasure in the distance. Worse, when those decadent sounds were no longer to be heard, she still couldn't help but recall, with perfect clarity, everything she had witnessed. And the images continued to arouse her beyond measure.

She fumbled in her pelisse for Oslo's broken lead and tied it clumsily around the dog's collar before she set him down and began to weave her way back to the house. With every step, she flashed to another heated image of Rothschild burying himself into the woman. Of him tasting her in the most intimate way. Of the moans. The slide of skin on skin.

"Oh, God," Miranda gasped. "I want that, I want that passion so very much. How could anyone ever settle for anything less?"

One

Three years later
1817

"Mama," Miranda Albright said with a sigh as she watched her mother hold up yet another silken gown to her younger sister Penelope. "Honestly, you should not have purchased these things without speaking to me first!"

Dorthea Albright turned her rotund form on her eldest daughter with a harsh frown. "This is *my* home, Miranda! I do not ask my children for permission for anything I do."

Miranda shut her eyes and counted to ten in her head very slowly. The hesitation wasn't nearly enough to keep her anger and frustration in check. Still, she somehow managed to maintain a calm tone when she replied.

"But, Mama, the cost of all these things!" she said through

tightly gritted teeth as she motioned to the pile of fabric and hats and . . . were those *jewels* stacked on the settee? "I have been managing the finances for six months and I know better what can fit into our budget and what cannot."

Her mother snorted as her eyes rolled heavenward. "You know better. Ha! You know how to keep us in rags."

Miranda gripped fists at her sides. "If you insist upon living beyond our means, at the very least speak to me so I can prepare for the additional cost. And perhaps together we can find ways to be more frugal. Our debts—"

Her mother held up a hand and waved off Miranda's words. "You would be better served by finding a rich husband to solve our financial problems than to spend all your time fussing over ledgers! When your father was alive, *he* managed to give us all we wanted and needed and more! Why should that change simply because he has left this world?"

Her mother sniffled, and despite Miranda's frustration, she felt a pang of empathy for the feelings etched across Dorthea's lined face. Whatever her father's faults, their family all loved and missed him terribly.

Penelope shot Miranda a brief, understanding look before she placed a hand on their mother's arm. "Mama, you know Miranda is only looking out for us all. And I do not need *three* green gowns. Perhaps if we return two of them—"

"Green suits your eyes the best," her mother interrupted. "They make it less obvious that they are too close together."

Miranda flinched. Good Lord, their mother had no tact. She'd spent a lifetime being picked apart. She could hardly stand to see that well-intentioned venom being turned on her sister.

"Penelope's eyes are perfectly spaced!"

Her mother glared at her. "She will need *all* the gowns when her Season begins. I won't have anyone saying my daughters are poorly dressed! That is the final word on the matter."

Dorthea gathered up the gowns and grasped Penelope's hand, shooting Miranda a glare before she swept out of the room with all the pomp and circumstance of a queen.

Miranda let out a moan as the parlor door shut behind them. If her mother was queen, it was over a shabby kingdom, indeed. Their father may have given them all they "wanted, needed, and more," but it had been at the expense of their financial stability. His gambling, coupled with a lifetime of poor investments and lavish living, had reduced their coffers to almost nothing. The upkeep of the house alone was putting them at the edge of ruin.

To make matters worse, as the third son of a not particularly wealthy Marquis, her father had no land to make up for their losses. All he had were bad habits, debts, and kind smiles.

"God rest his soul," Miranda murmured as she looked at the line of ciphers a second time. Nothing had changed. She rested her head against the desk edge with a sigh.

What the hell were they going to do?

"Miranda?" came a voice from the settee beside the window.

Miranda jolted up straight in surprise. Her middle sister, Beatrice, was staring at her, arms folded. She'd almost forgotten the girl was in the room. A rare occurrence, since the spoilt child rarely allowed herself to be anything but the center of attention.

"What is it, Beatrice?" Miranda asked on another sigh.

"You cannot deny us Seasons!" Beatrice declared, her slippered foot beginning to tap beneath the hem of her extravagant morning gown. "Just because *you* are determined to be a spinster doesn't mean the rest of us should be forced to follow in your footsteps."

Miranda flinched. "I can hardly be considered a spinster at twenty, Beatrice. And your Season will not happen for at least another year, so I wouldn't concern yourself yet."

"Ha!" Beatrice moved toward her in three long steps. "How can I not concern myself? You are already denying Penelope gowns! If you get your way, I will neither be fashionable nor desirable by the time I step into Society!"

Miranda opened her mouth to speak, but Beatrice extended a finger into her face and waggled it.

"And a spinster is made by her actions, not her age," Beatrice snapped. "You could have married a dozen wealthy men—"

"It was hardly a dozen," Miranda muttered.

Her sister continued, unhindered by the interruption, "—and saved us from this trial in the first place, but you refused. You don't want to be happy!" Beatrice's lip began to quiver and her blue eyes filled with tears. "And you refuse to let any of the rest of us be happy, either!"

Miranda sighed as her sister gathered up her skirts and flew from the room, slamming the door behind her with a jarring bang. If Beatrice didn't do the very same thing every other day, Miranda might have been moved, but today she was too tired to play her sister's childish games.

She stared at the financial figures again. God, by the time Bea came out, they might not have enough money for food, let alone gowns.

The door clicked and it took everything in Miranda not to set her head back on the desk and sob. She couldn't take one more tantrum. She simply could not.

But it was Penelope who stepped into the parlor, not Beatrice or their mother. The two girls exchanged a weary smile. At least Miranda could depend on Penelope. Her best friend and confidante . . . at least on *most* subjects. There was still one secret even Penelope didn't know.

And if Miranda had her way, she never would.

"I have tried to convince Mama to return the dresses, but she refuses." Penelope sank into the chair across from Miranda with a weary sigh. "I'm sorry."

Miranda shook her head. "I never believed she would acquiesce. And *I* should be the one apologizing, not you."

Penelope sat forward in surprise. "You? Apologize? Whatever for? Since Father died six months ago, you have been the only person keeping this family from being tossed out on the street as paupers. I realize that even if Mama and Beatrice do not. You have nothing to be sorry for."

Miranda pushed to her feet and paced to the window. She looked outside and bit back a curse as she watched three servants planting new rose bushes. When had *those* been ordered? Drat it all, that simply meant more money draining from their depleted resources for frivolous things that only her mother would dare call necessities. Her head began to pound.

"As Beatrice points out daily, I could have taken offers of marriage from several men who were all in the financial position to save this family from ruin. If only I had, our problems would not be as pressing now." Miranda continued to stare outside, but she hardly saw the gardens anymore. "Because of my decisions, your Season will not be what it should. And then there will be Beatrice, not to mention Winifred!"

Penelope got to her feet and came to wrap an arm around Miranda. She squeezed and Miranda was filled with comfort, albeit briefly.

"Ignore Beatrice. If you tell her the sky is blue, she argues it just to hear her own voice. And Winifred is only sixteen. She still has her head in the clouds. She isn't even thinking of a Season yet. As for me, I certainly do not blame you for not taking those offers. For one thing, they were all made long before you knew of our . . ." She hesitated. "Our situation. And two of the gentlemen were quite awful. The other was, well, you didn't love him. You want love."

Miranda winced. No, she wanted *passion*. But she wasn't about to tell her sister that. Nor was she going to tell her exactly how she knew so much about the subject of passion.

Erotic images began to invade her mind, as they did more and more often this time of year, but she pushed them aside. Not now!

"Women of our position cannot hope for love. I was selfish and now we are all paying the price." Miranda sighed. "I simply didn't realized how dire our situation had become until Papa died. By then I was already labeled as a woman who refused proposals. A spinster in training. I doubt I could obtain another offer even if I tried. Certainly not one from a man with the ability to help us."

Penelope squeezed her arm. "How bad is it, Miranda? Tell me plainly."

Miranda turned on her sister and frowned. She'd kept the bulk of the details from her siblings, but the weight of the truth was beginning to grate on her. And there would be no hiding it once she had to start altering the comfort of their everyday lives. Already she was beginning an inventory of items that could be sold without rousing her mother's suspicion. Sadly, there wasn't much left in the house that fit that description. Her father had done very well in clearing out those things, himself. If her mother realized just how much of her beloved jewelry was already paste. . .

"If we do not find a way to bring money into this family soon," she whispered, "we could very well lose everything, including our home."

Penelope paled. "Oh my. I knew it was bad, but I had hoped we were in a slightly better position than that." She paced away a few steps as she lifted a fist to her heart. "Oh, Papa . . . how could you be so foolish?"

Miranda nodded in silent agreement, ignoring the pain of loss that still troubled her when she thought of her father. Her feelings about the man were mixed, at best. Anger and grief, warmth and pain combined.

"What can we do?" Penelope's soft voice interrupted her musings.

Miranda rubbed her eyes. "A good marriage may be the only way."

"*My* good marriage, you mean," Penelope whispered.

"Yes, I'm afraid that is true." Miranda sighed. "I have failed, but there is still hope for you before the whole world learns of our troubles and our name is blackened. You need a Season. A spectacular Season. And I must find a way to provide it. Actually, I've been thinking about that lately and I believe I may have found a solution."

Penelope tilted her head in surprise. "Whatever do you mean?"

Miranda shook her head. "No. Don't you worry about that. Just go and try on those gowns and make Mama happy. If she is happy, she won't notice I'm gone."

"Gone?" Penelope's surprise turned to alarm. "Where are you going?"

Miranda flinched. That was one question she couldn't answer. "I-I have something to do."

Penelope gnawed her lip as she regarded Miranda with concern. But then she shrugged. "Very well. But be careful."

Miranda patted her sister's hand and slipped from the room. But as she gathered up her things, she couldn't suppress a shiver. The thing she was about to do could either help her or completely ruin her. It was the thing she feared and longed for most.

She was about to offer a bargain to the man who had taught her everything she knew about desire and passion. The man who'd never known he was her tutor.

Ethan Hamon, Earl of Rothschild, took a long sip of sherry, savoring the flavor. God, it was good to be home. Despite the life he enjoyed in London, the few months he spent here at Hamon House were what he looked forward to all year. He had his sport, he had his friends coming and going all summer . . . and normally he had a lover, a new one every year.

Except this one. No woman had struck his fancy enough to

make him bring them to his summer estate for long days and nights of decadent pleasure.

Truth be told, he was beginning to bore of the game. The flirting, mincing women. The pretended reluctance. The ultimate acquiescence. The manufactured passion. He wanted something . . . *different* this year.

Not that he knew what *different* meant. Perhaps he would recognize it when he saw it.

"My lord?"

Ethan turned to his butler with an arched brow. "Yes, Winston?"

"You have a caller, my lord. I told her you were not in residence, but she is insistent. She seemed to be very aware of your schedule."

The butler sniffed his disapproval of Ethan's lifestyle, but Ethan ignored that. He'd grown used to Winston's airs, and since he was a perfect butler in all other accounts, it was worth enduring the subtle censure and side glances.

"*She*? Hmmm, very interesting." Ethan set his glass down. "Do I know the lady?"

Winston's mouth thinned. "She has been here before, sir, if that is what you mean. She is Miss Miranda Albright, the daughter of your late neighbor, Mr. Thomas Albright."

Ethan's brow wrinkled. Miranda Albright was here?

"Is her mother with her?" he asked with a shiver. Dorthea Albright was his worst nightmare and he made every attempt to avoid her at all costs.

"No, sir." The butler wrinkled his nose before he said, "Miss Albright is *alone*."

At that, Ethan straightened up. Miranda was alone? He didn't think he'd ever been alone with the lady. Mostly because she was just that . . . a *lady*. She didn't go anywhere without a gaggle of chaperones to scrutinize her every move.

Despite that nauseating fact, Ethan had still noticed her. He was careful about the women he chose to pursue, of course, but that didn't mean he was immune to the charms of the ones who were out of reach. And there was no harm in looking.

So look, he did. Miranda Albright was a beauty. Blonde hair, bright blue eyes. And she was tall, with willowy limbs he had imagined wrapped around him quite a few times.

All those things drew him in, but it was something else that made her memorable. As was proper for a lady of her station, she hardly ever looked directly at him, but when she did, he always had the sense that she knew something secret about him. Something no one else was privy to.

It wasn't true, of course. A sheltered girl like Miranda could never even begin to fathom the life Ethan led, but still . . . the look was enticement itself.

And now she was in his home. Alone. Demanding an audience with him.

Intriguing.

"I'll see her," he said quietly.

Winston let out a loud sigh that left little doubt to his disgust at that decision. "She awaits you in the front parlor, my lord."

After the servant had bowed his way out, Ethan smoothed his coat. No doubt he looked a mess after a final week of debauchery in London and then a long carriage ride to the country. How would his little miss react when he strode into the parlor with the shadow of a beard across his chin and the scent of sherry on his lips?

Wouldn't it be interesting to see?

He grinned as he made his way down the hallway and opened the parlor door.

Miranda was sitting in a chair by the fire, her foot twitching nervously beneath her. When the door clicked open, she surged to her feet and turned to face him. For a brief moment, her face reflected nervousness and an awareness of the impropriety of the situation.

But then she *really* looked at him and everything changed. Her wide, blue eyes—such a bright color that almost put him to mind of the sea in warmer parts of the world than England— slipped up and down his body. And it wasn't a quick, nervous perusal. No, this was something else.

She lingered on every inch of his form and for a brief moment something flashed across her face that nearly set Ethan back on his heels.

Desire. Hot, heady, unabashed desire.

He realized in that moment that he was looking right at exactly what he had been searching for in every courtesan and widow in London while he sought out this year's lover.

And it was facing him in the image of a woman he could never have without a band of gold encircling her finger.

This was a mistake. A terrible, terrible mistake. And yet Miranda couldn't find the strength to run. All she could do was stand in the middle of Rothschild's parlor and stare at him. Drink him in. Think about every wicked thing she had ever watched him do.

By God, he was the most beautiful man she'd ever seen in her entire, admittedly sheltered, life. But she couldn't imagine that even the most experienced woman wouldn't look at him and lose her wits. In fact, she knew they couldn't. She'd seen so many of them surrender to his touch over the three years she had been spying on his trysts.

The things he had done to those willing women. The *ways* he had done those things. . .

Just the thought made her squirm as wet need flooded her thighs. No! No, she couldn't think of that now. Not if she wanted to talk to him and not come off as an addled ninny.

"H-Hello," she stammered, her voice cracking.

To her surprise, he left the door open wide and leaned against the entryway with one broad shoulder.

"What a surprise, Miss Albright," he said with a hint of humor in his voice. Like he was laughing at her. He always sounded like he was laughing at her. Hot blood flooded her cheeks.

"I realize I was not expected." She jammed her shaking hands together behind her back in the hopes she could somehow erase her nervousness.

"Nor invited," he interjected with a wide grin that seemed to flow over his entire handsome face. "But I did not say it was an unpleasant surprise. I do admit, I'm quite curious as to the reason for your call. Would you care to enlighten me?"

She shifted nervously, staring at the open door. Why hadn't he come inside?

"Er, it is a delicate matter I wish to discuss," she stammered. "I would rather the servants did not hear."

Rothschild tilted his head and looked at her closely. There

was something about the way he was examining her. Like he wasn't sure if he should eat her or indulge her. She wasn't sure which option she preferred.

"My servants have no ears, my dear," he finally said and remained in the doorway.

She frowned. "*All* servants have ears, my lord, even when they pretend they do not. You know that as well as I do."

"I had forgotten that you are a sharp little minx, too."

He smiled again, wolfish, but it was as if the comment were more for himself than her. She folded her arms across her chest as a barrier.

"Will you not close the door?" she asked, tilting her chin with pride.

His grin became less genuine. "No, my dear, I will not. I won't have your Mama saying I ruined you and demanding I take your hand in marriage. I won't be trapped, if that is what you came here for."

She moved forward without thinking. "How dare you! Of course I didn't come here to trap you! And my mother has nothing to do with this!" She stopped. "Well, she does, but only indirectly. She certainly did not send me here as part of some scheme."

He leaned back to examine her. "Sharp, saucy and beautiful, too. It is a pity." He seemed to ponder her statement for a moment, then shrugged as he stepped into the room and shut the door behind him. "Very well. But recognize that if you are lying, I won't marry you to salvage any blemish to your reputation. If you create a situation for yourself, you will live with the consequences."

If Miranda hadn't been so nervous, she might have laughed. Dear God, the man had no idea what she was about to propose. Well, he was too smug and self-assured for his own good anyway. It might be entertaining to see him completely shocked.

Terrifying. But entertaining.

"Speak Miss Albright," he said as he poured himself a drink. "You certainly have my attention, do not lose it by staring at me silently."

She started. She *had* been staring. It was hard not to with his shirt stretching over his arms when they flexed as he reached for a glass.

"Yes, of course." She stopped, clearing her throat as she thought about the words she had prepared. She'd practiced this speech at least a hundred times, yet it still came with difficulty. "I-I must be blunt, I'm afraid, for I have little time."

He laughed, that rich, husky sound she'd heard so many times before. Instantly her eyes fluttered shut and she stifled a sigh.

"Bluntness is my preference, for *I* have little patience."

Her eyes came open. He might say that, but she knew it wasn't true. Since the first afternoon she spied on him three years ago, how many times had she watched him lying out in that same spot by the lake and pleasure a woman for hours without slaking his own needs? That required patience and, if his groans of relief when he finally did enter his lovers were any indication, generosity.

"My, wouldn't I like to know what you are thinking right now," he said. His voice had gone low and soft and his gaze was focused and intense.

Miranda gasped as she turned away. Damn, this was harder

than she thought it would be. Shaking, she pulled herself to-gether. This was her last option. She couldn't throw it away.

"I'm sure you're aware my father died six months ago."

"Yes." His tone held no indication of his thoughts on the sub-ject and she didn't dare to look at him. It didn't matter what he thought of her father or her loss.

"Not many people know this, but my family is in dire straights." She forced herself to turn now, though she continued to stare at the floor to avoid his piercing, dark stare.

"I had guessed as much," he replied.

She glanced up in surprise. Was it too late? Had news of her family shame already spread so far?

"Oh, no," she whispered.

He shrugged. "Do not worry, my dear. I don't think your father's . . . problems are public quite yet. At least, not with those who do not have their own vices to contend with."

She let out a sigh of relief. "Then how do you know about them?"

Ethan tilted his head. "I do not want to reveal any secrets about your father that might pain you."

Miranda flinched. "You saw him gamble?"

He nodded, just once. "But what does your situation have to do with me? I am owed no money from his estate and even if I were, I doubt I would pursue the matter. I may have a reputation, Miss Albright, but it has never been one of a man who would make a woman and her four daughters destitute."

Miranda almost laughed. "Well, some men do not have your . . ." She shivered as she looked at him. God, most men didn't have *anything* like Rothschild. "Your kindness. There are many so-called gentleman and rogues alike demanding repayment for my father's debts. My mother does not seem to care that soon we will lose everything. She is determined that my sisters will each have the most spectacular Seasons society has ever witnessed. And she doesn't care if that goal ultimately puts us onto the street."

"While I am sorry for your troubles, I still don't know what it has to do with me."

Rothschild didn't look one bit sorry for her troubles, but he did look intrigued, so Miranda rushed on.

"You sponsored two of your cousins in very successful Seasons not long ago," she said.

He couldn't quite manage to conceal a shudder and she almost smiled. So, he hadn't enjoyed bringing the girls out into Society. She could hardly blame him. His cousins were pretty young women, but entirely empty-headed ninnies.

"Yes, they both managed to leg shackle two unsuspecting, and more importantly, *titled* men."

"That is exactly what I mean!" Miranda said with an enthusiastic nod. "That's the kind of match one of us will have to make."

"A titled, rich man." Rothschild folded his arms and looked at her for a long moment before horror dawned over his features. "Not me!"

Miranda flinched at his heated, appalled tone. Dear Lord, was she so unappealing as all that?

She arched a brow and hoped she would sound cool and condescending. "Of course not. I did not come here to throw myself or my sisters at you for a marriage."

It *would* solve all their problems, of course, but that was beside the point. She had no illusion that a man of such lusty appetites would want her, and the thought of handing over one of her innocent sisters to him was even less appealing.

Rothschild gave her an audacious wink. "That is more your mother's speed, eh?"

Miranda knew she should feign outrage, but couldn't manage it. Her mother's aggressive tactics when it came to pursuing good marriages for her daughters were actually in part why Miranda knew she would likely never find a husband.

"I hoped you might do my family the same courtesy that you did your cousins."

He blinked once, then twice, as if he hadn't fully understood her meaning. Then he frowned. "You want me to sponsor your Season?"

"Not me, Lord Rothschild. My sisters!" She clasped her hands together, praying he would do this. "I know it is so much to request when you are only vaguely affiliated with my family. But I *need* you to sponsor their Seasons. If you don't, I do not know what will happen to us!"

Two

Ethan stared at Miranda Albright. The woman might be everything desirable, but he was beginning to think her daft, as well.
He wouldn't doubt it, considering her mother.

How could Miranda think that he would ever willingly be the
sponsor of her sisters' Seasons? If he hadn't been conscripted
into duty by his beloved aunt, he never would have been a bene-
factor for his cousins! The months they had been husband hunt-
ing had been the most trying of his life, requiring sacrifice and a
propriety that made his teeth ache when he recalled it.

He couldn't think of anything that could tempt him to repeat
that process for three veritable strangers.

"Great God, woman," he said as he set down his drink with
a clink of glass on bare wood. "Why in the world wouldn't you
turn to your own family? Why involve me in your nonsense?"

Miranda's face flickered with embarrassment that she quickly covered. He admired that ability. Though he'd always seen her as a typical Society Miss, beautiful but empty, she was proving him wrong. She stood toe to toe with him, swallowing back emotions in a single-minded pursuit of her strange request, when most women would have been in hysterics by now.

"My mother's family does not have the means to assist us. They have no position and little wealth," she said quietly. "And my father grew estranged from his family the more he wasted away his life through gambling. I *have* tried to contact his elder brother, the Marquis, but he refuses to have anything to do with us. His response was, essentially, that my father had made our bed and it was not his responsibility to keep us from lying in it."

There was an underlying bitterness to her tone that was not reflected in either her face or demeanor. Ethan tried to remain immune to it, but it reminded him too much of his own broken upbringing and severed familial ties. He would never admit it to Miranda, of course, but he understood the pain she was trying to keep secret.

"And what of your family friends?" he asked, searching for one last way to escape this request she was making. "Surely one of them would be of greater assistance than a man you hardly know."

"Many of my father's supposed friends are the ones who are calling in his debts." Now she didn't make any attempt to mask her anger. Her blue eyes flashed with a rage and resolve that surprised Ethan. "And I don't wish to meet the terms some are requesting in order to cancel our obligations."

He arched a brow as he looked her up and down. He could well imagine the bargains those men would offer. Who wouldn't?

Miranda Albright was wholly unspoiled, but still maintained an air of innocent sensuality about her in everything she did, from her sultry eyes to the way she held her body. The man who claimed her would be wise to teach her in all the traditions of sin and passion and pleasure.

"They want you, eh?" he asked, unable to keep the wicked question from falling from his lips just to see her reaction.

For a moment, she seemed shocked by his forward words, but then her mouth thinned into a brittle line. "No. That would trouble me far less. My youngest sister was what one man requested. She is just sixteen."

Anger and disgust flooded Ethan and he clenched his hands at his sides. "Bastard."

She nodded once in agreement. "Do you see now why it is imperative that I host a good Season for my sisters?"

Miranda moved forward, lifting her hand like she was going to grasp his arm, but then she stopped. She stared at him and then to her hanging hand and he couldn't help but do the same. He found himself disappointed when she pushed her fists down at her sides instead of touching him.

"You keep saying you want Seasons for your younger sisters," he said, surprised at the husky tone of his voice. "But you are certainly still of an age. Why not simply find a husband, yourself?"

"I have had two Seasons," she said, her face becoming a stony mask. "If I could not find a suitable match by now, I certainly don't think my luck will change. And I am beginning to think a marriage would not suit me anyway. I am too independent."

Ethan stared at her. He'd heard the "independent" speech

before. Most of the time, it came from hardened spinsters and unappealing wallflowers. Women who could not find matches because of their looks or shrill attitudes. Women who had no hope of ever marrying, let alone marrying well.

But when he met Miranda Albright's eyes, he didn't see the disappointment often found in women who had surrendered their hopes of marriage. There was a true independent streak in her. A recognition that she might be able to find a marriage, but not one that would suit her desires.

And hadn't he heard she turned down at least two—perhaps it was three—very respectable offers, albeit before her father's death, when she might not have realized the full ramifications of that action? No, she was no wallflower.

He moved toward her, almost without thought. She watched him step in her direction and her eyes widened, but she didn't back away, even when he moved too close for propriety. A dark hunger stirred in him at her spirit. At the flicker of sensuality that she probably didn't even understand or recognize. There were so many things he could teach her. Things he could do to her. But a woman of her station and past would never allow for that . . . would she?

There was only one way to find out.

"Independence is all well and good," Ethan said with a smile his last mistress had called wickedness embodied. Of course she had said it just as her own sweet mouth encircled his cock. "But what of the pleasures you will miss by surrendering yourself to the path of a spinster?"

Miranda swallowed and her throat worked. Her mouth was lush, with full lips. How had he missed that fact before? It was exactly the kind of mouth a man wanted to feel trailing along his skin.

She shifted slightly and a charming dash of high color entered her cheeks. By the way her gaze darted away, she knew exactly what kind of pleasures he was talking about.

He inched closer. Now his body was almost touching hers, teasing him with what it would feel like if her skin brushed his. She smelled of just a hint of the heady scent of lilacs.

"I-I suppose there is the companionship," she stammered, blue eyes darkening as she fought to look anywhere in the room but at him.

"Not companionship. You can get that from a dog. No, Miss Albright, I am referring to the *physical* pleasures," he said softly. "Do you not wonder about what happens between a man and a woman? Those mysteries no one wants to reveal to you until you are married?"

She swallowed again, but then her shoulders straightened and she looked into his eyes directly. A flash of challenge lit up the blue, and that feeling that she knew his secrets flooded him yet again.

"I *know* what happens," she said softly.

He drew back in startled surprise. "Are you saying you have been with a man?"

She never looked away, never balked. Only the darkening blush of her cheeks gave away her feelings on the matter. "No."

Ethan looked her up and down. What was it about her that made him ache so? Normally he just wanted to fuck. To bury himself in wet and welcoming heat until he was spent. Who cared about the source of his pleasure? A pretty woman, one who could make him smile, was always nice but certainly not required.

But Miranda Albright, with her innocent blushes and hidden fire, made him want *her*. And he always got what he wanted.

One way or another.

"You think this is the only way?"

She nodded without hesitation. "I know it is the only way."

He stroked his fingers along his stubbly chin. "What if I told you I would provide your sisters their Seasons, but only at a price?"

Much to her credit, Miranda didn't even blink in surprise. "Of course. I never expected you would do this for free."

He drew back in surprise. "So you came here ready to bargain?"

She swallowed and her throat worked with the action. Once again, he pictured those full lips closing around his length and barely held back a moan. The little innocent had no idea of her charms.

"I thought to offer you some of my jewelry, but unfortunately I have recently discovered that it was all replaced with paste by my father." Her mouth drew down. "Including my grandmother's broach."

"I wouldn't have taken it even if it was diamonds," he retorted, enjoying the way her eyes snapped up to his. "What else?"

Her lips thinned with a flash of irritation and he barely suppressed a chuckle. Damn, it was amusing to rile her.

"And then I thought perhaps I could promise you some portion of my sisters' pin money if they found husbands' with means."

Ethan arched a brow. "A rather difficult promise to make. You're not only promising someone else's blunt, but only if your sisters are successful in their husband hunts. It seems like a poor investment."

"So clearly I have no money," she said with a sigh. "And I came here in the hopes that you would be able to suggest some kind of payment that would be amenable to you. What could I possibly offer you?"

Ethan groaned as his cock eased to attention beneath his breaches. Damn, she didn't know all the dark and dangerous images that innocent question inspired.

"My request is not much different from the other men who are trying to collect on your father's debts," he said softly. "However, I have a bit more sophisticated tastes than to want a child hardly out of the schoolroom. No, I want *you*."

Miranda blinked as Ethan's words began to sink into her system. Her? He wanted *her*? Like he had wanted those other women she'd watched him with?

But no, he couldn't mean it in that sense. Not Ethan Hamon. Not the wicked Earl of Rothschild who had his pick of willing, beautiful, experienced women. Not the man she'd watched pleasure two courtesans just one summer before and leave both women begging for more by the time Miranda snuck away home to relieve her frustrations alone.

He couldn't want *her*.

"You mean for . . ." She struggled to find some other explanation. He had money, he had servants, he didn't have children who required a governess. He would have no need for her.

Except for the one purpose that was so hard to accept.

She swallowed as she met his gaze. It was hard and hot and swept away any remaining doubt of exactly what he meant. Under that stare, she felt stripped. Naked. Desired. Owned. And he hadn't even touched her yet.

"You mean my innocence," she whispered.

Ethan flinched just a fraction, but then the reaction was gone. He took a step away and swept up his forgotten drink. He took a sip before he answered.

"At first, but that isn't all I want," he said. His gaze flitted over her from head to toe and she felt even more exposed the second time. "You are asking me to potentially host three Seasons, my dear, if one of the girls is not immediately successful. And considering your mother's tastes, that won't be inexpensive. And there is my time to consider. My sponsorship will mean I shall have to attend at least *some* tedious balls and parties over the next few years. I don't think your mere innocence is valuable enough to cover all that."

Miranda gasped. As a lady, she had been taught that her virtue was her most important possession. The one fragile thing that separated her from one life and another. Losing it meant losing any chance at the marriage her mother had long planned for her. It could very well mean a loss of respectability entirely if the truth were revealed.

"My innocence is all I have," she said.

Ethan stopped mid-sip and stared at her. His dark brown eyes were almost black and hard as steel. He set the glass down with a loud, echoing clink and moved on her.

"No, that is what the matrons tell you to keep you in line.

That one little barrier separates you from sin or sainthood. From good and evil. But you have so much more to offer than that."

He stopped just inches from her, invading her space for a second time. Just as it had the first, his nearness made her head spin. His hand lifted and one finger trailed lazily over the curls along her hairline. Miranda gasped. He had never touched her before. Not even her hand. And this . . . well, it wasn't the kind of intimate touch she had witnessed from him over the years, but it wasn't proper, that was certain.

She tried to draw breath, to remain calm as that one finger continued to trail down her skin until it skimmed her jawline. Little electric tingles rocked through her at the touch.

"So you—you want me three times?" she asked.

He barked out a laugh and pulled his hand away. "My, we do have a high opinion of our sexual prowess, don't we?"

Hot blood filled her cheeks, but Miranda forced herself to remain where she stood and endure Ethan's mockery. "I have no sexual prowess—"

"You'd be surprised," he muttered.

She ignored the dry interruption. "I am merely trying to understand the terms of the offer you are putting forth."

A sudden, small smile tilted the corners of his lips. "So very businesslike. Have you done this before?"

"Of course not." She folded her arms over her breasts and glared at him. "Tell me exactly what you are asking of me. Now."

He inclined his head in a sarcastic salute. "Yes, Miss Albright, of course. Here is *exactly* what I want. I will be here at my estate for several months, as I am every year at this time."

Miranda flushed as she thought of how well she knew that

fact. This was the time of year she looked forward to more than any other. As soon as she knew Ethan had arrived from London, she began her summer walks . . . her summer spying sessions where she watched Ethan take his pleasure, give pleasure, do shocking things. And she loved it. Every forbidden, stolen moment.

"What I want is for you to be my mistress this summer."

Miranda stumbled back a step and her arms fell straight to her sides. "You—your mistress?"

How many times had she longed for that very thing? Pictured herself spread out for Ethan's desires, waiting for him to have her in every wicked way his naughty mind could fathom? How many times had she touched herself while imagining it was Ethan stroking his hands and mouth and cock over her? And now he was offering to fulfill her fantasy for the entire summer.

"Yes." He shifted and actually looked a little uncomfortable. "Despite your claims that you know what goes on between a man and a woman, a lady like yourself may not realize that an unmarried man of my means and appetites often keeps a woman to fulfill his needs. I generally bring someone with me on my visits to the country, but this year I—" He stopped and his hot gaze settled fully on her mouth. "Well, I didn't. If I am to sponsor your sisters, I shall expect you to repay me by becoming my mistress. One month of your service for each sister I will sponsor. *Those* are the terms."

"So you want me for the entire summer?" she whispered, staring with unseeing eyes at the floor.

"Yes. Your days and nights will belong to me." His voice had gotten husky again and Miranda shot him a side glance. He was looking at her just like she'd seen him look at all those other women he'd taken. A look of wanting. Waiting.

So *this* was what being desired felt like. Like a thousand hot prickles up and down her spine that made her body weep with need. She squirmed a little under his scrutiny, but her shifting only worsened the throbbing ache between her legs.

What he was asking for was madness and she would be a fool to agree. Giving up her virginity and then becoming her neighbor's mistress would utterly ruin her for any other respectable man. If their bargain were discovered, it would probably also destroy her sisters' chances at marrying well. They would certainly never be accepted into good society again.

And yet, she found herself thrilling at the prospect. Ever since the first afternoon she watched Ethan make love to one of his mistresses, she had secretly longed for that kind of passion. For desire that overflowed until it could no longer be contained. She wanted a man who would take her, force her pleasure, teach her to give him his own.

Those dark, dangerous wants were the biggest part of why she had turned down any proposal made for her hand, despite all the other theories about her refusals. She wasn't cold, she wasn't snobbish or even mercenary. In truth, she had simply looked at each man who offered for her and saw that they would want a proper wife. They would be a proper husband. They would be gentle and detached and not press their suit too often or too vigorously. If she said no, they would let it be. And if she dared to ask for more, they would be shocked.

Those men would make love to her not . . . not *fuck* her, as she had heard Ethan call it so many times from her hiding place. She would never experience danger or daring at their hands.

With Ethan, she would. If she took his offer, if she gave herself over to him, he would teach her every sinful thing she had ever wanted to learn and more. He would make her shiver with release. He would never make her feel ashamed of her natural curiosities and desires. He would give her what she wanted.

And he would take whatever he desired in return. He would push her to her boundaries and far beyond.

That was the dangerous part of the offer. More dangerous, even, than having their agreement found out or being ruined.

"Do you have an answer, Miss Albright?" he asked softly.

"I have questions and stipulations of my own," she replied. Her legs shook, so she crossed to the nearest chair and sat down, praying she looked calm and cool, not frightened and painfully aroused.

He chuckled. "Do you? So this is to be a negotiation?"

Nodding once, she said, "It must be. I have a great deal to lose."

His taunting smile fell. "I suppose you do. So ask me your questions and we shall see if we can come to terms."

She thrust her shoulders back and willed her hands not to tremble. He couldn't see how much he moved her or else he would take more than she could give.

"Will you make our arrangement public?"

"No, of course not." He took his own chair across from hers and sprawled out with lazy elegance. "I want you in my bed, not my opera box. No one need know of our arrangement."

"Even your closest friends?"

He leaned forward and locked eyes with her. "No one, Miranda."

She jumped. That was the first time he'd ever said her given name. It seemed to roll off his tongue like a caress, stroking over her body in a strange, powerful wave.

She forced herself to remain focused. "What of your servants?"

"They are judgmental, but completely trustworthy. I've been certain of that. There have been other women here who would be, shall we say, *harmed* if their visits here were revealed."

Miranda nodded. That did make her feel better. Of course, Ethan would have to be discreet in the past. And if it came out that he had ruined her and then refused to marry her, that wouldn't exactly cast him in a fine light anyway. So she trusted his secrecy, if nothing else.

"Which leaves us with terms," she said with a sigh. "I cannot be away from home for an entire summer with no one suspicious of my whereabouts, my lord. I, unlike your widows or courtesans, have a quite overbearing mother."

"I am well aware." Ethan leaned back with a shudder. "How shall I receive payment on my investment, then?"

She drew a deep breath. "What if I were only to come once a week? But I would stay the entire day and all night. You would have me for twenty-four hours and I . . ." She hesitated, unsure of the prudence of her next statement. But there was nothing to be done about it. She had no choice. "I will agree to do whatever you wish, whenever you wish during that twenty-four-hour period."

Three

Ethan straightened up in the chair as his face darkened with hot blood. For the first time in years he was actually shocked. Not horrified, but utterly surprised. The worst of it was that an innocent, willowy country miss had been the one to set him on his heels. She had no idea what she was offering. Or just how tempting that offer was.

Miranda drew a harsh breath and continued before he could interrupt. "The rest of the arrangement remains the same. Every four weeks, I will earn a Season for a sister. Will my utter surrender, within the new confines of the agreement, still suit you?"

Ethan groaned at her choice of words. Utter surrender. What images that conjured. This young woman, spread out on his bed, arching beneath him. Covering him. Having her in every wicked way until she begged for more. Until he had his fill. Debauching her completely.

But that was the rub, wasn't it? Miranda wasn't just a lovely widow he could use and discard without doing any damage. He might not have much honor, but he knew what this arrangement could do to Miranda's reputation. The last thing he wanted was for her to come back to him later, making accusations and demands for reparation. If he was going to accept her proposition, something he couldn't believe he was even considering, he would have to be sure she understood exactly what surrender meant to him.

"Once you give me your innocence, you will severely hinder your choices in the future," he said, shifting in the uncomfortable chair. The damn erection this chit had caused was raging now, fed by all the images she was creating with her *offer*.

"There is more to be experienced in life than marriage," she said with a little shrug. "Once my family is situated, I could become a governess. Or a lady's companion. Or . . . or perhaps I'll even decide to remain a mistress, once my sisters are all married, of course."

Ethan shoved out of his chair hard enough that it rocked back. A mistress. So he would be training her to please other men, was that it?

"Do you even know what that means?" he barked, surprised by the tone and strength of his voice. "Do you have any concept of what you are proposing?"

She got up, too, and held out her hands in a motion of surrender that matched her earlier words. "Of course I do."

He stepped forward and grasped her elbows, yanking her against him until the entire length of her willowy frame touched his. She was taller than he had realized. Her forehead was even with his lips and he had a height advantage on most men.

"You don't understand anything," he growled, holding her firm against him with one arm while he tilted her chin up with his hand. "Once you do this, there will be no going back. You'll never be the same. I don't want you to come crying to me later with your regrets."

Her full bottom lip trembled, but she held his gaze evenly as she croaked out, "I stopped crying a long time ago. Once we begin, I won't wish to go back. I know what I'm doing."

"No, you don't," he said, unable to deny himself any longer. "But you will, little innocent. You will."

He crushed his mouth against hers as the last sentence slipped from his lips. She remained stiff for a moment in his arms, her hands trapped between their bodies, still fisted against his chest. Her entire body was like glass in his arms. Unbendable, only breakable. Despite all the passion he could feel pulsing below the surface, her reaction wasn't something that moved him. Not when it was clear she wasn't at all ready for what he had to offer.

He was about to pull away when something happened. In an instant, she let go of all the tension, the shock, the missish denials he was sure she wanted to say now that her resolve was actually being tested. All of that bled away and she softened. Her legs tangled between his and her hips molded to him. Her hands unclenched to caress his chest and slid up to his shoulders as her breasts flattened against him. And her lips, the lips that had been cold and flat and unyielding, suddenly parted.

Ethan forgot whatever lesson he was trying to teach her as he darted his tongue inside. She tasted sweet. A bit of tea, a whisper of mint, a hint of something citrus. All those things combined and burst on his tongue as he took her kiss and demanded even more.

But Miranda wasn't fighting him. Not like he had expected her to. And she wasn't allowing him to just take from her, either. Instead, as he swirled his tongue around hers, her fingers moved up to tangle in his hair, her mouth moved, her tongue teased and playing with his as the kiss spiraled deeper and deeper.

And finally, just when Ethan thought a first kiss couldn't be any sweeter, her hips thrust up and the juncture of her thighs stroked over his cock. His eyes flew open and he looked down at her, even as he continued to kiss her. Her eyes were shut and her face was utterly innocent. All the things she was doing came from pure instinct.

But how far would that instinct go? Would she truly surrender to him completely, despite the consequences?

There was only one way to find out for certain.

He cupped his hands over her backside, lifting her against him in a rhythmic motion. Somehow he expected her to bolt away, but instead she broke the kiss to tilt her head back over her shoulders with a long, shuddering sigh of pleasure.

His blood heated, churning wildly as he adjusted their positions and guided her toward the settee. They fell back against the lush cushions and his body weight pushed her far into the pillows. But still, she didn't demand that he stop. Instead, she settled back and simply looked up at him. Her expression was slightly dazed, a little dreamlike. As if she couldn't believe this was happening.

Neither could he. But he didn't want to stop it, either.

"If you do this, you'll have to surrender all the lessons you've been taught about prudence—"

He accentuated the statement by stripping open the buttons along the front of her dress with one skilled movement. The fabric parted and revealed a tantalizing glimpse of soft, pale flesh.

"All you believe about modesty," he continued as he slipped a hand into the gaping gown and stroked his fingers along the edge of her worn cotton chemise. Miranda's eyes went wide as his fingers danced below the chemise neckline and stroked across the swell of her breasts.

"I will *demand* passion."

He tugged and her chemise slithered downward, revealing the perfect globe of one bare breast.

Miranda's face flamed as Ethan stared at what he had exposed, but she didn't look away from his face. She made no move to cover herself.

He watched as his fingers, dark against her pale skin, circled around her flesh. Her breasts were small, but that fit her tall, slender frame better than large, heavy ones would have. He liked that he could cover the entire mound with one palm. As he did so, Miranda's eyes fluttered shut.

"Oh," she gasped, fingers clenching at the settee cushion beneath her.

"You cannot just lay there and 'endure' my touch, then expect I shall count that as payment," he continued, watching high color darken her cheeks when he massaged her flesh. So very responsive. He wondered what she would do if he flicked a thumb over her nipple just . . . like . . . so.

Her eyes flew open and she looked at him wildly as a gasp escaped her lips.

"Do you understand what I'm saying?" he pressed, stroking

his thumb over her rapidly hardening nipple over and over again. Her back arched. "I don't want some frigid martyr."

Not that she was turning out to be frigid in the least.

Miranda's breaths came in pants. "I-I'm no martyr, my lord. I may be doing this for my family, but . . . but there are other reasons."

He stopped plucking at her nipple and looked into her flushed face. "What other reasons?"

"I want . . ." She squirmed a little and her blush darkened. "I want *this*. I want you to touch me. I want to feel alive. I want to know pleasure. Please, please don't deny me that."

Ethan stared at Miranda, her face so open, so honest. This truly wasn't a game to her, as it was for so many of the women he had bedded over the years. She didn't make this request out of boredom or only because of her desperation. To her, his touch was . . . an awakening.

Her fingers came up to curl around the nape of his neck. A gentle touch as she stroked the skin revealed between his collar and hairline.

"Please," she whispered.

Ethan's mouth came down and silenced her further pleas. He pushed harder now, driving his tongue into her mouth and mating with her like he would soon mate with her body. He wanted to drink her in. Fill himself with her. Drown in that lilac scent and unique flavor.

Miranda rose up and tugged Ethan's hard body down upon hers even tighter. It was like heaven to feel his weight on her, just as she had imagined it would be so many times. It made her feel *alive* and that was worth any price.

His hand found her bare breast again and he resumed the gentle, rhythmic strumming of her taut nipple. Miranda had touched herself many times, especially after watching Ethan with his lovers, but she'd never spent much time on her breasts. She'd never realized how sensitive they were, or how the pleasure she felt when he stroked her nipple went down through her body. She could feel it between her legs, throbbing in time to his touch.

Ethan pushed at the rest of her gown, easing it over her shoulders and leaving it in a pool at her waist between them. Miranda arched her back to offer him free access. She wasn't ashamed. In fact, she was *proud* of the way he looked at her. Proud of the desire that lit up in his dark eyes. She aroused him, and considering his lengthy experience, that was a triumph.

A triumph soon forgotten when he gave her a wicked grin and dropped his hot lips to one of her straining nipples. He drew her between his lips and swirled his rough tongue over the exquisitely sensitive tips.

Miranda cried out at the pleasure this new exploration caused. Wet heat, hot tingles, focused pleasure . . . they overtook her, rushing through her. Her pussy clenched at emptiness and wetness flooded her thighs as he sucked hard, almost hard enough to hurt.

"No one has ever done these things to you?" he murmured against her skin before he gave her swollen nipple a little bite and moved to the other side.

"No, never," she moaned, thrashing her head on the pillows as he licked her like a cat.

He looked up and she couldn't tell if he was pleased or bothered by that confession. But he didn't stop pleasuring her, drawing out sensations that she'd never felt before. Doing things she'd only witnessed from afar and imagined in her darkest dreams.

His hands slid down as his mouth continued its wicked work. Long, warm fingers stroked her rib cage, her belly, and finally hooked her crumpled gown and began to shove it away entirely. She lifted her hips to aid the descent and quickly found herself entirely naked except for her stockings and slippers.

As Ethan pulled back to look at her, she flashed briefly to the memory of the first time she saw him by the lake. His lover had been similarly clad, white slippers thrown over his shoulders as he drove into her. Would Miranda soon be in the same position?

Her body clenched at the thought and Ethan's eyebrows both went up before his hands came back down on her skin. This time, he placed the flat of his palm on one thigh. She trembled at the intimate touch, but didn't recoil. She could see he was surprised by that, by her lack of shyness and shock. But, then, he had no idea of all the ways she had been tutored in passion. Of all the fantasies she had lived in her mind over the past few years.

He was gentle as he urged her legs open, wider and wider until she was on display before him. Miranda studied his face as he, in turn, studied her body. She loved how desire flickered in his gaze, making his face more alive with feeling. She loved how his shoulders tensed with the effort it was taking him to go slow. How she could see the harsh, insistent ridge of his erection pressing against the fine fabric of his trousers.

His hands slipped up from her thighs and he cupped her sex with one hand. Now that she was bare, the sensation was multiplied, powerful. No one else had ever touched her like that. Only her own fingers had explored her folds, burrowed deep inside.

His touch was far more pleasurable. Ethan teased her, stroking her with the flat of his palm first, light pressure meant to acclimate her to the intimacy of his hands. But as she parted her lips with a sigh of pleasure, the pressure intensified and changed.

Ethan parted her folds, opening her to his fingers. He glided one across the wet slit. Miranda's hips bucked of their own accord and the action forced the thick digit inside of her body.

They both froze, locking gazes. This was it. This was what Miranda had been dreaming about for years. And now Ethan had breeched her body with his own, not with his cock, no, but he was inside of her nonetheless. Nothing would ever change that. Nothing would ever take it away.

And nothing had ever felt so good. He slipped into her past his second knuckle and gently stroked, curling his finger toward himself like he was beckoning her to surrender.

She was helpless to resist the temptation. She let her head fall back against the settee pillows as she gave in to the foreign, powerful sensations. He stretched her untried channel, opening her, awakening her in ways she had only imagined. Every stroke of his fingers made her all the more aware of her body and of the tingling pressure mounting between her thighs.

He slipped another finger inside to join the first and Miranda gasped. God, she felt so full. So wickedly wanton, spread out naked on his settee while he pumped his fingers in and out of her body. The sensation was overwhelming, far more potent than when she did the same action herself.

Ethan could sense how close Miranda was to release. It was etched on the strained lines of her face and the glazed focus of her gaze. And her body spoke of her impending orgasm as well. Her pussy clenched like a vice and her juices flowed over his fingers.

His cock throbbed in time, needs whispering at him to take. Claim. Forget everything except burying himself deep inside of her.

But he managed to pull away. He stopped all his movements, kept her right at the edge of orgasm without taking her over as he stopped curling his fingers and stroking her clit with his thumb.

Miranda moaned in protest as she lifted her head to look at him. "Why—why—?"

He smiled, though the expression took a massive effort. "This is your last chance to change your mind, Miranda. The way you are surrendering to me now is just the beginning. And once this is done, it will never be undone. Once you say yes, you'll be mine. So you must mean it."

Miranda's eyes were wild, the pale blue reflecting emotions so powerful that Ethan almost wanted to look away. He didn't want to be witness to all her fear and worry and desire. It brought her too close.

But he stayed focused on her, waiting for whatever she would say.

"Yes," she groaned, tilting her hips. "Stop toying with me. You know I'm saying yes. For me. I want this."

Control slipped from Ethan's grasp at her begging. Slipping his fingers from inside of her, he scrambled to his feet and shed his clothing with little care to where the various items fell. All he cared about was being inside this woman. Now.

When he was entirely naked, he turned to take his place between her legs and found Miranda staring at him. She sat up a little on the settee, staring at the cock that was only a few inches away from her. She didn't seem at all shocked by the sight, as he imagined a normal virgin would. Did that mean she lied when she said she'd never lain with a man?

Not that it mattered. Virgin or no, he was going to have her. And not just this one time. Once this bargain had been sealed with the joining of their bodies, she would be his until the summer's end or he bored of her, whichever came first.

She tilted her head. "May I . . ." she trailed off, a blush darkening her cheeks.

"What?" he managed to grind out between clenched teeth.

"Touch it," she finished, darting her stare up to his face. "May I?"

"God, yes."

Her hand trembled as she reached for him. He tracked her fingers like a hawk on the hunt, waiting and anticipating the moment when her fist would come around him. When it did, it nearly unmanned him. Soft fingers curled around his length, stroking him from base to head in a timid, but utterly satisfying caress.

"Am I doing it properly?" she asked as she continued to gently stroke him.

His knees were starting to buckle from pleasure. "Perfect. And I look forward to expanding on your technique even further." He pushed her hand away, though his cock twitched in protest. "But not right now. Right now I want to do this."

He dropped down between her legs and threaded his fingers through her hair. Her lips parted in surprise and he took advantage by driving his tongue into her mouth. Immediately, her response shifted. She sucked him in, dueling with her own kiss that was raw and real and utterly erotic.

Perhaps he had been wrong to avoid virgins. If they could make him feel like this . . .

He nudged her back, covering her body with his own. She was so supple beneath him, her lithe frame molded to his, curving into the valleys of his body and fitting softness against hard. But he wanted more. More than just a superficial touch. He wanted to be inside, to be joined as one.

He pushed her legs open wider with one thigh, easing himself into position as he continued to devour her mouth like a ravenous man. He *felt* ravenous, so hungry for her that he could hardly contain himself.

The head of his cock found her entrance, wet and hot and ready. Just that grazing touch of skin against skin sent a shiver of pleasure up his spine. He reached around to cup her backside and slowly, gently pushed forward.

Ethan broke the kiss with a low, harsh moan as her inner walls pulsed around him, massaging him in greeting as he thrust home. Had any other woman ever been so damn hot? Suddenly he couldn't remember. All he could feel was this keen pleasure.

He caught his breath as he inched forward and opened his eyes. Miranda was staring at him, mouth open a fraction, eyes wide. She looked terrified and aroused at once, her chest rising and falling on ragged breaths.

"Almost there," he reassured her through grinding teeth.

God, he wanted to pound forward, rut with her like an untamed animal. But not yet. Not yet.

He drove further and encountered the barrier of her body. So she hadn't been lying. No other man had ever claimed her like this. All her innocence was real, just as her hot desire and tempting abilities were natural.

"God, I am going to enjoy teaching you," he murmured before he caught her mouth for another kiss, this time gentle.

She relaxed as he nibbled on her lower lip, sucked her tongue slowly. When she sighed with pleasure, he surged forward and broke the last barrier of her innocence.

Miranda stiffened, arching up in his arms with a gasp of pain. Though his cock was actually pulsing with desire, Ethan held perfectly still as she acclimated to the new feeling of his erection buried to the hilt inside her.

"I'm sorry," he murmured into her hair.

"No," she shook her head as she rested her forehead against his shoulder. "It's better now. Just . . . full."

She wiggled a little, squeezing him experimentally.

Ethan growled with the pleasure that shot up the length of his erection and tightened his balls. If she wasn't careful, she'd end up getting fucked and fucked hard this first time.

"Don't play games," he whispered as he swiveled his hips gently.

She pulled back and met his eyes with a decidedly wicked smile. "You *like* games, Ethan."

"Oh, yes, I do," he admitted as he swirled his hips a second time. "And by the time I am through with you, so will you."

He cupped her harder against him and thrust forward, driving into her with as much gentleness as he could muster when her pussy was already starting to flutter with the first hints of the release about to come. She clenched at his shoulders as he thrust, digging in her nails and giving little mewls of satisfaction as he took her.

Every time he drove forward it was like pleasurable torture. A balancing act where he tried to remain steady for her sake, even as his own body screamed for rough and wild claiming. He had never struggled with his own pleasure so keenly. Normally, he could set aside his needs to give his partner her release first. But with Miranda, he wanted to be rough and selfish.

But the fact that it was her first time kept him from surrendering to those base desires. He swirled his hips to be sure to stroke her clit with every movement. Her breaths came harsher now, harder and her hands dug deeper into his shoulders. She was trying to match his driving cock with her own hips, squeezing and lifting against him each time.

Finally, her eyes rolled back and she let out a gasping, keening cry that echoed in the room around them. Her body exploded in a mass of shaking, trembling, clenching heat that drove him over the edge of control into madness. He couldn't stop himself anymore. He pounded through her orgasm, reveling in the tightening of his balls, the building dam of pleasure that made everything that much sweeter, that much sharper.

With a roar of possession, he drove deep into her and came before he collapsed into her embrace.

Four

Miranda lay in Ethan's arms, half on and half off the settee, their panting breaths mingling in the quiet room. Now that the trembling of her body had subsided and her heart rate was returning to normal, she could finally comprehend what had just occurred.

She had surrendered her innocence, that commodity she had, from an early age, been taught was her only bargaining chip. And she'd given it to Ethan Hamon, the only man she'd ever fantasized about.

Did she regret the choice? No. It had been as powerful and pleasurable and life-altering as she had always dreamed it would be.

She stretched against his chest with a smile before she tilted her face up to look at him. His head rested on the arm of the settee and he was staring up at the ceiling with an unreadable expression.

"Is it always like that?" she asked quietly, studying the strong line of his jaw.

His lips thinned and he jerked his gaze down to hers. With a quiet curse, he maneuvered away from her body and got to his feet. Snatching up his discarded trousers, he said, "Yes. That is sex, my dear."

Miranda's teeth sunk into her bottom lip as she watched him dress with jerky, controlled movements. He never looked at her. He hardly acknowledged her at all except to occasionally hand her an item of her clothing that had become entangled in his own. He was cold, distant.

Her stomach sank with every silent moment that ticked by. What was wrong? Had she not pleased him? He had *seemed* to enjoy her touch. He'd found release with a shout much louder than any she'd heard from him in the years she spied on him. But now he didn't seem happy in the least about his conquest.

Perhaps conquering an inexperienced virgin hadn't been as satisfying as he'd thought it would be.

The heat of embarrassment flooded her cheeks as she quickly detangled her chemise from her wrinkled gown to pull it over her head and regain some semblance of decorum. Now the voices of doubt crept in, reminding her that Ethan Hamon was no man of honor. He could easily change his mind about the bargain they had struck, leaving her with no virtue *and* no hope for her family. He might even tell the world about her surrender, the consequences to them both be damned.

Struggling to her feet, she shook out her gown and stepped into the folds of worn fabric. She refused to look at him as she began to refasten her front buttons with shaking fingers.

"Here."

She jumped as Ethan's voice interrupted her work. She looked up to find him finally facing her. His shirt was half undone, his feet bare, and his hand was extended toward her, motioning her to his side.

Heart throbbing, she moved to him. "Yes?"

"Let me."

He caught the gaping sides of her gown and went to work on her buttons with the same efficiency as he had torn them open, but far less passion. The action felt sterile, distant, like she was some child he was assisting, not a lover.

Miranda bit her lip. She wasn't going to become upset in front of him. A man like Ethan wouldn't want some hysterical woman sobbing in his parlor. Doing that would only prove that she was more trouble than she was worth.

"Ethan," she whispered, hating how her voice broke just a little.

He hesitated before he slipped the last button into place. Slowly, his gaze lifted to hers and a flicker of heat stoked deep within his eyes. Dark and dangerous, but it gave her hope. He still wanted her.

As if he had read her mind, he cupped her chin and tilted her face, letting the rough pad of his thumb drift along her bottom lip. The passionate sensations that had just come to a sparkling, spectacular head a few moments before began again, teasing Miranda with the promise of release. She was shocked by how quickly she could want, despite her aching body.

"What now?" she whispered, darting her tongue out and slipping it over his questing thumb briefly.

"Damn it," Ethan muttered as his arm came around her waist. He yanked her flush against him and then stood there, staring down at her. His face was intense and still, his eyes and expression dark and indecipherable beyond that burning fire of desire.

"*You* are going home," he finally croaked out as he let her go and backed away. He held out his palms to her like a shield. "Go home, Miranda."

Panic gripped her as she sucked in a breath. "But we—our agreement—"

"Friday," he barked, his sharp voice silencing her protests. "Your Fridays will be mine this summer. Come back in two days time and we'll begin this bargain in earnest."

Miranda stared at him for a long moment. Part of her was relieved he didn't wish to break their bargain before it even began. Still, his attitude kept her from feeling any comfort about her future.

"Very well," she stammered as she turned away.

He wanted her gone and she had no leverage to argue that point with him. They had come to terms, they had sealed their arrangement, why wouldn't he become businesslike and cold? Ethan Hamon was known as a man of passion, not compassion. For him, this experience was not emotional. Desire was not overwhelming. And she would have to follow his lead in that view or find herself lost entirely.

She forced her tone to become as calm and detached as she could manage. "I will return Friday morning."

"Not too early," he said as she opened the door to step into the foyer. "And Miranda?"

She turned back.

He was watching her, his gaze focused firmly on her face. "A warm bath will ease the stinging. Have your maid draw one for you when you arrive home."

She stared at him, cheeks flaring. Perhaps there was some compassion to the man after all. "Thank you, my lord. Until Friday."

Then she shut the door behind her and fled.

The moment the door closed behind Miranda, Ethan went to the bar and poured himself a very tall, very strong glass of whiskey. He downed the first tumbler in two swigs and poured another before he went to the window to look out over the front grounds.

He pursed his lips. He couldn't deny he was looking for Miranda. And he found her, stumbling across his lawn toward the lake and the shortcut through the fields to her family home.

Even now, when she was little more than a diminishing figure heading toward the horizon, his body tensed and tightened and swelled at the thought of her. He could still taste her on his tongue, despite the drink. The scent of her, now mixed with the musk of sex, hung heavy in the room and taunted him with overwhelming images and feelings.

He downed the second drink and went for a third.

She'd asked if "it" was always like this. And he'd lied and made some callous comment about sex that had hurt and shut her down. He wasn't proud of that, but he certainly wasn't going to admit that the answer to her question was most decidedly no.

Ethan had been with many women over the years. Beautiful,

skilled lovers who knew exactly what to do with their mouths, their hands, their breasts, their pussies. Yet nothing in his experience had prepared him for what happened in this parlor today with a virgin. A *virgin* for Christ's sake.

He'd lost all semblance of control.

With difficulty, Ethan moved away from the window, determined not to stare like a lost puppy after Miranda's retreating form. He slumped into a chair across the room and looked at the rumpled settee instead. It served as a reminder of the way Miranda had surrendered to him.

Perhaps that was it. It was the combination of her total surrender and her virginity that intrigued him so. They were a novelty. He'd never deflowered anyone, in fact he'd avoided such things in the past. And he had already admitted to various friends that he was growing tired of the practiced passions of the more experienced ladies who offered him a place between their legs.

The real passion and the uniqueness of being Miranda's first had affected him more than he expected, but now that he understood why, he could fight it. Dear God, he certainly wasn't about to be mastered by an innocent. In fact, on Friday he would begin the process of utterly owning *her*.

Doing so would put an end to this off-kilter feeling he was experiencing now. And if, after this was over, Miranda did indeed want to become a mistress, his tutelage would be a kindness. He could teach her so much about desire. About passion. About pleasure.

He shivered at just the thought of it. And at the thought of Miranda being someone's mistress. He'd scoffed a little when she first proposed it, but now. . .

Now he was beginning to think she could be very, very good at it.

Miranda stood at the edge of the veranda stairway and looked up at the house she had lived in her entire life. For the first time, she was hesitant about entering. She wasn't the same woman who had left just hours before.

A few short hours and yet it seemed like everything had changed. Would everyone be able to see? Would they guess the truth the moment she met their eyes?

It seemed like that was possible. She *felt* different. Even now, her body ached from what she'd done with Ethan, like it was mocking her with the memory of his hands and mouth on her. His body invading and claiming her own in the most primal way possible.

She shivered at the memory and was shocked that behind the deep ache were tingles of pleasure. What a little wanton she was to still need more after all she'd already done. And now she would repeat that experience over and over again. Once a week for three long months. Twelve full days that would belong entirely to Ethan and his whims.

It hadn't seemed like so much to bargain away when she began . . . but now . . . now it was an overwhelming prospect.

"Miranda, there you are!"

Miranda jolted as her fog was pierced by mother's voice from the veranda above. She looked up to see her mother and sister Beatrice coming down toward her. Her mother did not look especially pleased, not that she had for months.

With a sigh, Miranda prepared herself for the onslaught just as the two women reached her.

"Where have you been, child? And why in the world do you look like such a wreck?" her mother barked.

Miranda's hands went reflexively to her hair. She'd done her best to smooth her appearance on the long walk home from Ethan's estate, but she'd known it wouldn't be enough.

"I know where she's been," Beatrice said with a smirk.

Miranda's eyes went wide as she shifted her gaze to her younger sister. Surely that wasn't true! Even Penelope didn't know where she'd gone, Beatrice couldn't! But if she did . . .

"Penelope said she went on one of her walks. Looks like she went through a bog," her sister finished.

Their mother pursed her lips. "For heaven's sake, girl, why do you insist on those long walks through the woods? You know you could better spend your time making calls and garnering invitations for us."

Miranda sighed, partly in relief and partly in annoyance. It seemed her secret was safe, but only in exchange for the same speech she'd heard a hundred times before.

"The fresh air is good for me," she argued as she made her way around her mother and sister and headed up the steps to the veranda.

"It makes you freckly," her mother insisted. "And what if someone had seen you looking like this?"

"Who could have seen me, Mother?" Miranda sighed as she stepped inside the parlor.

"What about Lord Rothschild?" Beatrice offered.

Miranda skidded to a halt and spun on her sister. "Lord Rothschild?" she repeated past a suddenly dry throat. Her head was beginning to pound.

"Oh, is he back?" their mother asked with a groan.

Beatrice nodded. "I heard from Susanna Carlton that he is back in the county for his annual visit. Sometimes *he* roams about the woods."

"Likely looking for unsuspecting young girls to seduce," their mother said with a tsking of her tongue. "You see, Miranda, if you had stumbled into his path, you might not think the outdoor air was so very good for you after all."

Miranda folded her arms, overcome by a sudden desire to defend Ethan against her family. "You dislike him, yet you always accept his invitations."

Her mother blinked like she didn't understand the point. "Of course. He may be a scoundrel, but he's a well-connected one. And until he has the decency to quit the country, why shouldn't we take advantage?"

"Oh, Mother!" Miranda cried as she began to rub her temples.

Her mother caught her hands and drew them together, squeezing almost to the point of pain. Miranda looked at her in surprise and caught just the faintest hint of fear in her mother's wild stare. She'd never seen that before, not in all the times they discussed their financial problems. Miranda had always assumed Dorthea really didn't understand the straights they were in.

Perhaps she did, after all.

"Miranda, you may judge me and my methods, but I do not want to wait for fate. We must take control of our own destinies." Her mother released her hands and the emotions were wiped clean from her round face. "Now, please go upstairs and tidy up."

Miranda nodded slowly and did as she'd been told.

As she moved up the stairs to her chamber, she thought of what her mother had said.

"We must take control of our own destinies," she murmured.

That was what she'd been trying to do today by asking Ethan for help. And by accepting the terms of his agreement. But she hadn't been in *control* at any point of their encounter. Ethan had seduced and pleasured and dominated her from the moment he entered the room to the moment he told her to go.

She had allowed him to do so, giving in to what he wanted with little argument except for her one stipulation of limiting their encounters to once a week.

If this were a courtship, she wouldn't worry about the issue of control all that much. It was expected that a gentleman would rule in a scenario where he would end up married to a woman.

But this arrangement wouldn't end in marriage. It wouldn't end with a trusting, or even loving, bond, despite the surrender of her body to his whims. If she allowed Ethan to control her at every turn, she could end up hurt.

"He could steal my heart," she whispered as she entered her chamber and rang the bell for her maid.

That was true. She felt it. She could almost taste it. After years of fascination with the man, surrendering to him had left her feeling . . . good. Happy for the first time in months. It wouldn't take too much more surrender to have those feelings turn to love. And loving Ethan was the most foolish thing she could possibly do.

"Miss?" her maid said as she pushed the chamber door open.

With a start, Miranda turned on the girl. "Maddy, I fell on my walk today and I'm a bit dirty. I'd like a warm bath."

The maid tilted her head in surprise. Normally the family didn't bathe in the middle of the afternoon. But finally, she shrugged. "Of course, miss. I'll make the arrangements immediately."

"Thank you."

As the girl left, Miranda moved behind the screen in the corner of the room and began to strip out of her gown. As she did, she couldn't help but notice little marks on her skin, tiny bruises that had been left by Ethan's hands and mouth. She stifled a curse. Already she was branded as his and they had only just begun together.

"I cannot let him take everything I am," she said as she wrapped herself in a worn dressing gown.

But how to keep that from happening? How could she manage to keep a grip on her "destiny," as her mother had put it?

Miranda sat down at her dressing table and began to brush her tangled hair. Her thoughts drifted to her encounter with Ethan. Every moment played through her mind in sensual, slow motion and her body reacted accordingly.

It had felt so good to be touched. To touch him.

Touch him.

Miranda straightened up. The only time she'd felt any kind of control was when she touched Ethan. When she stroked his cock, he'd been at *her* mercy, not the other way around. By giving him pleasure, she'd kept some of her power in the process.

That was it. She couldn't just allow herself to be seduced. She had to seduce him. She'd been watching him for years, hadn't she? She knew what he liked, what made him moan, in a way he didn't know about her.

If she could use what she'd seen, what she'd watched those other women do over the years, she could keep Ethan at bay. Keep her heart firmly in her own hands.

All it would take was seduction.

And just because she had never tried to seduce anyone before didn't mean she *couldn't* do it. Women did so every day, didn't they? Ones with far less intelligence than she possessed. And she had her years of spying on her side.

The door opened behind her and two maids came in carrying the tub, with two more following with hot water. As they prepared her bath, Miranda stared at herself in the mirror with renewed purpose.

She could do this. She had to. At this point, her only hope was seduction.

Five

A stroll through the woods was normally Miranda's favorite pastime in the summer months. Even before she'd become obsessed with spying on Ethan's sexual exploits, she had loved the quiet of nature, the feel of a soft breeze on her face. Time spent alone had helped her handle her overbearing mother's demands and the slow realization that her father wasn't the heroic figure she had believed him to be as a sheltered child.

Today, however, her walk was no stroll, but more akin to a death march. She hardly noticed her surroundings, let alone took peace in them, as she made her way over the rolling hills toward Ethan's home. Instead of quiet, an insistent refrain played over in her head. A skipping question about Ethan. What would he do to her? What would he say?

Today was the first full twenty-four hours of their agreement. With the barrier of her virginity gone, he would begin his promised debauchery in earnest.

As she stepped through the final veil of trees, Miranda shivered, though the air was warm. Across the lawn Ethan's palatial home rose up like a beacon. Or point of no return. Which, she wasn't quite certain yet.

But that was her destination and there was no going back. Not anymore.

As Miranda straightened her shoulders and tried to smooth the lines of nervousness away from her face, she forced herself to move. She wouldn't give Ethan the satisfaction of seeing her worries. No, she would remain in control. She would use everything she'd secretly seen against him.

At least she would try. It was her only weapon in this sensual war.

She climbed up the marble stairs leading to Ethan's front door and extended a shaking hand to knock. But before she could rap her knuckles across the shining surface, the door opened and revealed Ethan's stern-faced butler. As always, he appeared disapproving and Miranda felt the blood begin to move to her cheeks. Clearly, Ethan's servants were privy to her secret, or at least some of them were.

"Good morning, Winston," she managed to croak out with as much dignity as she could muster given the circumstances.

"Good morning, Miss Albright," he said with a small nod of the head. "*He* is expecting you. Please follow me."

Miranda shoved her shaking hands behind her back and trailed after Winston as he led her down a long hallway to the backstairs. She looked around as they ascended to the second floor.

For as long as she had known of his secret trysts, the appearance of Ethan's home had shocked her. Not because it was so very decadent, but because it was the complete opposite. The décor was elegant and masculine, done in dark colors with tasteful art.

It made all his vices that much more fascinating. Like he was two people. One the outwardly sinful lord with a reputation of seduction, the other a respectable gentleman who lurked under the surface and appreciated the finer things life had to offer.

Winston paused at a locked doorway halfway down the hall. He produced a key from his waistcoat and opened it, but didn't step inside. Instead, he motioned for Miranda to enter the room in front of him.

"You will find a door along the west wall," he explained with a frown. "Go through there and Lord Rothschild will join you in a few moments."

Miranda stared into the dim room before she shook off her thoughts and nodded to Winston. "Thank you."

"Good day, miss," he said as she entered and he pulled the door shut.

Miranda hesitated, waiting for the sound of the lock being slid back into place, imprisoning her like in some gothic novel where the wicked gentleman seduced the virginal heroine. But that never happened. Instead, Winston's muffled footsteps moved away from the chamber door. But, then, Ethan didn't have to lock her in, did he? She had entered into this bargain of her own free will. She could leave at any time.

As long she forfeited her prize of the Seasons for her sisters.

No, she couldn't afford to do that. Not after giving up her

innocence. As he had pointed out two days ago, there was no turning back now.

And when she was honest, she didn't *want* to turn back. Since their first encounter, she'd been thinking about the feel of Ethan's skin against her own, the taste of his lips, the way she was stretched and filled when he took her. More than once, she had awakened wet and swollen, aching to be with him. And her own attempts at relief, which had always been satisfying enough for her in the past, had fallen short when compared to the memory of Ethan's touch.

She took a brief glance around the room. Plain. Almost like a foyer to another chamber, rather than a room in itself. The only furniture present was a wingback chair next to the door Winston had instructed her to enter. It seemed like such a normal thing, but behind it awaited sin and pleasure and who knew what else.

Miranda held her breath. The final moment had come. The last instant between her life before this bargain and her life after.

She opened the door.

Inside, dark velvet curtains were drawn, so the light was dim. Only the fire and a few scattered lamps illuminated her way. As her eyes adjusted, though, she gasped.

If she had ever pictured what Ethan's home *should* look like, this room exceeded even her most wicked imaginings. A huge bed was the centerpiece, with a high canopy and gauzy draping that swooped down over the mattress. Through the filmy fabric, she could see the coverlet was done in sensual, dark velvet that would caress over bare skin.

Her gaze skittered around and she realized that the bed was

only the beginning. A table with various bindings rested directly across the room. Ones for the wrists, some at ankle level. She shivered at the shocking thought of being bound. It was something she'd never considered before. Would Ethan do that to her?

She darted her gaze away before she had to consider her increased arousal too closely. A huge mirror was along the opposite wall, its frame gilded with golden images of mythical beasts in various stages and varieties of copulation.

As she turned in shock to take in even more of the chamber, her eyes adjusted and she caught a glimpse of movement in a darkened corner of the room. She skirted back in surprise when a shadowy figure rose from a hidden chair and stepped into the light.

Ethan.

Miranda caught her breath. His shirt was open a few buttons and the firelight flickered against the tanned skin revealed there. He hadn't shaved that morning, so a dark slash of stubble made his jaw line all the more defined. He was barefoot, just as he had been the last time she saw him, right after they made love.

And just like the last time, his gaze was filled with desire, but lacking in any other emotion.

"Good morning," he drawled.

She straightened her shoulders with the silent reminder that she had to be as distant as he was. "My lord."

He gave her an indulgent smirk. "As much as I like to be referred to as *your* lord, I think we've gone far beyond those empty platitudes. You have called me Ethan several times." He hesitated and tapped his chin. "Actually you moaned it once. I prefer you call me that while we are alone together."

Miranda blushed at his plain reference to their first afternoon tryst, but managed to bob out a quick nod. "Very well."

"So, I am curious. What excuse did you give your . . ." He hesitated and Miranda thought he gave a little shiver. "*Mother* for your absence for twenty-four hours?"

She shifted uncomfortably. Although she had her own issues with Dorthea, as a general rule Miranda didn't like to lie. And coming up with an excuse to appease her prying mother had been difficult.

"She thinks Lady Ingleworth in Tipton has taken a liking to me and asked me to come each Friday to read and play the pianoforte for her, then spend the night. Since she is a Dowager Duchess, my mother wants to encourage the supposed friendship," she explained carefully.

Ethan leaned back with a low whistle. "Ingenious, my dear. Lady Ingleworth is practically a shut in. There will be no awkwardness of meeting with her in London and being caught in the lie later."

Miranda sighed. Ethan was clearly amused by the situation, but she was not. The idea of having her lie revealed and her mother pick and pick at her until the truth was uncovered kept her up at night.

"Yes, that is what I thought as well."

"Hmmm." He seemed bored of the subject already. "What do you think of my room?" He motioned around them without looking away from her.

She folded her arms. "It suits you far better than the rest of the house."

He chuckled. "How impertinent, but probably true. The rest of the house is for public consumption. One must make allowances for their prim expectations. But this is *my* room."

"Your chamber?" Miranda asked past a suddenly very dry throat. So this was where he slept. Dressed. Dreamed. Those mundane activities were ones she had wondered about, even though she knew the intimate details of his affairs.

He smiled again as he moved to a table that held a bottle of red wine and poured her a glass. "No, no. Even I can only live in such decadence for short periods of time. This is the room where I *entertain*, for lack of a better word."

Miranda took the glass he offered and sipped the wine. It was a fine vintage, not cheap and watered down like the kind served in her household. Her mother complained endlessly about it, but she'd somehow convinced herself that it wasn't really worse.

She had been wrong. The delicate liquid slipped down her throat with a heavenly bite.

"You don't entertain here that often," she said as she took a second sip. "I've never seen this room before and you've invited our family to several events over the years."

Ethan arched a brow. "If I had known what a delightful student you would turn out to be, Miranda, I would have invited you to this room long ago."

"You lie," Miranda said with a laugh. "You never even looked at me before I showed up here unescorted."

He stepped back, apparently surprised by her outburst. Miranda looked at her half-empty wineglass. She'd rather forgotten how little alcohol her body could take before she started saying things she didn't mean to say out loud. She set the glass aside before she blurted out anything else and made an effort to look comfortable despite her sudden embarrassment.

He tilted his head closer. "I don't make a habit out of ruining women who will want more than a few months in my bed, at best. I assumed you would want a lifetime commitment, so I stayed away. But I noticed you, my dear."

His smile was positively animal and he moved toward her like he was a cat and she a helpless mouse. Suddenly she felt like one.

"What did you notice?" she asked softly.

"Your eyes, your lithe frame, those pretty breasts of yours." His voice dropped lower to a seductive level that raked over her senses. "But mostly I noticed how you looked at *me*. Like you knew my secrets."

Miranda started. She hadn't realized her appraisals of him had been so transparent. Thank goodness he didn't know exactly what secrets she *did* know.

"I imagine you must have many secrets, Ethan," she countered, stepping out of his reach to pace across the room.

He laughed. "And I am beginning to think you have a few as well. I'm going to enjoy ferreting them out and exploiting them."

Miranda turned on him with a gasp and found him watching her intently. "You are a cad."

"Of course," he agreed with a good-natured grin. Then he motioned toward the wall behind her. "What do you think of my art work?"

She wrinkled her brow at the sudden change of subject before she turned to look at the picture he'd indicated. She sucked in a breath. From a distance, she had hardly noticed the sketches on the walls, but they, like the mirror frame she'd seen earlier, depicted a variety of sinful couplings.

The one before her portrayed a couple waltzing, which wouldn't have been so outrageous, except that both the dancers were totally naked. The man's cock was engorged, prodding the wet lips of his partner's sex. The orchestra and other dancers looked on as the two spun around the dance floor, lewd expressions on their faces as they groped their own partners.

She felt the whisper of Ethan's body heat as he slipped up behind her. "Well?"

"It's shocking," she admitted, her voice wavering. It was also arousing, but she didn't admit that to him.

"All these portraits will likely be shocking to you," he said, his lips moving close to her neck.

He brushed stray hairs away from her skin with the back of one hand before he pressed his mouth to her. She shivered as his lips parted and he teased his tongue over her flesh. The wet heat was mimicked between her trembling legs.

"But you should examine them well," he whispered. "They could easily be the blueprint of what is to come for you."

She stiffened. So Ethan would demand she participate in all the vices portrayed by the pictures on the walls. She let her gaze rove around the room again. It was a den of sensual delights that decent people didn't speak of. Things she feared she wasn't ready for, despite all she thought she knew.

She had been foolish enough to think that she could control this man, but she was far out of her element. Seeing all these images, all these devices he used regularly on his lovers, she wasn't certain she could do this. Not without losing her soul.

"Stop," she whispered as his arms came around her waist and he moved her back against his hard chest. It felt too good.

"Stop?" he repeated, continuing to rock her against his body so that she could feel the hard ridge of his erection pushing at her backside. "Do you mean that or are you simply afraid of your own desires? Afraid that if you do what I ask, you may never be the same? That I'll change your ideas of sensuality and lust so entirely that you'll forget what you consider 'proper'?"

Miranda pushed away from him and he immediately released her. She covered her hot cheeks as she spun to face him. His expression was bland, almost bored.

"I don't know," she whispered. "I don't know."

He held her gaze for a long, silent moment. Then he turned sideways and motioned to the door. "You are no prisoner, Miranda. If you cannot live up to the terms of our bargain, you're free to leave. But doing so nullifies the agreement. All of it."

Miranda stared at the door, just a few feet away. It represented both freedom and a whole different prison. By walking out, she would sentence her family to ruin. And worse, she would never explore the pleasures Ethan offered her. They might frighten her, but a life lived with only dull attraction terrified her even more.

"What will you do?" he asked softly.

She glanced at him. He didn't look like he gave a damn what she did. In fact, his smirk led her to think that he expected her to run like a ninny. That expression only strengthened her resolve even further.

"I'll stay," she whispered. "I'll hold up my part of our agreement."

★ ★ ★

Two feelings rushed through Ethan when Miranda spoke those trembling words. Both were equally disturbing. On one hand, he couldn't help but be impressed by her wobbling strength. Any other innocent facing the kind of debauchery he was tempting her with would likely flee without a backward glance. And yet Miranda stared at him with a power in her stare that hit him straight in the groin and made his erection even harder.

The other feeling was worse. Relief. He was *relieved* that she wasn't going to turn back on their bargain. Like he actually cared about her.

That wasn't possible. He had never cared about the women in his bed beyond a vague interest. He never knew about their pasts or their dreams or their goals. He didn't want to. He gave them pleasure, but that was as close as he cared to grow to them. One woman was interchangeable with the other, so it didn't really matter.

Yet, with Miranda, he didn't just want a warm body in his bed. He wanted her. Just her. At least for now. But the feeling would fade. It had to.

He folded his arms and looked her up and down. He took in the gown she wore, which was too high collared, too long sleeved. Too much fabric, too many frills. A woman like her should be dressing with provocative simplicity. He would love to see her in a gown that clung to her curves. Perhaps without anything beneath it.

Stifling a groan, Ethan mused, "You're wearing too many layers. I want you to remove your clothing."

Miranda stiffened a fraction, but then she acquiesced, lifting her hands to the buttons that fastened the front of her gown. As she slipped the first two free quickly, he shook his head.

"No. Slowly. I want to see you reveal yourself inch by inch. Seeing you undress is a pleasure I want to indulge in."

She hesitated, looking at him with the expression of a scared little rabbit. Her gaze flitted to the door behind him a second time, but she made no move toward freedom. Finally, she pressed her fingers down to the next button of her gown and flicked it open. Her hands shook as she spread the fabric apart, revealing a few scant inches of pale flesh.

Ethan licked his lips as he backed toward a chair beside the fire. He took his place, then motioned for her to continue.

Miranda moved toward him, her hips twitching as she popped the next button. Her expression was still filled with terror, but her body seemed to know what to do, even if those actions revolted against what her mind and propriety said was right. Somehow that made him want her all the more. He could teach her to listen to her body's desires over the voices that whispered to her not to be naughty, not to be passionate.

With a shiver, she opened the last button and spread the fabric wide, revealing an expanse of bare skin and the beginnings of a worn, cotton chemise. Ethan frowned. Clearly the family's financial troubles were deep, since both times Miranda had undressed for him, she had revealed old, threadbare undergarments. That was something he would have to remedy.

"Turn around," he ordered. "And slip your dress off. Slowly."

Miranda hesitated before she turned her back to him. He expected her to drop the gown at her feet in one motion, but instead she peered over her shoulder at him. Their eyes met and

he saw a little flame of desire in the bright blue. As uncomfortable as putting on a show of stripping was to Miranda, on some
dark, hidden level, she liked it. She liked revealing herself to
him, layer by layer.

His cock stirred.

"Take it off," he demanded quietly.

She slipped the gown off one shoulder, sliding it down her
arm at a smooth, slow pace. Ethan straightened up, staring as
she pulled her arm free while holding the bodice of her gown
against her chest. With her opposite hand, she freed her other
arm at the same slow pace.

Her gaze never left his face, bright eyes flickering in the firelight as she stared at him over her shoulder. Then she let the
gown go and it dropped around her waist. She hooked her thumbs
around the waistline and gave a little shimmy of her hips.

The fabric slipped over her body and she released her thumbs,
letting it drop around her feet.

Six

Ethan wet his suddenly dry lips. Miranda's chemise was worn, but it had its benefits. For one, it was too small and clung to her body, showing every single curve of her hips. It was also too short, probably the hem had been mended more than once. But that meant that it fell just to the top of her thighs, revealing the bottom swell of her backside.

"Turn around," he croaked, shocked by how shaky his voice was. How quickly his heart was beating. How hard his cock was and he hadn't even touched her yet. His body was out of control, wild and tense.

Miranda stepped away from her gown and kicked it aside before she followed his order and faced him. Her nipples were hard against the cotton, perfectly outlined by the firelight. The fabric was so worn that he could see the rosy red color through the white. God, he wanted to lick her, suckle her until she moaned and cried out. He was ready to come out of the chair, he was so on edge, so hard and heavy and ready.

Instead, he examined her further. The chemise clung to her stomach and thighs. He could even see the dark shadow of downy hair between her legs through the stretched material. The sight nearly drove him wild, making his cock twitch and his blood burn hot.

"Take it off," he murmured.

Miranda arched a brow and a wicked power came into her stare. "How, Ethan? You have to tell me what you want for me to please you properly."

Suddenly he was in no mood for a show anymore. He just wanted her naked. He wanted her beneath him. Over him. Around him. He wanted her panting and sweaty. He wanted her whimpering and clinging. He just wanted her.

"What would please me is to have that off. Remove it, whatever way is quickest," he growled.

"You just cannot make up your mind." she said softly, with a hint of nervous laughter to her voice. "Remove it slowly, remove it quickly . . ."

Ethan surged to his feet and Miranda drew back two steps, eyes widening.

"Very well," she said, raising a hand to ward him off.

She grasped the edge of the chemise and peeled upward, rolling the tight fabric over her hips, her stomach, her breasts and finally she tugged it over her head and let it drop to the floor near her discarded dress.

Ethan stared, unable to keep from showing all his interest on his face. God, she was lovely. Long, flowing limbs, smooth, soft skin . . . it was like she had been built to his every desire, his every fantasy.

He wanted to touch her. To lock her legs around his waist and rut with her right there on the hard floor. That wasn't like him. Slow seduction and drawn out pleasure had always been his preferred manner. That quiet building of desire was a way of ensuring his partners were at *his* mercy, not the other way around.

It could be no different with this woman. If he lost control and took her like an animal in heat, he would give her far too much power. Even if Miranda was too innocent to know what to do with it, that wasn't a risk he was willing to take. He had to remain calm, focused, detached.

He couldn't do that by touching her. Not now when he felt so close to explosion.

"Go to the bed," he whispered, his voice rough.

A visible shiver wracked Miranda and her gaze shifted away from him to the big bed against the far wall. He'd seen the way she looked at it earlier. Seen the fantasies and questions about what he would do to her slip through her mind like she had spoken them aloud.

He shifted, cock throbbing in time to his racing pulse.

"Go," he repeated.

She did as she'd been told, crossing the room to the empty bed like a woman condemned. When she reached the foot, she held out a shaking hand and brushed her fingertips along the velvet coverlet. Ethan swallowed as she let out a little sigh. She was completely attuned to sensation. Things like the brush of velvet, the swish of cotton, the stroke of silk . . . they could be made tools in his seduction.

He filed the information away for later and said, "Climb up."

She cast a quick glance over her shoulder before she stepped onto the small staircase beside the bed. As she crawled onto the mattress, he caught a brief glimpse of her sex as her thighs parted. It glistened in the soft glow of the firelight, already wet with desire. It wouldn't take much to put her over the edge.

"Lie back on the pillows and spread your legs," he ordered as he came to the foot of the bed. His fists gripped the footrest and he clung tight to keep from throwing himself on top of her and having her without preamble.

Miranda blushed, but didn't hesitate to crook her knees and part her thighs. Now he had a full view of her swollen lips, her hard little clit, the wet slit that was begging to be filled with every motion of her body.

"Touch yourself."

Miranda sat up in surprise and stared at him. "What?"

His fingers tightened on the footrest. "You heard me perfectly well. I said I want you to touch yourself. Pleasure yourself. You *have* done this before, haven't you?"

He expected her to say no. Ladies of her rank were almost always told that their bodies were meant for a man's use and that purpose only. Stupid mothers and spinster governesses told young ladies never to tend to their own desires. That sex was a duty, much like seeing to the day's menus in a great house. Necessary, but not especially pleasant.

"Yes, I have." Miranda turned her face away as heat darkened her cheeks.

"You have?" he repeated, shocked by her unexpected answer.

His erection was so hard now, he felt like he could bang nails with it. He couldn't remember ever being so aroused before. A strange realization considering just what kind of woman he was with.

She nodded, her gaze still focused on any place but his face.

"Show me," he groaned. "I want to see you pleasure yourself."

Miranda's breath came in little shivering gulps as she lay perfectly still for a long, silent moment. Ethan almost thought he had finally pushed her too far and that she would run, but just as he was about to remind her of her precarious position, her clenched fists opened and she slid one hand down to rest on her flat stomach.

Her slender fingers brushed her skin, stroking gently in a downward motion. Lower and lower, inch by inch, as Ethan clenched the footboard harder and harder. He leaned in, staring as her hand stroked her thigh, smoothing the flesh there before she covered her sex with the flat of her palm.

Miranda held still again for a brief moment, panting quietly. Ethan broke his stare from her hand to look at her face and found that she no longer looked embarrassed, but aroused. She stared at him, watching his reaction as she cupped herself. When their eyes met, she held his stare evenly, then lowered her lids and moaned.

Ethan's eyes shot down and he saw that she'd begun to stroke over her pussy. She parted the folds of slick flesh, massaging every one in slow, seductive time. The pads of her fingers swirled over her damp skin, opening and stimulating herself. She sighed as her body relaxed, growing wetter at the seeking touch of her fingertips.

Her clit swelled as she continued to stroke, darkening as it demanded her attention. She brushed over it lightly and sucked in a sharp breath, but then she skittered away. Ethan smiled. She was teasing herself, drawing her pleasure out until she could no longer bear it. That meant she enjoyed this exercise, didn't just do it to relieve her needs.

Damn, but there was a wild vixen trapped inside the shell of this sheltered young lady. A woman of fire and passion and heat. Ethan wanted to draw her out, crush the shell, leave Miranda with nothing but her desires. Leave her wanting and willing.

But as much as he longed to do just that right now, he held back. Her passion was almost overpowering and if he tried to harness it now, it might sweep them both away. He had to be patient. He had all summer to revel in her awakening. To mold her. To introduce her to every vice in his repertoire and ruin her for regular, boring men and regular, boring sex forever.

He almost moaned with the thought. It was going to be so fucking good.

Miranda's back arched as her fingers worked in earnest. She drove her forefinger inside her clenching body while she ground her thumb down on her clit. Moans erupted from her throat as her hips thrust and a slash of pink color arose on her chest.

She wailed out her release, shaking and quivering, her head moving back and forth on the pillow as she came. Then the tremors eased and her body relaxed. Her eyes came open.

When she looked at Ethan, it was almost too much. With a growl, he released the footboard and stalked toward her.

Miranda's breath came in uncontrollable gasps as her aching body began a slow descent from the utter pleasure of release.

She had indulged in such activities before, alone in her bed, especially after she watched Ethan with his paramours and her body was empty and wanting. But her experiences had never been like this one.

Alone, she had been ashamed of her furtive actions. In her mind, she could always hear the echo of other's voices, telling her to never let her body come to shame. To never *want*, to never *need*. Her attempts at self pleasure had been furtive, under the covers, through her chemise.

But this was totally different. Touching herself like this, spread out naked on Ethan's bed of sinful pleasures, while he stood watching her . . . that had been earth shattering. At first she had been embarrassed, yes. But when she saw just how much her desire moved him, it had made her forget her self-consciousness and the rules others had instilled in her. Ethan would never judge her harshly for her desires and right now Ethan was all that mattered.

Feeling and sensation had taken over the moment she surrendered her fears and the explosion she'd experienced was almost as powerful as the one she'd felt when Ethan was buried deep within her body a few days before.

Almost.

She looked up to find him staring at her, but something in his gaze had shifted. Ethan was dangerous now. And . . . out of control.

He was out of control. *She* had done that to him with her little show. A surge or triumph rushed through her, tinged with hope. Perhaps she wasn't entirely out of her element after all.

Ethan let go of the footboard he'd been gripping and started around the bed. All Miranda's thoughts of control fled instantly. In her rush of victory, she had forgotten that an out of control man was often a hazardous man. From the look in his eyes, all Ethan wanted to do was pound into her, take her, claim her.

She shivered as he reached for her, ready for an animalistic, demanding touch. But despite the glow of passion in his dark eyes, when he cupped her shoulders, his fingers were gentle. With a tug, he moved her further down on the pillows and flipped the coverlet around her until her body was wrapped in velvet heaven.

He said nothing as he moved to the center of the room where all this had begun. He caught her long forgotten wineglass in one hand and downed the remaining liquid in a gulp, then poured her a fresh glass.

"Here, drink this," he said, his voice low and rough as he returned to the bed, arm outstretched. "I'll have food brought. I'm sure you're hungry."

Miranda looked at the little clock on the mantel and was surprised by how much time had passed since she left home. It was past the luncheon hour. She had been too nervous to eat breakfast, and even if she hadn't been, that meal was one she'd taken to skipping to scrimp funds. Her stomach rumbled softly at the mention of food.

"But, don't you—" she began, than cut herself off as heat flooded her cheeks.

"Want to fill your body with mine and make you scream?" Ethan asked benignly as he went to the door and rang for a servant.

"Yes," Miranda said, forcing herself not to look away. If he was going to be so blunt, she couldn't be missish in response.

He didn't reply as a servant appeared at the inner door. Miranda couldn't see the person, but the two talked for a moment before Ethan shut the door and returned to the bed. He perched next to her and looked down into her eyes. His stare was intense, like he was trying to read her character, delve into her soul and see her secrets.

She turned away instinctively, unwilling to allow such an intimacy. Ethan growled his displeasure a moment before he bracketed one hand on either side of her head. He leaned over her, his face mere inches from her own. Hot breath stirred her cheek as he cupped her chin and turned it back to look at him. Their noses were an inch apart, his lips were delectably close. But he didn't lean in to kiss her. He didn't touch her at all.

"Miranda, there is nothing I would rather do than fuck you." She flinched at his bluntness and Ethan's frown darkened. "Don't recoil from that word. It is exactly what I want. I don't want to make love to you like a gentleman. I want to spread you wide and pound into you. I want to tie you down and make you beg. I want to lick every inch of your body until you're so wet with need that I almost slide out of you on every damned stroke. That is *fucking* and you shouldn't be afraid of it. It's what you were built for, perhaps more than any woman I've ever met."

Miranda could hardly breathe through the heat that suddenly coursed between them. Her body, still wet from the teasing and pleasure it had been given earlier, sparked to life at his frank, dark words. They should have frightened her, but instead they excited her.

"Then why won't you?" she asked, hating how her voice shook.

He hesitated, but then he pulled away, sitting up so she was no longer trapped. It should have been a relief, but it was a disappointment instead.

"You're not ready for that yet. You hardly understand your own sensuality, you're not anywhere close to accepting mine." He leaned back against his hands and smiled, wicked and filled with promise. "So, for a little while I'll hold back. The waiting will make everything else all the better."

Now it was her turn to frown. As much as she couldn't admit it out loud, she didn't *want* to wait. She wanted him to do all the things he had described as "fucking."

"But—"

"Eroticism is about more than mere taking, Miranda," he said softly, cutting off her protest when he reached into the folds of blanket and found her left leg. He pushed the coverlet aside until it was revealed and let his fingers stroke up the length lazily. "It's about your senses."

The only sense Miranda could concentrate on was touch as Ethan's long, rough fingers glided over the slope of her calf and he cupped her knee.

"To fully enjoy passion, you must use *all* your senses. Sight to watch what you are doing and what is being done to you. And to uncover what you would like to try."

He smiled as he massaged her knee and elicited a gasp from her lips.

"Taste. From the flavor of your lover's skin to the way a grape explodes on your tongue. Touch, to feel not just the way you're filled by a man's cock, but the way your fingers thread through his chest hair or the rough slide of his tongue when it mates with yours. Hearing. The way your lover says your name. The way a moan echoes in a quiet room. Even smell to savor the scent of rose petals as they stroke your skin or the scent of a man who wants you."

Ethan fingers lingered at her knee, stroking a light pattern on her kneecap that had her shivering. She watched him touch her and his words about the senses sunk in. His tanned fingers were dark against her pale skin and the contrast was both shocking and pleasing. His thumb was rougher than his other fingers. When it brushed the inner curve of her knee, it created a cascade of tingling sensations that ricocheted through her entire body.

"First, focus on sight."

Miranda jolted as he pulled his hand away. Now that he was no longer touching her, it was as if a lifeline had been taken. She felt a little . . . lost. Which was very bad.

She watched him walk over to an ornate, carved chest that sat in the corner of the room. He removed a few items from the box and returned to set them beside her on the bed. Books.

"What are these?" she asked, fingering the pages as he crossed over to the door and opened it. When he turned back, he was carrying a tray with a plate covered in food. Miranda's stomach rumbled at the faint mingled scent of sharp cheese and light fruit. Again, she thought of Ethan's admonishment to use all her senses to uncover the true nature of eroticism. Who knew sandwiches could be so sensual?

"Look at them." He motioned to the books as he placed the

tray on the bed next to her. "Study them. Be aroused by them. Be shocked by them. I will even leave you to do just that for a while."

"What?" Miranda asked, forgetting the books when Ethan leaned down to press a far-too-brief kiss against her forehead.

"I don't want you influenced by my preferences." He smiled, wicked. "At least, not yet. I shall return in a while."

Before she could argue, Ethan left the room and shut the door behind him. Miranda stared at the barrier now between them as she heard the second door shut in the distance. She had come to be seduced and debauched and he left her with food and books and her own hand! It put her on her head and left her reeling.

Damnable man!

With a sigh of frustration, she propped herself up on the pillows, popped a grape between her lips and sinfully savored the explosion of flavors on her tongue as Ethan had instructed, then she opened the first book. What she saw nearly made her upset the tray.

It was an erotic story, complete with detailed sketches to illustrate what she was reading! Miranda flipped through the other books, only to find them to be similar tomes.

Ethan had left her with books to arouse her and make her even more frustrated and achy for his touch. Miranda scowled. Here she was trying to keep some control over the situation, but he didn't do the things she expected.

Still . . . she looked at the food and then the book in her hand.

What was the harm in just looking? Perhaps she would learn more skills to use in her arsenal.

★ ★ ★

Ethan stood in the darkened outer room that led back to the bedroom where Miranda waited for him. He stared at the door, hand outstretched, but didn't enter. Not just yet.

It had been two hours since he gave her a pile of his extensive collection of erotic works and left her to explore on her own. Oh, he'd given her some long explanation about awakening her senses and learning her hidden desires, and that *was* part of why he had done it. But there was another part. A troubling part. A part he'd been trying to forget ever since.

Something about this woman erased his control.

That had been his only constant for years. Control. The only thing separating him from being casually debauched and the total animal his father had been. Ethan knew he couldn't avoid his predilection for sin and sex, those desires were in his blood. His father had reminded him of that fact regularly.

But Ethan knew just as well that if he allowed it, those desires could consume him. Change him. Make him unable to choose and steal whatever thin veil of respectability he continued to cling to.

Who would have guessed his desires would overwhelm him in the package of a slender, poor, country miss?

It was ridiculous.

He shoved the door open with a bit more violence than he had originally intended and stepped inside. Immediately, he came to a halt.

Miranda lay on the bed, but she wasn't reading. She wasn't waiting to tempt him with innocent passions. She was curled up, sound asleep.

The velvet coverlet was still around her, though it had slipped down to reveal one small breast. Her long, lithe leg was crooked on the outside of the cocoon she had created for herself.

She made a delightfully erotic picture, lying there like that. Like something out of a legend, where a god found an innocent waiting for him and took her.

That's what Ethan should have done. Awakened her with deep, lush kisses starting from her parted lips and leading down, down to a much sweeter place.

But he didn't. Slipping up beside her, he picked up one of the books he'd left for her. It was open to the spot where she'd been reading before she fell asleep. A part in the story where a man was taking his willing partner right out in the open, daring to be caught, exposed.

He shook his head. That was one of his favorite fantasies. One he had acted out more than once in various public areas on this very estate. Perhaps he would do the same with Miranda. Later.

Hesitantly, Ethan reached for her. With the back of his hand, he brushed a lock of blonde hair away from her face. She smiled in her sleep at the touch.

So damned innocent. So sweet. Those things had never appealed to him, yet he was moved by them now. An ache started deep down inside of him, one he hadn't felt since he was a boy, watching his mother sob into a bottle of wine. He had wanted to help her then and he couldn't.

He wanted to hold Miranda now and he shouldn't.

Instead, he backed away. And left her to her sleep and whatever dreams she was having.

Seven

"Miranda, what in heaven's name is wrong with you?"

Miranda jumped at her mother's sharp question. Shaking off her musings, she looked across the breakfast table with something she hoped resembled a smile.

"I'm sorry, Mama. Just woolgathering."

"You have been doing that very thing for three days," Dorthea grumbled as she slathered butter across her toast.

Miranda shrugged halfheartedly and that seemed to appease her mother, as she turned her attention to Beatrice and Winifred, who were sitting on the opposite side of her. Miranda sighed.

Yes, she *had* been doing "that very thing" for three days. Since her first full day at Ethan's home.

She shivered slightly at the thought. How could she have fallen asleep in that den of sensuality he had created? Yes, she had been exhausted since her father died and she had taken up the task of juggling her family's troubles. And that bed had been so luxurious and comfortable. Lounging about in the middle of the day, indulging in decadent food and wicked reading . . . it had made her forget her troubles. Allowed her to relax.

But what a ninny Ethan must think she was. That had to be why he hadn't come back and claimed her.

Oh, he had been kind enough the next morning. He'd kissed her cheek before she left and whispered that eroticism was often also about waiting and wanting.

Well, she'd been *waiting* and *wanting* ever since! And wondering if Ethan was even interested in her any longer. Had he already bored of her?

Why wouldn't he? She certainly wasn't sophisticated like his former lovers had been. She might have seen some of the wicked things he liked, but she had no skill at them. Perhaps he hadn't been as aroused by her little show of undressing as she thought. Or he already regretted the bargain they made after she failed his expectations so completely.

As their mother chattered in the background, Penelope reached over to place a hand on Miranda's knee beneath the table. She jumped at the touch and her sister's eyes widened at the way her body jolted.

"Dearest, you do seem very distant since you returned from Lady Ingleworth's," her sister whispered, casting a quick glance at their mother to make sure she wasn't eavesdropping. "Did the old dragon give you trouble?"

Miranda flinched. Lying to her mother was difficult enough, but doing so to Penelope was torture. Being only two years apart and having a similar disposition, they were friends as much as sisters. And now Miranda was keeping so many secrets from Penelope that she could scarce keep them all straight in her mind.

"No, I apologize if I've been distant." She squeezed her sister's fingers for reassurance. "My visit was . . . educational, if nothing else."

"Educational?" Penelope repeated, wrinkling her brow. "Whatever do you mean?"

Before Miranda had to explain herself, their butler entered the morning room. He stopped in the doorway with a small bow and announced, "A letter for Mrs. Albright, from the Earl of Rothschild."

The table fell into silence for a moment as all five women stared at the servant. The others seemed surprised, but Miranda's heart leapt into her throat. Why was Ethan writing to her mother, who he had made clear he felt nothing but disdain toward on more than one occasion?

Dear God, was he going to expose Miranda for a wanton?

Nausea churned as she watched her mother stagger to her feet and reach out her hand.

"The Earl of Rothschild? To me? Give it here, Adams!"

The butler sighed almost imperceptively and allowed the letter to be snatched from his fingertips before he exited the room. Miranda's mother threw herself back into her chair and stared at the letter, addressed in Ethan's large, even scrawl. Lazy handwriting with lazy elegance. But an underlying strength.

Miranda rolled her eyes. Dear God, she *was* obsessed with the man if she was reading his personality into his handwriting, of all things.

"Why in the world would *he* be writing us?" her mother muttered as she flipped the letter over and broke the seal. "Wicked, wicked man."

Penelope laughed. "A *wicked, wicked* man whose parties you and father attended every single summer."

Their mother shot a pointed glare in Penelope's direction. "Your sister is a bad influence on you, for she said exactly the same thing to me! And as I told her, I don't have to like the man to benefit from his position in society."

Miranda shut her eyes and stifled a sigh. Her mother had always been such a social climber, trying to find any opportunity to elevate their family's position. Though she didn't want Dorthea to uncover the truth, Miranda almost wondered what her mother's reaction would be if she knew the bargain that had been entered into on her sisters' behalves.

Would her mother even care that she'd sold herself if it meant a chance at a good marriage for Penelope or Beatrice or Winifred?

Then again, perhaps she didn't want to know.

"Oh!" her mother gasped as she read the letter.

Miranda's heart sank as she tried to decipher her mother's shocked expression.

"Oh, girls! Listen to this!" Her mother got to her feet and began to pace around the room, reading out loud. "'My dear lady, it has recently come to my attention that I owed your late husband a kindness I was unable to repay before his recent passing. Therefore, I feel it is only right to make reparations to his remaining family. I would like to offer you my assistance, both financially and socially, in providing a Season to your second eldest daughter, Miss Penelope. If this would be agreeable to you, please send word to me here at my estate. Yours, Rothschild.'"

Miranda let the air out of her lungs in a burst as relief shot through her body. He hadn't revealed their arrangement. Thank God.

The relief was followed close behind by confusion. Why had Ethan already offered to sponsor Penelope?

She was jolted from her musings when the room erupted in feminine squeals and chatter. Her mother let out a whoop more befitting a schoolboy than a lady and her two youngest sisters began talking at once, prattling on about gowns and balls and whether they, too, would find sponsors.

"There now, Miranda," her mother said with a triumphant glare in her direction. "You may cease your constant haranguing about our financial position. The *dear* Lord Rothschild will take care of us."

"A moment ago you were condemning him as wicked," Miranda said mildly as she set her napkin aside and pushed away from the table. She paced to the large set of streaked windows that looked down over the gardens.

"I said no such thing!" her mother snapped. "And even if he is, what do we care? His money and connections will surely give your sister better luck in her Season than you experienced in yours."

Miranda clenched her fists and kept her gaze focused firmly outside. Her mother's hypocrisy was difficult to stomach, but she was in no position to cast stones.

Penelope cocked her head. "But I don't understand this, Mother."

"He is offering to sponsor you, ninny!" her mother laughed. "What more could there possibly be to understand?"

"But why?" her sister pressed, reaching for the letter that still dangled from their mother's fingers. "He says he owed Father a 'kindness'. Does that mean he was in our family's debt? If so, why doesn't he just give us financial reparation? Hosting a Season seems like an almost limitless expense, not to mention a social imposition." She turned to Miranda expectantly. "Did you find such a debt owed to Papa when you went through the records?"

Miranda turned slowly to stare at her sister. She could almost feel the lies beginning to bubble on her lips and they were bitter, indeed.

But before she had to speak them, their mother interrupted by snatching the letter away. "Who gives two figs about the circumstances? You shall have a wonderful Season, Penelope! That is all that matters, so don't argue the point."

Penelope didn't seem moved by that statement. "I simply wonder at the cost. Lord Rothschild has never been close to our family and he is certainly not known as giving."

Miranda stepped forward, driven to defend Ethan against her sister's condemnation. Especially considering how "giving" he had been to her in their last two encounters, always thinking of her pleasure before his own. And not even taking his the last time.

"Yes, he is!"

The room fell silent for a second time, but it was Miranda who everyone was staring at this time. Even her mother, who was mostly studying Ethan's letter with a focused smile, wrinkled her forehead in confusion.

"What are you talking about?" Penelope asked, her hands

coming to her hips. "You have only met the man a few times, yourself. And you know his reputation!"

Miranda shifted, silently berating herself for her outburst. She had no need to defend Ethan and the action only foolishly brought attention to her.

"I-I only mean that he must be generous in some fashion or he wouldn't have made such an offer." She shrugged and kept her gaze away from Penelope's. Her sister could read her too well. "I agree with Mother. Perhaps it's best not to argue or explain away this unexpected gift, Penelope. We must accept it and try to make the most of this Season he wants to give you."

Penelope stared at her like she had sprouted a second head. "You *agree* with Mother?" she repeated blankly.

Beatrice chuckled. "This is a first."

Even Winifred looked incredulous.

"It's the first sensible thing she's said in months," her mother sniffed. "I must begin making arrangements. There will be new gowns to order, we must find a flat in London for the Season. Oh, it shall be beyond wonderful!"

"Mother!" Miranda threw her hands in the air. They'd had the promise of money for all of two minutes and already her mother had spent it all and then some. "We do not even know how much he intends to—"

Their mother waved her protests off and made for the door. "Come along Penelope, Winifred, Beatrice."

Her younger sisters followed immediately, but Penelope stayed where she was, continuing to stare at Miranda with an incredulous expression. Miranda fought to keep her own countenance free of any emotion. The last thing she wanted was for Penelope to ferret out the truth. No doubt her sheltered sister would be shocked if she knew the lengths Miranda had gone to.

"I'll be along in a moment, Mama," Penelope said softly. "I wish to talk to Miranda first."

"There is so much to do. Don't be long!" their mother ordered before she swept from the room and left the two older sisters alone.

Penelope tilted her head. "Did you know of this before Mama received Rothschild's missive?"

Miranda's eyes went wide. "Of course not, why would you believe that?"

"Your reaction, Miranda! You *agree* with Mother, who dashes headlong into all circumstances without thought for the consequences? Surely you cannot think Rothschild will host this Season without expecting *something* in return." Penelope shivered. "Remember what Mr. Stephanson wanted."

Miranda winced. He was the man who had asked for their youngest sister, Winifred, in order to repay the debt their father owed him. Even their mother had not been ready to stoop so low.

"Lord Rothschild is not anything like that . . . that . . . " She bit back a slew of curses. "That *person*. If the Earl says that he owed father something, why not allow him to repay it in this fashion? It will solve so many of our concerns."

Her sister shook her head and worry was bright in her eyes. Miranda sighed. Penelope was only thinking of the family's good with her protests and Miranda could hardly blame her. In any other situation, she would have been asking the very same questions.

If only she could explain, but that wasn't possible. Her sister would be horrified if Miranda admitted the truth.

She took her sister's hand instead. "This is what I want you to do, Pen."

Penelope smiled at the childhood nickname. "What, Mir?"

"Take this Season you're being offered. Enjoy every last moment of it. Dance. Laugh. Maybe even fall in love, if you can—though if you can fall in love with a rich man, it would be better."

Penelope laughed.

Miranda's smile fell a little. "Whatever you do, don't worry yourself about Lord Rothschild or anything else. Let *me* take care of him."

Her sister sighed. "Just be wary of the price he wants us to pay for his 'kindness'. It may turn out to be too high, Miranda."

With that, her sister pressed a brief kiss to her cheek and slipped from the room, leaving Miranda to rub her hands across her temples. In just a few days, she would be back at Ethan's home, paying the price Penelope had mused about.

That was, if Ethan even still wanted her. If he didn't, that might be the highest price of all.

Ethan paced his chamber, hating how his gaze slipped to the clock on his mantel. Time seemed to inch forward, tormenting him with every tick of the seconds.

It was Friday.

Normally, the days of the week were meaningless to Ethan, especially in the country. But now, in short order, Friday had taken on a different meaning to him. It meant Miranda.

Never before had he been so obsessed with a woman. Especially one who he had only been with once in over two weeks. Normally, he would have been with his mistress a dozen or more times already. In fact, he would already be bored and restless, driven to more and more outrageous sex to slake his desires and hold his interest.

But Miranda . . . Miranda was different. She had been on his mind every moment, every hour since she left just a week ago. He found himself wondering what she was doing or who she was with. What she was wearing and if she was thinking of him.

Those wandering thoughts often came up at the most inopportune moments. While doing some business with his estate manager, for example. Or during a visit with an old friend who had passed through the shire a few days earlier and commented on Ethan's shocking lack of companionship. Even an offer to visit a local courtesan had held no appeal to him. Not when compared to Miranda.

He didn't want this need to be with *her* more than any other woman. He didn't want this . . . this strange caring about her welfare. And today he would regain control over his emotions and her body.

His door opened and Winston put his head into the room. "Miss Albright awaits you in the, er, *other* chamber, my lord. Will you require anything this morning?"

Ethan's blood roared hot at the fact that Miranda was here in his home, waiting for him in the room he'd built for sex and sex alone. God, he wanted to touch her. Taste her.

"Privacy," he said as he marched to the door and past the butler. "All we shall require is privacy unless I call for you."

He didn't hear Winston's reply over the rush of blood in his ears. His body and mind were too occupied with getting to Miranda to pay attention to anything else.

He thrust open the outer door to his special chamber and came to a halt at the inner one. Calm. Control. He had to remember those things. He could have his pleasure and he intended to do just that. But he couldn't let Miranda's innocence corrupt him, for lack of a better word.

He threw open the door, letting it fly back to collide against the opposite wall. Miranda was standing in the middle of the room, staring at the bed, but she jumped at the loud crash of wood on wood and spun to face him.

Ethan took a deep breath as he stared at her.

He had always been the kind of man who found himself crossing rooms to speak to women who were blatant. Even the proper widows who had graced his bed had all been daring in their attire. Low necklines and bold colors were normally his siren song.

But with Miranda, things were different, as seemed to be the theme. Here she stood, surrounded by black velvet and tools of sex, yet her demure sensuality attracted him more than anything else. She wore an icy blue gown that matched the stunning color of her eyes, but it wasn't the kind of outfit meant to summon men to her side. The neckline was fashionable, but didn't reveal her cleavage. The fabric wasn't sheer in any places, nor did it scream out to be touched.

So why did her mere appearance make his erection spring to life?

Perhaps it was the very fact that her gown *didn't* proclaim her intent and desire. She wasn't on display for any man to ogle at. She was his. *He* was the only man who knew what her breasts looked like as her gown fell away from them. The only man to have touched her in an intimate way. The only one who had experienced the searing passion that masqueraded under her exterior of a proper miss.

Those facts were surprisingly powerful.

"Hello, Ethan," she said, tilting her head to look at him.

He realized he had been standing completely motionless, staring at her for at least a full minute.

"Good morning," he managed to say as he pulled the door shut behind him.

Her gaze shifted to the door and he thought he saw *relief* in her expression.

"I admit, I was nervous about coming here," she said softly as she watched him move toward her.

He stopped. "Nervous? Why?"

"Your note to my mother on Monday made me worried that I had displeased you in some way," she admitted after a pause. Her cheeks turned a charming pink as she looked away from him to stare at the floorboards.

He drew back in surprise. "I am living up to my part of the agreement. I offered to sponsor your first sister's Season. That was what you wanted, was it not?"

She shifted slightly and continued to stare anyplace but his face. "Yes, of course, but I have not . . . that is, I've only come here one Friday. I haven't yet earned her Season."

Ethan shrugged. "You have earned one quarter of our arranged price. As long as you continue to come and do as we agreed you would, I see no reason why I shouldn't render my payments as we go." He stepped toward her, unable to keep himself from being near her. "You don't intend to renege, do you?"

Her gaze finally met his and she caught her breath, almost like she'd forgotten what he looked like and was reminded when he came closer. His blood burned as her lips parted on a tiny sigh.

"No, Ethan," she whispered.

"Were you upset when you believed me to be disappointed?" he asked, reaching for her. He caught her forearm and pulled her against his chest, molding her body to his own.

She caught her breath and her pupils dilated with desire. "Y-Yes."

"Because you thought you had lost the chance to help your family?" he pressed as he threaded his fingers into her blonde hair and let the pins holding her style clatter to the floor around her. "Or was it because of some other reason?"

She let out a little whimper as her hair fell around her shoulders in a fragrant wave. "Ethan—"

He cupped the back of her skull and tilted her face up. "Which one was it?"

Her throat worked as she swallowed and he watched the delicate movements in fascination. How could he find her every little activity, even the benign ones, erotic?

"I was upset," she whispered, her voice trembling. "Because I thought you might turn me away if you didn't want me anymore. I was upset because I thought we wouldn't—that we wouldn't—"

"I have, in essence, purchased you for three months, Miranda," he growled as he brought his lips down to the curve of her throat. Her pulse pounded beneath his lips. "I have no intention of turning you away."

He darted his tongue out to taste her flesh and Miranda's hands came up to grip his shoulders as she let out a low moan. The sound was infinitely arousing, a noise of pleasure-pain that echoed the frustration he had been feeling since their last parting a week before. Without words, it spoke of Miranda's desire, her fears, her fantasies.

And it stripped away his intentions to be cool and collected as he took her. Need pounded up behind him like an inferno and he had to have her beneath him. He had to taste her.

He had to do it now.

Eight

Miranda sensed a change in Ethan as his kisses against her throat grew hungrier, wilder. It shocked her that she could be so attuned to him when she hardly knew him at all. It seemed *wrong* to feel any kind of emotional connection to him while understanding nothing about his family or his past or his dreams. The rational part of her told her to pull away, but her body wouldn't allow for that. Instead, she leaned into the curve of his body, arching toward his seeking lips.

"God, you are drugging," he murmured, almost more to himself than to her. "So sweet."

His dark gaze came up and snagged hers. There was so much sinful promise in that one look that her knees began to tremble and she felt the telltale wetness of desire begin to overflow from her shaking body. All that with a look. What power this man wielded over her in such a short time.

"I wonder, Miranda," he said as he backed her toward the settee in the middle of the room. "Do you taste as sweet everywhere?"

"What?" she breathed, hardly able to think, let alone speak when he was tugging at her buttons, pulling her dress away, her undergarments. Leaving her utterly naked.

Her cloudy mind tried to process what he had asked and suddenly it became clear. He wanted to lick her, to taste her just as she'd seen him do dozens of times to other women. An intimate kiss.

He lowered her to the settee, laying her head back against one of the pillows as he dragged her backside to the edge of the couch. He palmed her thighs with his hot hands and they fell apart like she had been born to offer herself to him.

Just as he had the first time they were together, Ethan looked at her for a long moment. She realized how much he *liked* witnessing her arousal, and how much power he took in seeing how wild he could make her.

"A taste, Miranda," he whispered as he dropped to his knees on the floor between her legs. "It will be so good for you, I swear it."

Miranda could hardly manage to give a jerky nod. He had no idea how many times she'd fantasized about this very experience. About watching his dark head dip down between her pale thighs, about feeling his mouth latch on to her pussy.

But he didn't simply press his mouth to her. He leaned in closer and blew a hot gust of breath over her ultrasensitive outer lips. Her body clenched, gripping at emptiness as her already slick folds grew wetter in readiness for the pleasure about to come.

He slid his hands higher until his thumbs brushed her folds. Miranda shuddered and couldn't hold back a moan. She had been waiting for him to touch her ever since the last time they made love. It had haunted her thoughts for days. And now that the moment was here, just the slightest touch made her aching body quiver on the edge of a powerful release.

He stroked her lightly and then peeled her open, exposing her wet slit and the aching nub of her clit. Ethan let out a low curse, so quiet she couldn't make out exactly what he'd said. Then his rough tongue stroked over her opening in one long, languid lick.

Hips arching helplessly at the focused, spiraling sensation, Miranda cried out.

The touch lived up to all her fantasies and more. It was heavenly. So focused. So hot. It was like Ethan had found every part of her body that could experience pleasure and united their attention to one place with his tongue.

The rough texture stroked over her clit, making it swell and tingle with each stroke. She couldn't help lifting to meet each caress, nor could she silence her wanton moans of encouragement. Pleasure spiraled throughout her body, her nerves tingled and her muscles contracted out of control. She could feel release coming, building like a wall before her. And it was going to be intense, it was going to be powerful. She reached for it, longing for the explosion of sensation.

The pleasure crystallized in an instant, overpowering her as her cries turned to screams and her hips rocked helplessly as her body shook out of control. Ethan continued to torment her with his mouth, tasting, licking, sucking until she was weak from release and could hardly move to meet his strokes any longer.

He pulled away, a wicked smile tilting his lips as he stared at her flushed face.

"I could watch you come all day," he said. "In fact, perhaps I shall do just that."

Miranda's eyes widened as he pushed to his feet and shed his clothing with practiced efficiency. When he peeled his trousers away from his cock and it sprung free, she sat up.

As much as she had been fascinated by watching Ethan pleasure his lovers with his skilled mouth, she had wondered what it would be like to do the same to him. Now his erection was right before her, offered up.

She reached for him before he could cover her body, taking him in hand just as she had the first time they were together. He sucked in a breath at the touch and braced his legs apart like he was trying to keep from pitching over.

"Ethan, I want to," she hesitated, uncertain as to how to explain what she wanted to do. "I want to do to you what you just did to me."

His eyes widened and he stared at her like she'd just offered to tup the entire serving staff.

"And what would you know about that?" he asked, watching her swirl her thumb around the mushroom head of his cock. He stifled a groan at the touch.

She swallowed. The last thing she wanted to do was admit her predilection for spying on his sexual exploits all these years. "I-I saw it in one of the pictures on your wall."

That explanation seemed to appease him. "Very well. No teeth, please."

She nodded, but she was no longer looking at his face. Instead, she stared at his erection. He was hot and hard in her hand. His member curled up toward his contoured stomach, a proud declaration of his virile power.

Miranda inched forward, closer and closer, and finally, gently, she stroked her cheek against him.

Ethan bit back a moan as he stared down at her in surprise. Her mouth he had been expecting, perhaps a daring touch of her tongue, but not the caress of her cheek. No woman had ever done that before. The brush of her skin against his cock was so . . . so tender. Sensual, but still personal. And it made him come to attention even more.

Miranda looked up at him and met his gaze briefly. Her blue eyes were bright with wanting and tinged with a bit of inexperienced worry. But there was also determination and hot desire.

Miranda turned her attention back to the work at hand. Darting her tongue out, she stroked it experimentally across the swollen head of his erection. Ethan jerked at the heat of her mouth, the intense pleasure the fleeting touch caused. But it was nothing compared to the explosion of sensation that ricocheted through his body when she wrapped her lips around him and slowly eased him into the hot cavern of her mouth.

She moved gradually, testing out what his girth felt like, taking him in at a painfully slow pace that only served to torment him. If she had been any other woman, he would have believed she was doing that on purpose, toying with him. But not Miranda. Everything she did was so unpracticed, so natural. Like she had been built to pleasure a man.

To pleasure *him*.

She began to withdraw, moving back until he had almost left her mouth, but then she stopped. Her tongue rolled, wrapping over him and back under with a firm pressure that made his vision blur with the absolute ecstasy of her touch. His knees almost buckled and he reached forward and caught her shoulders to keep his knees from going out from under him.

"Was that wrong?" she whispered, pulling away to gaze up at him.

"No," he managed to grind out through clenched teeth. "Perfect. Just do that again, but a bit faster."

She nodded and repeated the action, following his directions about increased speed. Ethan could hardly see through the fog her mouth created in his mind.

A quick learner and an immediate study in seduction, Miranda sucked on him like she knew all the intricacies of a man's pleasure. And if her little vibrating moans were any indication, what she was doing gave her as much pleasure as it brought to him. Which made the act all the hotter since not every woman found enjoyment in the activity. Some of his lovers had even used it as a bargaining chip in the past.

Ethan tangled his fingers in her hair, guiding her strokes with gentle urging as he dipped his head back over his shoulders and savored every sensation.

But as her mouth moved faster and she instinctively added the smooth strokes of her hand, enjoyment turned to something more potent. His pleasure mounted, burning hotter, faster until his release bore down on him like an out of control stallion.

"Miranda," he groaned, tugging back to keep himself from spending in her mouth. "Enough."

She ignored his order, clamping one hand around his backside to keep him in her mouth.

"Miranda!" he protested, though the sound was weak indeed.

She hummed out a noise of pleasure and Ethan groaned, trying desperately to hold back the flood of release, but it was fruitless.

With a harsh, loud cry he lost control and pumped hot. He expected Miranda to recoil from the burst, but she stayed where she was, taking every drop of his essence until he softened and slipped from her lips.

Ethan gasped, trying to catch his breath. As his heart rate returned to normal and his vision cleared, the full ramifications of what had occurred rushed through him. He stared down at Miranda, who had flopped back against the settee cushions with her arm over her face. He flinched. She was probably traumatized, though she had no one to blame but herself. He'd tried to warn her.

"Are you all right?" he asked, his voice sounding strangely stiff and unnatural. He wasn't accustomed to comforting his lovers.

She uncovered her face and looked up at him. While he'd expected tears or shock, instead she smiled. Her face shone with pleasure.

"More than all right. Was I . . ." She hesitated with a pretty blush. "Did I please you?"

He frowned, turning away. Please him? Fuck, she'd nearly take his head off with the intensity of his pleasure. Oh, he'd come like that before, but never because he lost control. He'd always taken great pride in being able to manage when he found release.

But Miranda had swept that all away with a few hot swipes of her pretty mouth. She had taken his control. Again.

He spun on her. "Yes. Quite lovely," he said with a benign smile.

Immediately her cat-in-the-cream grin fell, replaced by an embarrassed flash of hurt.

"Lovely?" she repeated, her face twisting like the word was poison on her lips.

He nodded. "Yes. But I don't think we have anything else to do today. So you may return home."

She stumbled to her feet. "But it's just after noon! I only arrived a few hours ago. I am yours until tomorrow."

He turned away with a frown. That reminder conjured such powerful images of all the things he wanted to do to her. But in every scenario, he couldn't see himself doing anything less than losing control again and again. Taking her, but being unable to keep himself slightly distant from the pleasure.

Worse, he found himself wanting more. Wanting to *talk* to her. Comfort her and make that flash of self-doubt he'd seen in her eyes go away.

Impossible.

"Don't you understand? I don't *want* you here any longer, Miranda," he barked, spinning on her. "Consider today a free day toward your debt!"

She stumbled back like she'd been physically struck and pain flashed so clearly on every single line of her face that it was palpable in the room around them. But then she quietly cleared the pain away. Pushed it back, far back. A familiar thing to Ethan.

He had been practicing the same method for so many years he'd lost count.

She nodded as she reached for her clothing. "Very well, Lord Rothschild. If that is what you desire, I'll go."

Miranda turned her back as she dressed, covering up all the curves he'd taken such pleasure in revealing. Watching them disappear beneath the worn fabric of her gown gave him far less enjoyment than unwrapping her body.

When she had fastened her last button and used the large mirror beside the bed to fix her tangled tresses, she turned back to him. Though she was trying to hide it behind a façade of calm, the muted hurt still sparkled in her stare.

"Good afternoon," she said softly. "Send me word if you do not wish to see me again."

Then she left, without so much as a backward glance.

Ethan stared at the door she'd shut behind her. Self-loathing washed over him, covering everything in a dark cloud of self-directed anger and out-and-out hatred.

He'd hurt her. He shouldn't care that he'd done so. After all, she was just the woman he was sleeping with and he'd never given his lovers' emotional well-being much thought in the past.

But Miranda was different. Which was the problem, after all. Something about her made him want to care. To forget about the past and all the things he knew he was capable of doing that would ultimately destroy a woman like her.

He had to do something about this. Something to regain his power.

He could break the bargain.

A flash of horror rushed through him. No. That wasn't the

answer. He wanted Miranda and the only way to purge that want was to have her until he bored of her. But he couldn't let her natural, unpracticed passions make him lose his head again. The next time she visited him, he would not *let* it happen.

He would become emotionless. He had done it in the past, he could bloody well do it again.

Miranda hurried through the woods until she was certain she was out of sight of the house. Not that she thought Ethan was actually watching her go. He could hardly look at her when she was in the room with him, why would he care enough to stare as she stumbled away?

Humiliation rushed through her. She had been so thrilled by what had happened. She'd *liked* giving Ethan pleasure, feeling his famous control waver. But afterward, his dismissal had been so cold and emotionless.

Tears pricked her eyes, but she blinked them back ferociously. She wasn't going to cry! Not over this. Not after everything else that had happened to her.

In the distance, she saw her own home approaching. She smoothed her gown and swiped a hand over her face. Calm. She would remain calm. Raising the suspicions of her family would only make things worse.

She slipped from the clearing onto the lawn with a smile that felt frozen on her face. She nodded to a gardener, waved to one of the stable boys in the distance. Yes, everything was fine. Everything was wonderful. She just had to get to her room. Once there, she could let all her emotions overwhelm her.

Reaching the house, she opened the door and slipped into

the foyer. The staircase leading to the family quarters was only a few feet away. She just had to sneak across the hall and she would be—

A floorboard creaked beneath her slipper, echoing in the hallway. Immediately, her younger sister Winifred's blonde head stuck out of the parlor and her face broke into a smile.

"Miranda!" she cried, stepping into the hallway to give her a hug. "We thought you'd be with Lady Inglewood until tomorrow!"

"Hello, Winnie," Miranda sighed, making her tight smile all the broader for her sister's sake as she stroked Winifred's blonde hair lightly. "I—er—"

"Miranda is back?" her mother's sharp voice echoed from the room. Miranda's eyes fluttered shut. Damn. "Why in the world are you home so early? You're meant to be with Lady Inglewood until tomorrow!"

Miranda entered the parlor like a prisoner condemned. Her mother sat having tea with Penelope and Beatrice. When Miranda nodded in greeting, her mother's gaze slipped up and down her form with a sniff.

"You made a poor impression on her, didn't you?" Dorthea pressed.

"Your hair *is* a mess," Beatrice offered helpfully, setting her teacup down with an expression of glee. Clearly she knew her comments would only spurn their mother on more.

Miranda gritted her teeth. "Lady Inglewood caught a cold. When I arrived, she was out of sorts and wished to rest, so she sent me home early."

"Just as well. She is probably only laughing at our misfortunes down her nose anyway." Her mother scowled. "Perhaps you shouldn't go back there at all."

Miranda's eyes widened. "Mama, you cannot mean that."

Dorthea responded by folding her arms with a petulant sigh. "Now that we have Lord Rothschild's sponsorship, do we need her airs?"

Miranda's head was throbbing. If her mother refused to allow her to continue her ruse, she had no idea how she would explain her absences while she paid her debt to Ethan.

If he still wanted her. She shoved that thought away with violence.

"We need all the good influence we can get, don't we?" she asked.

Her mother seemed to ponder that for a long moment. "I suppose it cannot hurt to have another potential patron for our cause. For now, I will allow it to continue. But let us not talk about that any longer. Come, sit down."

Her mother motioned to one of the empty chairs, with a look filled with expectation. It was an order, not a request.

Miranda looking at the door with a sense of longing. She wasn't certain she could handle tea with her entire family. Not at the moment. If only the floorboard hadn't creaked.

"Mama, I am tired from my walk. I would like to go upstairs and lie down for a while. After I've rested, I'll be happy to share supper with you all." She searched her mind for some carrot to offer her mother in return for a few hours peace. "Perhaps afterward we could play whist."

She flinched at the thought. She hated playing cards with her mother.

"Posh! You may rest here and have your tea with your family," her mother insisted. "*Sit down.*"

With a shudder, Miranda did as she had been told, too tired and emotional to face a drawn out argument. Penelope stared at her from across the table, concern plain on her face. Miranda struggled to keep her emotions from her expression in the hopes her sister wouldn't press for information on her upset later.

It was a losing battle.

"Speaking of our new sponsor, we were just discussing Lord Rothschild before you arrived," Beatrice said with a grin. "Mama is planning to host a huge ball in a fortnight to launch Penelope's Season."

"A ball!" Miranda repeated and thoughts of her own hurt and confusion fled. "Mama, the cost!"

Their mother glared at her. "It isn't our money, my dear, so don't begin your miserly ways. A ball will be the perfect thing. Your sister will be the center of attention and Beatrice and Winifred will even get to make a showing. We might as well use Lord Rothschild's kindness while we have it."

Miranda shut her eyes with a groan. Her mother might be correct in some ways. After today, her fears about Ethan's intent were back with a vengeance. She hadn't broken her word this time, she hadn't pulled away. But they had never discussed the terms if *he* reneged on their deal. For all she knew, he would tell her never to come back again. If he did, they would all be lost.

Except that wasn't the consequence that troubled her most. If she were honest with herself, the most upsetting part of to-day's events was that she might lose her time with Ethan. She wanted more. More of his touch, more of his body. More of everything.

Stupid, stupid girl.

"Is there any way to change your mind?" Miranda asked on a sigh.

"No," her mother snapped. "This is for the best."

She pushed away from the table. There was no way to contain her frustration any longer, not when she was already on edge. "Then do what you like. I cannot argue with you any more after such a trying day. I will see you all at supper."

She turned from the room, well aware of the gaping stares of her family at her back. She had never been so dismissive of their mother before. It should have made her feel guilty, but she was too emotionally wrung out to feel any more than the humiliation and fear and longing that already gripped her heart.

Trudging to the staircase, she heard footsteps behind her. Turning, she expected to see her mother at her heels, ready to chastise her for her behavior, but it was Penelope who followed her.

Which was actually worse.

"What has come over you, Miranda?" her sister asked in low, concerned tones. "I have never seen you so lost!"

Miranda flinched. Lost. That *was* how she felt.

"I am simply tired," she lied, turning away.

Penelope caught her hand and held her steady. "It is more than that, Miranda! You're my best friend. I can tell when you are troubled and pained and hurt. What is going on? Please, confide in me like you used to."

Miranda yanked her fingers away. "I don't want to talk about it. Just leave it be, Penelope."

"Leave it be!" her sister said with a shake of her head.

Miranda caught her breath as a sudden sob wracked her. "Yes. Leave it be. Leave me be."

Then she spun on her heel and rushed up to the privacy of her chamber.

Nine

Nearly a week had passed and Miranda had heard nothing from Ethan. She waited each day for some kind of sign as to how he felt about her, about their arrangement, about *anything* that had transpired the week before. But he had been tellingly silent.

She paced her room Thursday afternoon, practically leaping out of her skin with the waiting. If she didn't hear anything from him, she had no choice but to go tomorrow just as they had originally agreed. She didn't relish the idea of being dismissed by him in person or worse—she shivered—by one of Ethan's servants, but it was a risk she would have to take.

She'd taken so many in the past few years, what was one more?

The door behind her opened and the lady's maid she shared with Penelope and Winifred, Angelica, entered the room. Beatrice had insisted upon having her own servant and their mother's intervention had allowed their younger sister that foolish expense. Miranda ground her teeth every time she thought of it.

"Good morning, miss," Angelica said with a quick bob of a curtsey.

She had a strange expression on her face, like she was keeping a secret and about to burst with it. Miranda sighed. The servant could get in line, there were plenty of people with secrets in this house and *she* was at the top of that list.

"I think a simple twist will do for my hair today," she said as she took a seat at her dressing table and faced the mirror.

The girl nodded, but made no move to approach and begin her duties. She simply stared at Miranda in the reflection, her lips twitching.

Miranda sighed. There was no escaping it, she supposed. If she wanted to have her hair fixed and help with her gown, she would be forced to ask Angelica about her strange expression.

"What is it?" she asked with a forced smile as she turned back to the servant in her chair. "You look as though you have something to say."

The young woman nodded as she dug a letter from her pocket. Miranda's brow wrinkled. Was she resigning? She was certain the maid's salary had been paid and the girl didn't have to deal with pouty Beatrice. She couldn't imagine either Penelope or Winifred causing her any trouble.

"Miss, I have"—Angelica stopped, chewing her lip nervously before she continued—"I have a letter for you."

Miranda shut her eyes. So she *was* resigning. Perfect. Another item to add to her never-ending list of things to fix. "Won't you give me a chance to rectify whatever grievance you have?"

"Oh, no, miss!" The maid took a step toward her. "It isn't a letter from me. A . . ." she giggled. "A gentleman gave it to me and asked me to deliver it to you."

Miranda was out of the chair before she even realized she'd decided to stand. "A gentleman?"

"Well," Angelica blushed. "The servant of a gentleman."

Miranda snatched the letter from her fingers and turned it over. It was Rothschild's crest that sealed the papers together. Her heart began to throb as she looked at the note, knowing it could contain either her doom or her salvation.

"Thank you, Angelica. Why don't you go and help Winifred or Penelope first and come back for me in a while?" she said without looking away from the seal.

The servant nodded, backing toward the door. But before she exited, she stopped. Her stare was hard enough that Miranda broke away from the note and looked up at her.

"What is it?"

"Miss, I know it isn't my place. But I must tell you to be careful. A young lady such as yourself might not know about what kind of man Lord Rothschild is. I like you, miss. I wouldn't want to see any harm come to you." The servant blushed bright red. "I'm sorry to be so forward, but you've been good to me."

Miranda nodded. She was actually touched by her maid's concern. Though the fact that another person had some knowledge, however vague, about her relationship with Ethan made her heart skip faster with nervousness. The more people privy to her secret, the more likely it would be exposed.

"Thank you for thinking of my well-being, Angelica," she said with a smile. "But you have nothing to be concerned about.

I am well aware of Lord Rothschild's reputation. I would not allow myself to be hurt."

She flinched as she thought of just how hurt she had been since his dismissal, but shoved that away. Deep in her heart, she knew she could expect nothing from Ethan. If she kept a tight hold on that fact, he wouldn't disappoint her when he finished with her and sent her away. It was inevitable, and she would be prepared.

"But Angelica," she continued, crossing the room to take the girl's hand. "It would make things very complicated for me if my family were to discover that he had sent a private note to me through such unorthodox channels. May I depend upon you to keep this a secret, even from my sisters? And certainly from my mother."

The young woman hesitated and Miranda could see her concern was genuine and growing by the moment. But then she nodded.

"Seeing as you're the one who makes sure we're all paid, I'll keep your secret. I wouldn't want you to have any trouble."

Miranda's body went limp with relief and she squeezed Angelica's fingers before she released her. "Very good. Now go and help Winifred. You may come back to me after you've finished with her and Penelope."

With a quick curtsey, the servant left. Immediately, Miranda rushed to the fireplace where she would have the best light and tore open the missive from Ethan. Her hands trembled as she unfolded the sheet of paper.

"'Dear Miss Albright,'" it began and she frowned at the proper address. "'I hope you are not considering backing out on our arrangement. The terms still stand and you have much to lose if you do not come tomorrow at our appointed hour. I expect to see you then. Yours, Rothschild.'"

Miranda stared in shock at the terse, almost threatening words. Here she had been waiting and worrying that Ethan would throw her aside, but instead he sent her such a cold letter that it seemed he didn't even recall their emotional exchange a week before. He acted as if *she* were to blame for their early parting, when *he* had been the one to push her away.

Her emotions began to bubble inside her chest, but they had changed with just a few sentences from him. Where she had once felt regrets, she now felt anger. Nervousness was replaced by indignation. Anticipation with irritation.

How *dare* he? How dare he play with her like a cat with a mouse? How dare he make veiled threats and quiet accusations when she had followed his every direction to the letter?

Well, she was finished with his games. And tomorrow she would make sure he knew it.

"Miranda, did you know that Angelica began with Winifred this morning?" Penelope asked as she pushed her sister's door open and stepped inside. "Are you well?"

Miranda turned from the fireplace with a start, Ethan's letter still dangling from her fingertips. "Penelope, you gave me a fright."

Her sister cocked her head. "I'm sorry. What's that?" She motioned to the missive.

All the blood drained from Miranda's face in an instant and her hands began to shake. "Nothing," she lied, pulling the note behind her back. "Nothing."

Penelope came forward, hand outstretched. "You're lying. What is it? What's wrong?"

Her sister reached around behind her, as if to snatch the note away and Miranda pulled back.

"You needn't concern yourself," she insisted before she tossed the note far back into the fire.

Penelope's eyes went wide at the action and she stared as the note disintegrated into nothing more than ash. Then her gaze moved to Miranda.

"What is *wrong* with you? You have been acting so strangely for a few weeks now. You won't talk to me, you won't explain yourself, and now you burn a letter rather than let me see it." Penelope's voice trembled. "We have never kept secrets, Miranda, not from each other. But now it seems all your life is a mystery to me. I'm afraid for you. Afraid for us. What was that letter? Was it more bad news about Father?"

Miranda shifted. She hated that she was troubling her sister, making her worry, when all of Miranda's actions were designed to reduce Penelope's anxiety and make her life more comfortable.

"Please, Penelope." She gripped her sister's hands in a lame attempt to comfort her. "It is nothing. Let's pretend as if this never happened."

Penelope shook her head and her blue-green eyes grew even darker with increasing alarm. "I cannot do that. Was the letter from one of father's debt holders? Are they threatening you? Trying to make more despicable bargains?"

Miranda swallowed past the bitter taste of one more hateful lie. "Y-Yes. It was from one of father's debt holders. A horrid man who doesn't . . . he doesn't know what he wants."

Penelope backed away and scrubbed a hand over her face. "Let me help you," she whispered. "Let me at least council you so you don't have to do all this alone."

Miranda sighed. "You cannot help me, Penelope. Not with this. But I promise you, the matter will be resolved quickly enough."

Her sister pursed her lips, clearly upset that Miranda refused to allow her help. She couldn't blame her sister. She could well imagine her own upset if Penelope were the one shutting her out after so many years of close friendship. But it was for the best. Her sister didn't need to know what kind of bargains Miranda had made on the family's behalf. She could only imagine her sister's reaction if she ever found out.

Penelope shook her head as she moved to the bedroom door. "Miranda, I know all you do is to protect our family, but I fear you will sacrifice yourself in the process. That is why I know that I must find a good marriage, as quickly as possible. I promise you that I'll succeed and take some of this pressure off of you." She opened the door, but turned back before she departed. "I fear that my marriage will be the only way I get to see my sister . . . my *real* sister again."

"I am your real sister," Miranda protested. "But everything is changing now and I have no choice but to change with it if I am to keep our family together. Sometimes that means doing things that you might not understand or approve of. But in the end, what I do will help us all, I promise you that."

Penelope regarded her for a long moment. "For your sake, I hope you resolve whatever it is that is troubling you. And do it quickly. Nothing, not even the family, is worth seeing you suffer."

Then her sister slipped from the room and shut the door behind her. Miranda stared at the place Penelope had stood with wide, unseeing eyes. Yes, this situation had to be resolved quickly. And she intended to do just that. Tomorrow.

Ethan was sitting in his chamber down the hall from the room where he knew Miranda was waiting. She had been waiting for nearly half an hour by his pocket watch. By now, she was probably pacing, worrying. Wondering.

It was all part of his plan to show her, and himself, that *he* was in control of this bargain, not her. Just as his disagreeable note yesterday had been. And as unpleasant as it was, he would continue to exert that control once he went to her.

He shifted his weight, staring at the door and then his watch again. Just five more minutes and he would join her. The seconds ticked by and he checked the clock.

Four minutes, thirty seconds.

This wasn't control. It was mind-shaking anticipation. If he couldn't keep himself on a leash in his own room, how could he expect to maintain his calm when he actually came face-to-face with Miranda?

"Damn it," he grumbled as he strode to the door, wrenched it open and made his way down the hall to the other chamber. He went inside, thrust his shoulders back and passed through the second door.

He was shocked when, the moment he entered the chamber, he found Miranda waiting for him. Her arms were folded, slipper tapping beneath her faded skirt, her face a cool mask of anger.

Not what he was expecting at all and he came to a sudden

halt at the sight of her. Dear Lord, when she was angry, she was even more beautiful. She wore all passionate emotions best, and he found himself wondering how he could keep her in this state constantly just to enjoy the fire in her stare.

"You," she breathed, one finger coming out to point at him. "How dare you?"

"Make you wait?" he said blandly as he pulled the door shut behind him. "Your time is mine today. I may waste or use it as I see fit."

She shook her head. "I don't give a damn about the time, Ethan. I mean your treatment of me this week."

He arched both brows. "My treatment of you? I don't recall encountering you this week. How could I have offended you?"

She stepped forward, hands clenched at her sides. "Last Friday you sent me out of here like you could hardly stand to see me in your presence. And then you let me linger all week, wondering if I had displeased you so badly that you wouldn't want me back. When you *did* contact me, it was to imply that I might not return and would back out of our arrangement. Well, I am tired of your behavior."

He tilted his head, utterly confused. "What are you prattling on about?"

She gritted her teeth. "Do you want me or don't you?"

He stepped back, surprised by her candor. He liked this bold Miranda, though her question took him aback completely.

"Because if this is all some twisted game you delight in playing, than you can keep your money and forget our bargain. Good day, my lord."

She stalked toward the door behind him, but as she passed by, Ethan snaked out a hand and caught her elbow, drawing her up short.

"It *is* a game, my dear," he said as he yanked her against him. She glared up at him, though he could see the trembling beginnings of desire in her stare. "I never claimed this arrangement was anything but a game."

She yanked against his grip to escape, but he held fast.

"I don't like being your pawn," she all but hissed. Anger came off of her in waves, but there was also desire. "We made all kinds of agreements about what would happen if I refused to fulfill your desires. But what if you refuse to fulfill mine?"

Ethan stared down at her, utterly shocked. "Are you saying you have been left unfulfilled?"

She swallowed hard, but that was the only indication she gave of her nervousness.

"Yes, that is exactly what I'm saying," she said, her voice low and even. "Last Friday you sent me home before I was, er, ready."

Ethan blinked. Not since his first sexual encounter over fifteen years before had anyone complained about his lack of sexual prowess. No woman had ever expressed any displeasure about his performance. Miranda's implication was a slur against the one thing he knew he was proficient at.

With a little growl, he caught her other elbow and brought her flush against his chest. Her soft body molded against him, her warm curves settling into his and setting off a firestorm of reaction in his ready body.

"Well, I shall have to endeavor not to make the same mistake again," he said softly before he dipped his head and claimed her lips.

The kiss was harsh, hard, punishing, but to his surprise the punishment was as much to him as her. Touching her, tasting her, it made his already hard body even more achy and wanting. It certainly did nothing to give him the control he so desperately sought.

He speared his tongue between her lips, driving into her with all the hunger he had been building up for nearly a week. He felt Miranda fighting to keep herself distant, and he gave her credit for as long as she did. She remained stiff for a few swipes of his tongue before her body began to melt against him. Her tongue began to tangle with his.

God, she tasted good. And her touch, which was growing bolder with each encounter, stoked the powerful needs deep within him. The ones that stole his control. The ones that told him that he needed to be deep inside this woman. That he needed to claim her in every animal way possible.

He pushed her backward toward the bed step by step, thrusting his tongue into her mouth the way he'd soon thrust his cock into her clenching sheath. But before he could reach their destination, she pushed against him with a groan.

"No, no. This is just part of your game," she whispered, her voice harsh and low with desire. "You're toying with me."

He nodded as he continued to back her against the bed. "I intend to toy with you, Miranda. And by the time I'm finished, you'll take back what you said about being unfulfilled. I'll have you begging me before you leave here tomorrow."

Her eyes widened and she pushed back harder. "No—"

He cut her off with another kiss as he lifted her onto the bed and quickly covered her body with his own, pinning her down with his weight. She arched, fighting him, but he could feel her body's surrender even as she struggled.

He broke the kiss. "Still no? Now who is playing games? Your pretty little mouth says no, but the rest of your body says yes."

"No," she whispered, but she stopped lifting against him. Her stare held his, filled with confusion, interest, and just the barest tinge of fear.

He flicked the buttons on the front of her dress open and peeled the fabric away. He tugged at her chemise and bared one breast. The nipple was hard, thrusting toward him.

"Look, Miranda." He nodded his head toward her revealed flesh. Miranda's gaze flitted down and a blush darkened her cheeks. He smiled. "As I said, your body says yes."

He rolled his thumb around her nipple before he stroked his tongue across the nub.

"No," she said, but it was on a moan as her eyes fluttered shut.

He continued to suckle at her breast, drawing her nipple into the hot cavern of his mouth as he let his hand slip down the apex of her torso. Her body shook and quivered beneath his fingertips, driving him on until he cupped the mound between the legs. She shivered and her fingers clenched against his upper arms. He bunched her gown up, pulling at the layers of fabric until he managed to slip a hand beneath. He glided his hand up her inner thigh and found the heated slit there.

Despite their battle, she was already wet. Ripe and ready for the taking. He stifled a groan as he stroked her. He wanted so badly just to pull his cock free and plunge into her. Take her until he was spent and satisfied.

But this encounter was about control. Control over her and control over himself.

She moaned, turning her head to the side as his fingers parted her slick folds, seeking the nub of her clit. He found it, stimulating her with his thumb as he worked one finger deep inside her. She fluttered around the digit, her body sucking him further into her depths.

"Still no, Miranda?" he whispered as he let her nipple slip from his lips with a quiet pop.

Her eyes opened and snagged his gaze. Her pupils were dilated with hot want and from the way her body clenched at his fingers, it wouldn't take much to drive her over the edge. But she continued to fight him.

"No," but it was a whimper now. Weak and unbelievable.

"Hmmm," he chuckled. "Well, I won't take you until you admit you want me. Until you beg for my cock."

She shook her head. "I won't."

He curled his finger, stroking over the hidden bundle of nerves within her wet body. Immediately she shivered on the edge of release.

"You will," he promised.

"Why are you doing this?" she choked out as he thrust his finger in and out with a lazy, tormenting rhythm. Her skin was beginning to flush as the pleasure overwhelmed her.

He smiled. "You asked me if I wanted you or not."

Leaning in closer, he nearly let their noses touch. She caught her breath at their suddenly close proximity, but she didn't try to turn away from the stir of his breath against her cheek.

"I want you, Miranda Albright. I want every part of you. I want to make you surrender *everything* to me."

She squeezed her eyes shut. "I cannot. I can't give you everything, Ethan. It's too much."

"There's no such thing as too much," he murmured before he let his lips brush ever so lightly across hers.

She moaned as he increased the pace of his fingers and he took advantage of her open lips to kiss her even deeper. Miranda relaxed a fraction beneath him and it was enough to send her body over the edge.

Ethan was taken off guard by the power of her release. After all her resistance, it seemed that being controlled by him gave her as much pleasure as anything else he'd ever done. Her body pulsed wildly, clinging to him, gushing wet heat over his fingers. Her back arched, pushing her breasts against his chest as she broke the kiss and cried out his name in the quiet room.

She went limp beneath him as her orgasm faded away and he withdrew his fingers from her body. Rolling over so that he was on his side, Ethan looked down at her.

"You've proven your point," she said quietly. "That you can satisfy me. Even when I don't want you to. Are you finished with your games now? May I leave?"

He frowned. "Only if you wish to forfeit the bargain."

He lifted his finger to his lips and sucked the sweet nectar of her arousal away. Miranda's eyes widened, but he also saw her exposed nipple shoot to attention again at the action.

"Miranda, I have not yet begun to prove my point. Or end my games."

She shivered. "What do you want from me?"

"Get up. I want you naked."

She pushed herself to a seated position and looked at him. "You want to watch me strip my clothing off for you again?"

A shudder of lust moved through him at the memory of the first Friday they shared.

"No, Miranda. This time I want the pleasure of unwrapping your body myself."

Ten

Miranda stared at Ethan for a long moment. For the first time since making the bargain with him, she realized just how dangerous an agreement it was. Even when he took her virginity, even when he ordered her to touch herself for his pleasure, even when he sent her away . . . she had never felt so vulnerable as she did now.

He had been forceful when he touched her. Demanding. It should have made her recoil, but being trapped beneath his body and having him draw out her pleasure, almost against her will, had been more arousing than anything she'd ever seen or experienced. And yet that wasn't enough for him. He wanted more. He demanded full surrender.

Even as he fully admitted that everything between them was nothing more than a game.

Well, it was a game she had agreed to play. There was no turning back. Tonight she would experience the full ramifications of being Ethan's lover.

She slipped from the bed and turned to face him. What a sight she had to be with her dress twisted at her waist, one breast revealed, her hair half down around her face. She was certain she looked every inch the wanton. Ethan's eyes narrowed as he watched her and she wasn't certain she liked what he saw.

But then he came down from the bed to stand before her and it became clear. He wanted her. A powerful, driving desire was present in every fiber of his being. It practically poured off of him in the form of body heat. It surrounded her and made her body ache with renewed desire.

Miranda shivered, waiting for whatever would happen next.

He reached for her and she steadied herself, ready for him to simply grab and take. But instead, his fingers threaded through her hair, finding the pins and loosening her locks until they tumbled down around her shoulders and her back.

He grasped a lock and brought it to his nose, where he drew in a deep breath.

"Lovely," he murmured, then brushed her hair away.

He slid his hands beneath her dress and eased the fabric down. It swished to the floor and left her in her cockeyed chemise.

"You need new undergarments," he said softly. "New gowns. You should use some of the money for your sister's Season to buy things."

Hot blood flooded Miranda's cheeks. He'd commented on her clothing before and it was something that embarrassed her, certainly. Of course she wanted gowns and chemises and slippers. There was a point when she loved wearing pretty things and fussing over her appearance. Over time, though, she had come to accept that what she wanted really didn't matter. Not until her family was settled.

She shrugged. "It is tempting, but I can't. My time has past. The money must go to Penelope now. No one will be looking at me, at any rate."

Ethan let out a bark of laughter as he hooked his fingers under the straps of her chemise. "If they don't look at you, they're fools."

"You never looked at me," she whispered, her voice cracking as he pulled her chemise down around her waist and then pushed it over her hips to leave her naked.

He shook his head and his hungry stare moved over her body before he met her eyes. "I told you before, I always noticed you. Always."

Something came into his face. Something she'd never seen before and she wanted to turn away from the intensity she didn't understand.

"And you should look, too," he said, placing his hands on her shoulders and turning her around.

She found herself facing the big mirror along the wall beside the bed. The one whose frame she'd found so stunning her first day in this room. Now it was the reflection that shocked her.

There she was, utterly naked, her skin still flushed from desire and release. And if that wasn't astonishing enough, behind her stood her ultimate fantasy: Ethan Hamon. His big body was visible around her and his tanned hands stood out in stark contrast to her pale skin.

"Look at yourself, Miranda," he said, leaning close to her ear.

The sight of him moving in toward her was erotic and her body grew wet in response. She saw her nipples become hard.

She blushed and tried to turn away. "I can't."

"Look," he ordered, holding her steady. His voice was so gentle, so seductive. "Look."

One hand slipped away from her shoulders and she watched, mesmerized, as his fingers caressed her collarbone then lower to swoop across her chest, then cup one breast. She couldn't stifle a moan at the sensation and the sight. Together they were almost too much. Her knees began to tremble, but he held her steady and upright as he continued his wicked torment.

His hand kept roving downward, stroking over her stomach until her sensitive skin pricked and tingled with every touch. She tensed in anticipation, not able to look away as he cupped her mound. She leaned back against his chest with a heavy sigh of pleasure.

"No man could look at you and not picture doing this," he whispered, his breath coming harsh against her neck as he parted her folds and revealed her wet sex in the mirror image.

He fingered her gently, letting her see her body's reaction even as wild sensations raced through her, heating her blood and melting her bones with intense pleasure.

"No man could look at you and not picture doing more," he added before he slipped his fingers from her sheath and backed away.

She watched him in the mirror, trying desperately not to beg. He'd said that he would force her to ask for his cock and she didn't want to give him that satisfaction, though it took enormous effort not to do just that. Her body practically hummed with desire, with the need to feel him buried deep within her. It was all she had wanted for three long weeks and she wasn't certain she could take one more denial.

He dragged a chair over before the mirror and turned it slightly sidewise so that whoever was sitting in it could see the reflection perfectly. Then he motioned to the cushion.

She hesitated, meeting his gaze with a questioning one.

"Sit," he ordered, though there was no cruelty or anger in his tone. "Please."

She had no choice, so she did as she'd been told. It was a strange thing to see herself sitting primly in a chair when she was utterly naked. Especially since Ethan remained fully clothed as he stared down at her.

He took her off guard by dropping to his knees before her. He parted her legs before she could question or resist him and spread her wide. Despite the fact that he was in front of her, the way he'd positioned the chair gave her a clear view of the scene in the mirror. She stifled a moan at the vision of him leaning in toward her clenching pussy.

He puffed hot breath over her trembling lips and she arched toward him with a helpless cry of need. Her eyes squeezed shut at the intensity of the pleasure.

"Look," he ordered again. "Or you get nothing."

She forced herself to open her eyes and watch in the mirror. Ethan slipped his hot hands beneath her backside and lifted, dragging her down a fraction and bringing her to within easy access of his lips.

He met her gaze in the mirror. "Watch."

She gave him a few jerky nods and gasped as he brought his

mouth down on her. What had only been an exploration of sensation before was now an erotic vision like those she had secretly witnessed in the past. Only this was so much better because she could *feel* while she saw. She could touch Ethan and be touched in return, not just fantasize about him.

His tongue danced across her, finding every single place where pleasure could be brought. She watched as her clit swelled beneath his skillful mouth, her folds flushed and her slit grew slick and ready for more than just his tongue.

She tangled her fingers in his hair and was stricken, yet again, by the contrast of her pale skin against his dark locks. It seemed those were their predestined roles in their encounters. Light and dark. Innocent and skilled.

He sucked her clit and she arched helplessly, crying out as intense pleasure spiraled to the edge of control. Just as she felt herself begin to fall, he pulled back, keeping her from release.

"Beg, Miranda," he rasped, his lips vibrating against her body. "Tell me you want me."

She clenched her fingers into fists in his hair, lifting her hips silently as a plea. He ignored it, holding her steady and only coming in for the occasional, teasing nip against her quivering flesh.

"Tell me," he repeated.

"I want you," she cried, her breath bursting from her lungs in loud gasps.

He smiled and stroked his tongue over her as a reward. "What do you want?"

"I want you—" Her voice shook. "Inside of me. I want your . . . cock."

She flinched as the word left her lips. She'd never said it out loud before. It gave her a naughty thrill to be so bold.

"Thank God," he muttered as he got to his feet, pulling her with him as he went.

She staggered on shaking knees, but he caught her, keeping her upright as he maneuvered the chair so the back was to them instead of the cushion. He turned her until she faced the chair.

"Hold on," he said as he pressed a hot kiss against the back of her neck. "And watch."

She grasped the back of the chair and looked over her shoulder at him. He was shedding his clothing. First his linen shirt, then he toed off his boots, then his trousers fell away. She sucked in a breath, awed once more by how alluring his body was. How hard and masculine in all the right places, but especially the steely erection that curled upward, announcing his desires perfectly.

He positioned himself behind her and tilted her face for a hot, probing kiss against her lips. She melted into that kiss, clenching the chair back with trembling hands. He opened her legs a fraction and she felt the swollen head of his cock against her slick opening. He rubbed it back and forth over her slit and she groaned.

"Ready?" he whispered as he placed a hand on her back and urged her to bend over.

"Yes," she whispered.

Before she fully got the affirmation out, he entered her. This time there was no pain. Only tight, hot pressure as he filled her, took her, claimed her. She gasped as he pushed in all the way until his balls hit her backside. She felt wanton and womanly as she clenched experimentally around his girth.

"Fuck," he ground out, his fingers digging into her hips. "Keep doing that."

She obliged, squeezing and releasing as he began to pull back. He slammed forward and she cried out as her body spasmed around his.

"Look in the mirror," he panted. "Look at how beautiful you are."

She turned her head and started at what she saw. Her blonde hair fell around her shoulders and the chair. Her face was flushed and reflected all her pleasure. She looked wicked and desirable bent over the chair with this man, this handsome, complicated man, behind her. When he pulled back, she saw the hard stalk of his erection glistening from her arousal and it was the most erotic thing she had ever seen.

Her orgasm exploded almost immediately. She cried out, slamming back against him with as much speed and strength as he pounded into her. His hands came around to cup her breasts and his face contorted with his efforts to remain in control as he took her. But it was a losing battle. As her release roared on, she saw the moment he found the peak of his own pleasure. He groaned, long and low, his back stiffened and she felt him pump hard and hot into her body as the last tremors of her release faded to mere pleasing twitches.

Miranda sighed at the feel of his weight across her back, of his cock still buried within her. She looked at them in the mirror, both spent from pleasure, tangled up in each other and wondered at how right the image looked.

And how brief it was destined to be.

★★★

Miranda smiled as Ethan put a tray of food on the bed between them. It was overflowing with fruit, cheese, sandwiches, a meal fit for kings.

"Eat," he ordered with a grin as he grabbed a sandwich. "You need to keep your strength up."

Her stomach growled as she popped a grape into her mouth. "You're not done with me yet, are you?" she teased.

His face grew serious and he leaned over to press a brief, hot kiss against her lips. "Not even begun."

She shivered as he leaned back against the pillows and crossed his bare ankles. He was wearing a black silk robe, while she was wrapped only in satin sheets. It reminded her of the first afternoon she came to this hidden room. Only this time, Ethan seemed to have no interest in abandoning her to wicked fantasies. She hated to admit it, even to herself, but she was glad of that fact. The idea of him leaving her now actually caused her physical pain. After the intensity of their earlier encounter, she needed his presence.

He rolled onto his side and leaned on one elbow as he polished off his sandwich in two big bites. "Does your mother ask you many questions about your time with 'Lady Inglewood'?"

She flinched at the question and set her own sandwich onto her plate with a sigh. "My mother doesn't ask me about anything unless she thinks she can obtain something from the answer."

"She *is* mercenary," Ethan growled before he grabbed a grape and popped it between his lips.

Miranda sighed as thoughts of her mother invaded her mind. She felt a strange urge to explain Dorthea, explain herself. "She wasn't born into the same class that my father inhabited, you know. She spent most of her life on the outside looking in. Maybe . . . maybe her behavior is just her way to cling to what she fears she'll lose if she doesn't strangle it with her grip."

He shrugged and a frown creased his lips. "It does you credit that you can be so fair-minded toward a woman who has done nothing but berate you." Miranda's lips parted and he met her gaze. "I told you I watched you, didn't I? I've heard what she said to you. Her whisper is not very effective."

Her face burned with embarrassment. "No, it is not."

"You are nothing like her, though," he said softly and lifted his fingers to brush them along her jawline. Miranda caught her breath, but the touch was brief. He dropped his hand away. "I don't even know how you could possibly be related to her."

With a shrug, Miranda stared at her sandwich with unseeing eyes. No one had ever talked to her about her family like this and really made her think about their ways. "You don't like her, I know. And she can be difficult to handle, I admit. But I think we are very alike in many ways."

He snorted. "How?"

"We're both willing to go to great lengths to protect our family. Perhaps not for the same reasons, but the results are similar." She glanced at him to find him staring at her, a pensive expression on his normally relaxed face.

"She manipulates, though, and you don't," he said softly.

She sighed. "A manipulation is only a twisted lie. And I've been lying aplenty lately."

He shook his head. "No, a manipulation is a game with the prize being winning your objective by any means. There is a huge difference."

She didn't answer for a long moment. Ethan was the master at games, manipulations. He admitted freely that the bargain between them was a game. *She* was a game to him. A prize to be won and played with until he bored of her. She knew that, but the idea still stung.

Especially since currently she felt close to him. This conversation was perhaps the first *real* one they'd ever had. And she liked it. She liked being able to speak openly to a person who wouldn't judge or scold her.

With a light laugh to play off her suddenly somber mood, she said, "She's having a party, you know. This coming week."

He took a sip of wine. "I know. I received an invitation this morning before you arrived. According to her flowing prose, *I* am to be the guest of honor." He shuddered.

Miranda couldn't help but laugh. "Yes, my mother is quite taken with you now that you're assisting us financially. I'm sure she'll fawn over you all evening."

He downed the remainder of his wine in one swig. "Dear God, now I wish I hadn't accepted the invitation."

She giggled at his twisted, pained expression. "Oh, of course you must come. Drink the wine, appreciate the orchestra. After all, you're paying for it."

Ethan's expression went from a playfully pained one to a truly pained one for a brief instant. His frown drew down and he looked at her evenly.

"No, Miranda. I believe it is *you* who are paying," he said softly.

She tilted her head to look at him. Although his face was now unreadable, she could have sworn she heard regret in his voice.

But that was impossible. The Earl of Rothschild lived his life with no regrets. She'd heard him declare that fact many a time while she spied on him. He did what he did and dealt with the consequences, but he never looked back. He never apologized for who and what he was.

But now he looked at her like he wished . . . she didn't know what he wished for. But there was a longing there that she completely understood, even if the cause was unclear. She was familiar with longing.

"Ethan," she said softly, reaching for him. She cupped his cheek. "This is what I agreed to. I can't complain. I don't want to."

He looked at her for a long time, then took the tray and pulled away to set it aside. When he returned to the bed, there was a new look in his eyes and she shivered at its implication.

"Ethan—" she began, but he rolled his body on top of hers, silencing her with a kiss that melted her resistance and aroused her senses. She was confused by his sudden ardor, but didn't fight it. There was no purpose to that anymore. He knew he held enormous power over her.

In truth, she liked that dominance. That he could take any time he liked. That she would grow weak and wanting with just a fleeting touch.

He pushed the sheets away and opened his robe. Instantly, she wrapped her legs around his waist, lifting herself to his cock and moaning against his lips as he slipped inside. Her thoughts melted away and she surrendered to his touch.

Surrendered to him, forgetting any cost. Forgetting everything but how good he felt as he drove her over the edge of pleasure.

★ ★ ★

Ethan sighed as he slipped his arms from around Miranda's body. In her sleep, she let out a little grumble, then arched against him before she rolled over.

Just that little action brought his body to rock hard and ready attention, but instead of taking advantage of her slightly parted legs, he slung the blanket over her naked, tempting backside and got to his feet.

He paced to the fire and stared into the dying flames. Tonight, something had changed between them. Oh, he had succeeded in reclaiming his power over her. He had dominated Miranda, taken her, made her beg even. But then something had shifted.

Afterward, when he normally itched for escape, he had actually enjoyed lying beside her, sharing food and conversation. Thanks to that, he understood so much more about her family. And he hadn't garnered that information just as a weapon in this erotic war, either. He just wanted to *know* her, beyond her body.

That realization should have horrified him, but instead he felt a . . . peace about it. He *liked* Miranda, as much as he lusted after her. And why not? She was . . . interesting.

So long as he recognized the pitfalls to getting too close to her, there was no reason why he couldn't enjoy their affair on every level. And when it was over, he would let go. He was certain of that.

Except, when he turned back to look at her, all that certainty faded, leaving him with only lust and something more troubling that he couldn't define.

Eleven

Ethan caught Miranda's hand and pulled her back into the bed. She laughed as she hit the mattress and the sound pierced into his very soul. It was an uncommon sound, and after hearing more about her life, he understood why. Still, when Miranda laughed or smiled, he couldn't help but do the same. He liked to see her playful side as much as her passionate side.

Well, almost as much. Rolling, he covered her body and kissed her. Her laughter was smothered and the giggles turned to moans.

She allowed him his pleasure for a few, too short, moments, then he felt her pushing against his chest.

"No, no," she protested between groans as he suckled her neck and nipped her earlobe. "My mother expected me home a quarter of an hour ago as it is. If I am too late, she might send someone with the carriage to find me. If they discover I'm not affiliated with Lady Inglewood, all will be lost."

He rolled away with a noisy sigh. "Very well."

She struggled to her feet and returned to buttoning the dress she'd retrieved from her small portmanteau. Another worn gown that wasn't anything like what she deserved to wear. Ethan briefly imagined her in a shocking red satin with a plunging neckline and high waist. Something he could easily tug and reveal her . . .

"Ethan, are you listening?" she asked with a laugh.

He shook off the fantasy, though the raging erection that now tented the sheets wouldn't be erased so quickly. "What is it?"

"I was saying that I shall see you in a few days at my mother's gathering."

He nodded absently as he watched her put her hair up. Her neck fascinated him. Her hair fascinated him. *She* fascinated him and he wished she didn't have to go.

The realization jolted him and he pushed it away with a scowl. It was just lust, of course. Nothing more than lust. Soon it would fade.

Wouldn't it?

Yes, yes. Of course it would. It had always faded before.

"Goodbye," she said as she moved toward the door.

He flew out of the bed before she could leave and caught her arm. Spinning her around, he pushed her back against the wall and crushed her mouth with a kiss that left little doubt that he wanted her. She melted, hips arching against his naked ones, hands clenching at his bare back. Just as the desire became too much, he set her aside with a wicked smile.

"I will see you at the party."

She nodded, dazed, and staggered out. As soon as she was gone, Ethan rested his head against the door with a curse. He should have been pleased that he could so easily control her desire. Control *her*.

And yet, he felt no triumph at conquering her. She might not have known it, but he had been conquered as well. When she spiraled out of control, he had, too. When she begged for his cock, it felt more like redemption than conquest.

And now he was standing by the door like a fool, wondering how he would survive the time before he next saw her.

Well, he knew one thing that would help him pass the time. With a grin, he grabbed for his dressing gown and headed into the hallway to find Winston. He had a plan for Miranda and if he wanted to be ready by the day of the party, he would need to move quickly.

"Do you know how much money Mother is spending on this party?" Penelope asked as she followed Miranda into her bedchamber and shut the door behind her.

Miranda sighed. She'd been home from Ethan's for all of ten minutes and already her Mother had created new problems.

She sat at her dressing table and began to take down her hair. She blushed at her reflection, remembering the last time she saw herself with blonde hair tangled around her shoulders. Ethan had been behind her, driving into her clenching body and forcing her toward powerful, overwhelming pleasure. Even now, her body gave a little quiver just from the memory.

"Miranda?" Penelope said, stepping into the mirror's reflection.

Miranda shook away the image. "I'm sorry, I don't mean to be distracted."

Her sister examined her face. "You look tired."

Hot blood rushed to Miranda's cheeks. If she looked tired, it was because she'd spent the night beneath Ethan's sweat-slicked body, writhing in pleasure as he took her over and over again.

"Miranda?" Penelope's voice was sharp enough to shock her from her pleasant memories.

"I, er—I didn't sleep well last night."

"Does Lady Inglewood put you in some horrid servants' chamber?" her sister asked with a frown. "I wish you didn't have to sacrifice a day a week just to get into the dragon's good graces."

Guilt stabbed Miranda. Damn these lies that seemed to multiply every time her sister spoke to her.

She chose her response carefully. "You needn't be upset. I don't mind what I'm doing, really."

"How can you not mind?" Penelope sighed. "You're forced to sacrifice your time, your company, even your very body for us when I'm sure you'd rather be doing a hundred other things."

Miranda gave a small smile. "I can't think of anything I'd rather be doing." Then she shook off her soft emotions. "At any rate, if it helps our family in the long run, I can put up with a great deal. Now, let's not talk about my activities. Are you ready for the ball?"

Penelope pulled a face. "I suppose. I've been pinned and fitted and lectured and tested until I think I might lose my mind. But Mama seems satisfied that I won't disgrace the family completely." She sank into a worn chair beside the window with a frown. "So much rides on my success."

With a start, Miranda realized that while she had been so caught up in Ethan, her sister had been having her own difficulties. Now that she was focused on Penelope, she noticed how pale her sister was. And if her own face was tired, Penelope seemed to be teetering on the edge of exhaustion. She was pale and dark circles marred the skin beneath her pretty eyes.

How could she have been so selfish as to miss all the signs?

Miranda pushed to her feet and came to stand beside her sister. She placed a hand on Penelope's shoulder and squeezed. "Don't pressure yourself so much. You needn't find a husband right away. And if you don't like anyone who approaches you, for heaven's sake, don't go accepting any proposals and sacrifice yourself on the alter of our family problems."

"But if my Season fails—" Penelope began.

Miranda shook her head. "Then you will have another. And Beatrice will have one. And Winifred will have one."

Her sister flinched. "I know we cannot afford that kind of expense! Mother has already spent through the amount Lord Rothschild put into our accounts."

Miranda stepped back in shock. "What?"

Penelope's gaze came up to hers. "I tried to tell you when I came in. Mother has all but thrown the money away. She's gone positively wild buying new gowns and preparing the house for our guests." She shook her head. "And since we don't know how far Lord Rothschild's kindness will stretch, this might be our only chance for me to find a husband."

Miranda covered her eyes. Poor Ethan had no idea what he'd gotten into when he vowed to pay for her sister's Season. Surely he would be horrified when he realized his generous first payment toward her introduction to Society was already gone. Miranda could only hope he wouldn't back out on the deal.

Although, after last night, he didn't seem to be in any hurry to do so. Still, could her body really be worth so much to him? Especially since he could and *would* easily find another woman for his amusements. One who wouldn't be such a drag on his purse.

The very thought pained her.

She pushed the feelings aside. She could do nothing about that situation now. She would simply have to discuss the finances with him later. Perhaps at the party.

"I will speak to Mama," Miranda said on a sigh. "Though I don't know how much good it will do. She refuses to be reined in. In fact, my admonishments only seem to drive her on to more outrageous expenditures."

"I know. I tried, as well." Penelope threw up her hands in frustration. "Why does she do this?"

Miranda paced to the window and looked down below over the grounds. "Perhaps it is her way to keeping hold of Father's memory. He kept her in a fine fashion. If she faces the reality of how he lived, it will destroy her image of him. It will force her to admit that Papa wasn't the sun and moon. He was only human, and a flawed one at that."

Penelope shook her head. "I would think the truth would be more important to her than the false image of a dead man. I loved Papa, too, but I recognize his failings."

Miranda looked at her sister over her shoulder. She had always seen Penelope as her equal, despite the two years separating them, but at that moment, her sister seemed very young. Innocent.

"The love between a man and woman is different than the love between a father and daughter," she said softly. "Sometimes we see what we want to see."

Penelope shook her head with an incredulous laugh. "As if you know anything about love."

Miranda flinched. No, she'd never been in love. She felt something for Ethan, though. Something powerful and seductive that went far beyond the mere pleasure she received from his touch. Something that made her want to forget that he was playing a wicked game with her. That he was simply enjoying utterly debauching an innocent and that he would discard her as soon as he bored of the challenge.

"You're right," she said, forcing a brightness to her tone that she didn't feel. "I know nothing about love. I certainly shouldn't claim to understand Mama's motives. But I doubt anything I say will keep her from doing whatever she wishes. So we'll just hope that there is a wonderfully handsome, fabulously rich, perfectly kind gentleman who arrives at the party and is so charmed by you that he cannot stop himself from offering for your hand before the clock strikes midnight."

Penelope laughed as she got up from the chair and moved to the chamber door. "You sound like you're telling me a fairy tale. We both know that there are no happily ever after endings. I'll leave you to refresh yourself before luncheon. You'll need the rest to endure Mama's endless chatter about the food for the ball. I'll see you in a while."

Miranda nodded after her sister, but when the door closed behind her, she faced the lawn outside again. No happily ever after endings.

The reasonable part of her knew that was true. She'd witnessed the muck their father had made of their lives. When she realized the double life he'd been perpetrating, it had crushed any illusions she had about knights in shining armor and love that trumped all vices.

But in the past few weeks she'd begun to hope, in some secret part of her mind, that there was still a little bit of a fairy tale left for someone. Her sister's words reminded her not to count on wishes and princes.

Especially princes who made scandalous offers and overpowering demands that left her body aching and her heart longing for things she could never have.

"Ethan, it's so nice to see you."

Ethan got to his feet as Cassandra Willows entered her parlor. She held out her hands and kissed each cheek before she stepped back to look at him from head to toe. Her gaze was utterly familiar. After all, she had seen him wearing far less.

She smiled. "You always do cut a fine figure. But tell your tailor to put you in more blue. It's always suited you most."

She motioned to the seat he had vacated upon her entry and took her own place on the settee across from him.

Ethan laughed as he settled back into the chair "I will tell my tailor that the finest seamstress in all the country has that advice," he reassured her.

He looked at Cassandra. Not long ago, he would have been trying to find a way to get her out of that lovely fitted frock she was wearing. But though he enjoyed the view of the swell of her breasts enormously, he was surprised to find he had no interest in seeing anything more.

Not that she wasn't beautiful. Cassandra's dark auburn hair, petite frame and heavy, round breasts were still perfection. And he could tell by the way she smiled at him that she wouldn't be opposed to sharing a free afternoon of pleasure.

He just . . . didn't want to.

"Did you receive my note?" he asked, clearing his throat in the hopes that his discomfort would go away.

She nodded. "Yes. And I have done my best to make what you asked for as quickly as I could. It's difficult to design a piece for a woman who I don't know and cannot measure."

He frowned. "Whatever you made for her, it cannot be worse than what she is wearing now, I assure you."

"Hmmm, that bad, eh?"

"Wretched," he admitted as he thought of Miranda's worn clothing. "And what about the, er, *other item?*"

Cassandra smiled. In addition to creating beautiful gowns for ladies and courtesans alike, she had a thriving side business with toys and trinkets of a sensual nature. One that catered to a very select clientele.

"That is ready, as well." She got to her feet and crossed the room to ring a bell beside the door. As she waited for her assistant, she turned to examine his face closely. "Since I received your summons yesterday, I have been nearly overcome with curiosity about who these gifts are for. I heard you didn't take a lover with you to the estate this year."

Ethan shrugged. He'd promised Miranda not to reveal her

identity and he didn't intend to do so. "Rumors are a tricky beast, are they not?"

She smiled. "I told Richardson that he was wrong!"

Ethan didn't answer one way or another, and before she demanded more information, Cassandra's servant arrived with a box. She took the gift and nodded the girl away.

She turned back and held out the present with a smile. "Here."

Ethan took it with a bit more interest than he wanted and opened the gift. He smiled at what he saw. "Perfect, thank you Cassandra."

"You are very welcome. I'm glad I could oblige. Especially for the exorbitant fee you're going to pay me." They both laughed. "You must be bored with the young lady already, though. Are these things a goodbye gift?"

Ethan frowned. "No."

Cassandra pulled back and surprise was plain on her face. "Really? I don't think I've ever known you to buy a gift for a woman when it wasn't a consolation for your parting. Tell me more about the lady who has inspired such generosity, my lord."

Ethan pulled the box shut and held it closer to his chest. "There is nothing to tell."

Now Cassandra's eyes went impossibly wide. "Are you in love with this girl, Rothschild?"

He nearly dropped the box in shock. "What?"

"There is something in your look. Tell me you have not finally succumbed to the charms of a lady."

He scowled as he marched to the door. "Of course not. What

kind of fool do you take me for? Your payment will arrive by day's end."

Cassandra folded her arms as she watched him yank the door open. "Very well, Ethan," she said softly. "I think I understand perfectly."

"Understand!" he scoffed. "There is nothing to understand. Good afternoon."

But as he strode out of Cassandra's comfortable house and climbed up on his horse to ride back to his estate, he wondered that Cassandra would even guess such a foolhardy thing. Normally, she was so observant. Surely he wasn't showing that kind of ridiculous emotion on his countenance.

The kind of emotion that would not end well for anyone concerned.

Twelve

Ethan paced around his parlor, checking the clock every time he made a turn about the room. Almost time.

He shook his head at his own eagerness, but had given up trying to quell it. Soon he would be with Miranda and he could think of nothing else.

It had been two days since he last saw her. Two long days where he had been distracted by thoughts of her. Her scent still lingered on the pillows in his secret chamber. How did he know that?

Because he kept returning to the room to breathe her in.

But all the waiting was nearly over because she'd be arriving at his home in a few moments. Even though it wasn't Friday, even though she wouldn't be staying. But he had plans for her.

He shouldn't. He knew that. If he was smart, he'd stick to the terms of their deal. But he couldn't. He wanted her too much. More than he could remember wanting any woman, even his favorite mistresses. No one had ever stoked the fire in his belly like Miranda could with just one unpracticed look.

Cassandra thought he was in love with her. But that wasn't it. Since he left his old friend's home yesterday, he'd all but convinced himself that Cassandra was seeing things that weren't there. Foolish, romantic woman.

The door to the parlor opened and Winston stepped inside. "Miss Albright, sir."

Ethan's pulse leapt and he made a concerted effort to keep his face calm as the servant stepped aside and made way for Miranda. She stepped into the room with a brief nod for the man, but as the door closed, her gaze fell on Ethan and she smiled.

By God, she was beautiful. So fresh and honest and alive. And the longing he felt to touch her nearly overwhelmed him. He wanted to breathe her in, soak her in, own her in every way.

"Good afternoon," she said, peeling off her gloves. "I was surprised to receive your summons. How in the world do you keep arranging these notes directly to my maid?"

Ethan shook off his reaction to her with a grin. "One of my footmen has been, er, *visiting* your little maid for a few months. And he's happy to have an excuse to go to her and deliver my notes."

"Angelica?" Miranda gasped. "Really? My, she always seemed so innocent!"

Ethan stepped toward her and drew in a long breath of the scent of her hair. "So do you, my little minx. But I know better."

Miranda gave a pretty blush that started at her hairline and disappeared beneath the scooped neck of her gown. She looked away. "I suppose you are correct in that regard."

"I hope you won't terminate her now that you know her secret," Ethan murmured as he slipped behind her and wrapped his arms around her waist. She leaned back immediately. "It is very convenient to be able to pass messages to you whenever I like."

She sighed as his lips came down on her neck. "It would be rather hypocritical of me to end her employment for doing exactly the same things I am doing."

"Exactly the same?" he murmured as he bit her neck gently.

She shivered. "Probably not exactly the same."

He chuckled as he slid his hands up to cup her breasts. Her knees were trembling now and she leaned fully against him.

"Why—why did you call me here?" she gasped as his thumbs rubbed over her nipples, making them stand at attention even through the fabric of her gown.

"Thank you for reminding me," he whispered and turned her around to face him. She stared up at him, gaze clouded with desire. His cock was rock hard already but he knew there would be no release for him. At least not now.

But he was going to enjoy this particular "gift" for her.

"I have something for you," he said.

She cocked her head. "What is it?"

With a wicked smile, he dropped to his knees and began to lift up her skirts.

Nothing Ethan did should have shocked Miranda anymore, but having him drop down in front of her and slide his hands beneath her skirt surprised her nonetheless.

"Ethan," she cried, her hands fisting against his shoulders.

He glanced up at her with that wicked, calculating grin that was always her undoing.

"Shh," he soothed as his fingers glided over her trembling knees, past her damp thighs. He lifted her skirt as he went until he held it up to her waist and left her utterly exposed.

"Hold this," he said, motioning to the fabric.

She released his shoulder with one trembling hand and took the bunched gown, unsure of what else to do.

"What are you doing?" she breathed, her words ragged.

"This," he murmured, before he pushed her chemise aside and opened her legs. She shut her eyes and anticipated the brush of his mouth. He didn't make her wait long.

His tongue probed her, awakening her senses and making her utterly aware of the scene anyone would see if they entered the room. But she didn't object. She couldn't have cared less if disapproving Winston threw open the doors and brought in tours of onlookers. She wanted Ethan's mouth, she wanted Ethan's tongue, she wanted release. Everything else be damned.

He sucked her clit, not teasing her as he'd done in the past. The explosion of release was his intent and almost immediately waves of pleasure built low in her stomach and spread needy, out of control heat through her pussy.

"Ethan," she moaned, clenching his shoulder with one hand while she twisted her skirt in the other. "Ethan."

"Let go," he said against her skin and the vibration sent her over the edge in an explosion of forbidden sensation.

She thrust her hips to meet his mouth, moaning his name over and over as he forced more and more pleasure from her aching body. Finally, the tremors began to subside and the wracking tingles faded to a mere whisper.

"Here is your first gift," he said from below her. Then she

felt a sharp, pleasurable pinch on her clit that made her knees buckle.

He cupped her backside, stroking the globes as he held her upright and looked at her. She knew her eyes were wild as she stared down at him.

"What—what is that?" she panted, swallowing hard as the steady pressure on her clit made her tingle in dangerous, sensual ways. It was a constant reminder of her arousal, a touch that brought her to the edge, but never allowed her to go over.

He pulled her chemise back down over her thighs and then gently extracted her skirt from her grip. He let it fall over her and stood up.

"It's a special toy, designed to keep you on the edge, to keep you ready for me," he explained as he turned away to pour her a swallow of sherry.

He handed her the glass and she stared at him. He looked so calm. Like they were discussing the weather, not the clip he had just attached to her most private parts.

He smiled. "Drink it."

She downed the sherry in one gulp. The burn of the liquor only reminded her more of the heat that now pulsated between her thighs, taunting her with pleasure without allowing it.

"I want you to wear it the rest of the day," he explained as he took the empty glass. "And tonight to the party."

She shook her head, fighting for reason so she could manage to form coherent sentences. "Why?"

He leaned in closer. "Because I want you to know, every moment of the rest of this day, that you're mine. Every time I look at you across the room, I want you to feel that bite of pleasure. I want you to anticipate everything I intend to do to you the moment I have you alone."

Her head spun with that admission and with the possessive gleam in his eyes. "But—but this isn't Friday," she said. "You don't own me today."

He tilted his head and looked at her for a long, heavy moment. Then he reached out to cup her cheek. The expression in his eyes shifted, ever so slightly. The possessiveness was still hot in his stare, but there was something else there now, too. A tenderness. Something she'd never seen in this man before.

"Miranda, I want you to wear it because you want to feel that sensation even though we won't be able to explore it until later. I want you to wear it because it would bring me pleasure to know you had that reminder." He swallowed. "Please."

Her eyes widened at the "please". He wasn't demanding she take his gift, he was asking her. Giving her some of that precious control he snatched at every opportunity.

She couldn't deny him. And she wouldn't deny herself. "Yes."

"Good."

Without looking away from her, he reached behind him for a brightly decorated box. Holding it out, he said, "And here is your second gift."

She shivered as her clit throbbed mercilessly. What other wicked toys was he offering her?

"Take it," he urged, waggling the box back and forth.

Her fingers trembled as she reached for his gift. She almost felt like Eve with the snake, like she might be breaking every rule she'd ever made for herself.

"What is it?" she murmured past dry lips. How could he be so calm? Her whole body was on fire.

"Open it and see."

She shivered as she tugged at the ribbon and removed the box lid. Reaching inside past expensive, fragranced paper, she withdrew a soft, filmy chemise.

"Oh, Ethan," she breathed. "It's beautiful."

He wet his lips. "Wear it tonight as well."

She stared at the garment. It was so sensual and lovely. The sheer fabric was finely made and of the highest quality. It certainly didn't match the rest of her wardrobe.

"But, my mother, if she—"

He shook his head. "You will wear it beneath your clothing. Only you and I will know, as long as your ladies maid is as discreet as you claim."

He stepped forward and brushed his fingers over her jaw. "Wear it tonight, Miranda."

With a shaky nod, she whispered, "I will."

He backed away. "Now you had best go back before your absence is noticed. I'll see you in a few short hours."

She nodded as she turned toward the door. But before she could step away, he caught her arms and pulled her back. His mouth came down and he brushed his lips, ever so gently across hers. She opened and he glided inside, tasting, testing, but never fully possessing. It was a tender kiss. But an arousing kiss nonetheless. Between her legs, her constricted clit pulsed and her sheath grew slick with renewed desire.

"Run away, Miranda," he whispered as he turned her toward the door. "Before I forget myself."

She did as she was told and hurried from the room.

★ ★ ★

Ethan strummed his fingers along the side of his wineglass, watching the Albright ball spin at full tilt around him. Laughing gentlemen and ladies, the same ones who had been giggling at the family's misfortune mere weeks ago, were now dancing to the talented orchestra's music. They were eating the food, drinking the drinks, calling it the celebration of the summer.

He shook his head. How fleeting their loyalty was. Of course, he was no better. A month or two ago, he would have been doing the exact same thing. But now it somehow rankled him, for he knew that within a few more weeks, the *ton* could very easily return to shunning the Albrights. He could only hope his money and support would keep that from happening.

He scanned the crowd, ignoring friends and the occasional flirtatious stare of his former lovers. Just as had been the case with Cassandra a few days before, none of those women appealed to him in the slightest. It no longer mattered that if he approached them, he was certain to have a rollicking good time in a quiet study or garden pathway.

He wanted the good time, for certain, he just wanted it with one specific woman. At that exact moment the crowd parted to reveal her.

Miranda.

He took a step toward her before he realized what he was doing, then stopped. Jesus, he didn't *chase* women! Even if just the sight of her profile, as she chatted with a small group of ladies, *did* arouse ridiculous feelings and fantasies.

She turned as if she felt his stare and started when she found him watching her. Their eyes met and he saw the arousal in her expression. So, she still wore his little gift. She was still ready for him, right on the edge of release. She dipped her chin and blushed. He couldn't help but smile. She knew his thoughts.

He took another step in her direction. If he could maneuver this correctly, he could get her alone. He could ease the ache in both their bodies. Even just a quick tryst would be better than the driving want that made him so utterly aware of her every move.

Ignoring everything around him, he began to edge toward her in earnest. But before he'd gotten even three steps, he heard his name being screeched.

"Lord Rothschild!"

He froze. He would recognize the sound of Miranda's mother's voice anywhere. He'd been hiding from it for years, trying to keep out of the woman's line of sight. But since this was *her* party and he had paid for it, he couldn't exactly give her the cut direct.

Plastering a false smile on his lips, he turned toward her. "Ah, Mrs. Albright. How nice it is to see you. I am sorry that my late arrival kept us from greeting each other properly at the door."

"Oh, posh! We're just so happy you could come at all."

She smiled at him, her eyes shining. He didn't think he'd ever seen Dorthea Albright look so happy. He tilted his head as he subtly looked her up and down. He'd never taken much notice of her before, but now he wondered how this woman could have produced Miranda. She wasn't tall or willowy, rather of more average height and slightly rounded by age and childbirth. She didn't have silky blonde hair, but a mousier brown. However, there was one thing Mrs. Albright had given her daughter. Her bright blue eyes.

And suddenly she didn't make Ethan shudder so much.

"I know that I wrote you a letter, Lord Rothschild, but I wanted to thank you in person for your generosity to my daughter, Penelope." Mrs. Albright patted his arm clumsily. "I have been remiss in not calling on you before now."

The shudder was back and Ethan had to work to keep his smile. Dorthea Albright was speaking so loudly that everyone around them was now staring. Miranda's tact, along with her other more appealing attributes, must have come from her father. Or a grandmother. Or a distant cousin. Anyone but her mother.

"Your note was more than enough thanks, dear lady," he said with a slight bow. "We do not need to speak of it any longer."

She shook her head. "No, no, but we must. I beg a moment of your time, my lord, where we could speak more privately."

Ethan gazed across the room toward Miranda. She was standing with a man now. A handsome man, too. Ethan fisted his hands at his sides as unexpected jealousy rushed through him, especially when the bloke took a long look at Miranda's cleavage.

Not that Miranda noticed his appraisal. She was hardly attending to her companion. She had noticed her mother's approach and was staring at them now. Her blush was one of mortification rather than arousal. Damn it. Ethan hated that the desire he had cultivated was now dashed.

"My lord?" her mother repeated.

He sighed. "Yes, Mrs. Albright. Of course we may speak alone."

He motioned for her to lead and followed her from the ballroom and down the hallway to a private study. As she shut the door behind him, he looked around. What had once been a sophisticated room was now shabby. The fabric on the chairs was worn, the wallpaper peeling. All proof of what Miranda had already stated and he had guessed. Her father had put the family in dire straights.

"I apologize for the room," Mrs. Albright said with a grimace. "Miranda has been quite stingy about maintaining the house. She tries to act like it is for our own good, but it is trying to have to endure her miserly ways. Especially when her father kept us in such a fine fashion. I'm certain her tightfistedness is unwarranted."

Ethan pursed his lips. So this was what Miranda had to endure. These constant criticisms from her mother, who refused to face reality. No wonder Miranda always looked tired. No wonder she thought of her own clothing last.

"I'm sure your daughter is thinking of what is *best* for your family," he said, trying desperately to meter his tone when what he wanted to do was tell her to shut her mouth.

Mrs. Albright shrugged. "Perhaps. Though I doubt Penelope would have had a Season at all if not for your intervention."

Ethan clenched his fists. "As I said, we do not have to speak of that any longer. I will supply the funds for Penelope's debut. Simply have the bills sent to me."

Her eyes lit up and Ethan stifled a curse. This was going to be far more expensive than he had originally thought.

"You are too kind, my lord. And I feel we must do something to repay you." Mrs. Albright stepped forward and rubbed her palms together. "I wonder if there is some deeper reason for your kindness than whatever debt you owed my darling Thomas?"

Ethan cocked his head. What was she on about? She certainly couldn't know the truth about his bargain with Miranda. Dorthea Albright was mercenary, for sure, but he doubted she would approve of a daughter trading her virtue. At least, he hoped she wouldn't.

"I have no idea what you could mean, madam." He kept his tone bored and bland.

Mrs. Albright smiled conspiratorially. "Come now, Lord Rothschild. I wonder if perhaps you have taken a fancy to my darling Penelope? And you desire her to have a wonderful coming out so that Society can see what a gem you have uncovered?"

Ethan flinched, though he almost felt sorry for her, she looked so hopeful. "A fancy for Penelope? No, my lady. She is a lovely young woman, but I have no designs on her."

Her smile fell. "Beatrice, then? Or Winifred." Her brow wrinkled. "Winifred is a bit young for you, but I would approve the match in a few years."

"I have no intentions to pursue any of them, I assure you," he said. "There is no ulterior motive to my support of their Seasons."

That was a lie, but he wasn't about to reveal the truth.

Mrs. Albright gnawed her lip for a moment, as if she were reevaluating the situation. Then her smile returned. "Perhaps if you spend some time with them, your regard would grow. After all you've done, offering you the hand of one of my daughters is the least I can do."

Ethan staggered back as panic gripped him. He had cultivated a certain reputation and that kept some portion of the groping Mamas away. But there were always others who gave his status in Society more credence than his questionable character. Dorthea was clearly one of the second group, willing to overlook his less savory elements in trade for the privilege and power of his title.

"Penelope, Beatrice, and Winifred are all very lovely and accomplished," she pressed.

He stared at her, still too shocked to reply. And then he realized something.

"You do not mention your eldest daughter, Miranda," he said. "Except to criticize her."

She sighed as she turned away. "Miranda is, of course, very pretty and proficient in many things. But she is too spirited and independent for her own good. She inherited the trait from her father, I fear."

Ethan held back an unkind snort of laughter. Miranda was far more sensible and controlled than her father had ever been. "And you think I would not want her because of this?"

Mrs. Albright faced him with a shrug. "She has already turned down enough suitors that no man wishes to pursue her. But if she was the one you wanted to marry, I wouldn't discourage you. As I said, she has many positive qualities."

"Marry Miranda," he repeated.

The words sank into him, buzzing through his system like a thousand bees. A marriage would mean Miranda would be his. There would be no parting after a sinful night of pleasure. No limitations to their time together. She would be his, not just for one night a week, not just for a month or a summer . . . *forever*.

The concept of forever had always shaken him and this time it was no different. A future with Miranda would be wonderful, at least for a while. But then he would bore of her. She would be hurt, grow sullen. They would quarrel. He would be unfaithful. Perhaps she would be driven to drink like his mother had been.

That was no life for her.

"I'm sorry, Mrs. Albright," he said. "As charmed as I am by your offer, I have no intentions to wed."

She drew back, stunned by that statement. "No intentions? But you are an Earl. You must marry to insure your legacy."

He sighed. If he wanted any peace from this woman, he was going to have to play up that reputation he'd created for himself. Enough to keep her away, but insure she would continue to take his money.

"My legacy, dear lady," he drawled. "I'm sure my legacy will be continued through some means. Why would I need *legitimate* heirs? I can enjoy everything this title brings me, and leave the insuring of the legacy to my younger brothers or a cousin."

Mrs. Albright's eyes widened and her face turned red as a tomato. "Why, I never! Excuse me."

She turned on her heel and stomped away to the door. When it slammed behind her, Ethan was left alone. Yet it gave him little satisfaction because it meant his only company was his troubling thoughts.

"Mama!" Miranda hissed as she stepped out of a doorway near the parlor where her mother had been conversing with Ethan.

Dorthea turned and looked at her. Oh, dear. This wasn't good at all. Miranda recognized that look. Her mother was offended, outraged, and *she* wasn't going to escape hearing all about it.

"What were you doing?" Miranda whispered as her mother

came to stand before her, huffing and muttering. "I saw you take Lord Rothschild aside."

"*Lord* Rothschild, indeed," her mother said, foot tapping wildly as she tossed a glance over her shoulder at the closed parlor door. "The man is nothing more than a cad!"

"What happened?" Miranda groaned. "Or do I even want to know?"

"I simply wanted to thank him for his generosity," her mother huffed. "And make him an offer of one of your sisters' hands in marriage as a reward."

Miranda's heart sank. "What? You didn't truly offer him a marriage!"

"Why not?" Her mother tilted her head as if she didn't understand the problem. "I believed him to be a fine catch for Penelope, especially, since she is coming out into Society. I even thought he might have helped us in order to gain access to your sister. But he disabused me of that idea quickly. He said he had no interest in *any* of my daughters!"

Miranda blinked as pain roared out of no where and hit her straight in the stomach. "He said that, did he?"

"Yes." Her mother glared behind her again. "He admitted he intends to be a complete wastrel while he is Earl and not even marry and produce heirs! Can you imagine? What a waste of a good title."

Miranda nodded, but she was hardly attending. She was still reeling. She knew Ethan had said that to put her mother off. He would never be so cruel as to say it so harshly to her face, but it was a reminder of his intentions, nonetheless.

"I would have given him a good piece of my mind, if he wasn't providing us with so much money. And it should be *more* after that little encounter." Her mother scowled. "Well, we should return to the ball. No use wasting any more time on the man."

Miranda shook her head. "You go, Mama. I will join you shortly. I—er—I wanted to speak to the footman about something."

Her mother was already looking toward the ballroom. "Very well. Just be careful of yourself. Who knows when that horrid man will come back into the hallway. I wouldn't want you being compromised by that ne'er-do-well."

"Of course, Mama. I will be careful," she whispered, staring at the parlor door.

She waited until her mother had disappeared back down the hallway before she straightened her shoulders and made for the parlor where Ethan remained.

He was probably disgusted by her mother. He likely didn't want to see *her* at all. Yet, she couldn't stay away. Despite her pain and embarrassment, there was still a tingling ache driving her to him. A need made more sharp and defined by the clip he had put on her clit hours before.

So she opened the door and stepped inside.

Thirteen

"Ethan?" Miranda said softly as she pushed the door closed behind her. The room was dim and it took a moment for her eyes to adjust.

Then she saw him. Ethan was standing by the window where he had apparently been looking outside. But now he faced her, eyes glittering in the light of the fire.

"Hello, Miranda," he said, his voice alone a seduction to her raw senses. It seemed to dance over her skin and settle at her pulsing, empty sheath.

She stifled a moan and tried to remember why she'd come here. Focus. She had to focus.

"I—I'm sorry about my Mother," she whispered, voice cracking as she moved toward him, almost against her will. Her ready body was overwhelming her resistant mind. "She told me what she said to you. She never should have tried to offer you a marriage as some kind of reimbursement for your sponsorship."

She blushed as she thought of what she was already giving as "reimbursement."

"I wanted to tell her that I was already earning more than enough for my 'kindness'." He smiled wolfishly as she neared him. "But I restrained all my worst urges. I didn't think she would be happy to hear of our arrangement. Especially since she's so foolish that she doesn't see the truth when it is standing right before her."

"The truth?" she repeated, forcing herself to stop just out of his reach. What truth? That he didn't want *any* of the Albright girls? She tried to push the sting of that thought away and focus on his reply.

"Yes. Your mother is an utter fool, far worse than I first imagined," he said. "She thinks her future lies with the proper marriage of one of your younger sisters, but that isn't true. Her future lies with you."

He pushed off the window sash and stalked toward her, circling her, but never touching her. His body heat and the subtle scent of his shaving soap surrounded her, taunting her with the very essence of him. She so desperately wanted to take his hand and force it to her breast. To rub against him like a cat. To steal his kiss if he wouldn't give it to her.

But the things her mother said still rang too harshly in her ears.

"What do you mean her future lies with me?" she managed to ask on a shaky breath.

"I saw you tonight. Saw other men looking at you. You could easily find a way to get back in the good graces of the proper gentlemen of the *ton*. You could choose to be wife or mistress to any one of them."

Miranda swallowed, her throat suddenly constricted as her pulse beat wildly between her legs. His words were shocking, but she was determined not to react like some missish innocent. Affecting boredom, she said, "Could I? Perhaps I should try once our bargain is over."

He stopped moving and she realized she'd made a mistake in goading him. She'd said that to hurt him as she had been hurt by his statement that he wanted nothing to do with any of the Albright women. Instead, she had stoked that possessiveness that lurked just below the surface. The one that was darkening his face now.

"When you were with them, did you think of that clip I put on you?" he asked, voice harsh.

Miranda's first reaction was to ignore the question and bolt for the door, but it was too late for that. He wouldn't let her go. He'd have her in his arms before she made it two steps. There was no choice but to answer and answer honestly, no matter how hard it was to do so.

She nodded as heat filled her cheeks. "Of course I was thinking of it. You knew I would, that's why you gave it to me. You wanted to remind me of you, no matter who I was with or what kind of benign topic we were discussing. It was a constant reminder of—" She broke off.

"Of what?" He slipped a hand around her waist and pulled her closer. "Of me? Of my cock buried deep within you? Of the way you cry out my name when you come?"

She nodded, her motions jerky as she tilted her face up for a kiss. She ached for it now, and feared she would do almost anything to have even a brief taste of what she craved. *That* was the power he wielded over her.

"And did you think, for even one moment that any other man could ever make you as satisfied as I do?" he asked, harsh as his lips hovered just above hers.

She parted her lips and a jagged cry escaped them. "No," she admitted.

His mouth came down and crushed hers, punishing her with his rough kiss. Pleasuring her with it. Her body pulsed wildly, so close to orgasm even with this comparatively mild touch. She groaned, arching against him, trying to give herself the relief she'd been eager for since that afternoon.

"And you don't want any other man but me?" he urged, pushing her up against the window until her backside hit the glass and she felt the coldness through her satin gown. For a brief moment, she realized someone from below might see them, but she didn't care. If anything, that idea thrilled her even more.

"It has always been you," she admitted on a broken breath. "There's never been anyone else, there will never be anyone else that will make me *want* like this. Please, please!"

Her declaration seemed to surprise him. He drew back, his gaze still hot, but now startled. But then his mouth covered hers again and he cupped her backside, lifting her up, spreading her legs.

She cried out with pleasure as her nerve endings fired out of control. She had been stimulated by his gift for so many hours now that she was wild with desire. So needy that it frightened her.

"Take me," she groaned against his ear, pressing hot kisses to the straining column of his neck. "Please just make me come. I need to come."

His movements grew jerky at her request. He yanked at her skirt, bunching it up and up until the cool air in the room brushed over her sensitive skin. She was so utterly aware of every touch, every change of temperature, everything.

But especially him. Mere brushes of his knuckles as he shoved her chemise aside were enough to make her hips buck wildly. His breath on her skin made her so aware of how swollen and wet and ready she was.

And then, just as she was about to burst, he stopped moving.

"You're wearing it," he moaned.

She panted, uncertain for a moment what he meant. Then it dawned on her. "The chemise? Of course. You gave it to me."

His gaze jerked up and a small, sinful smile tilted his lips. "Later, I am going to strip you down and see you in it. But for now—"

He yanked at his trousers, unhooking buttons with frustrated groans. And then he sprang free, fully erect and ready. She licked her lips. She'd never wanted him more. She didn't want tenderness, she just wanted him. Heavy and hard and fast. She wanted him to take her over the edge. To own her. Maybe it wouldn't be forever, in fact she knew it wouldn't be. But it would be tonight and no one could take that away from her.

He cupped her and she cried out.

"Dripping," he moaned. "So ready."

"Please," she whispered, arching toward him. She didn't care that she was begging. "Please, please, please."

"Yes, right now." He positioned himself and pushed up. Her wet sheath offered no resistance and he filled her to the hilt in that one driving thrust.

Miranda clung to his still-clothed shoulders as pleasure threatened to make her lose consciousness. Her vision blurred around the edges and her entire body shook with the power of their joining. He continued to pound into her mercilessly, grinding his hips so that her swollen clit rubbed against him.

He locked gazes with her, never slowing his thrusts, then slipped his hand between them. He found the clip he had attached to her earlier and with a flick of his wrist, pulled it away. The reaction was immediate.

Miranda screamed as potent pleasure roared through her body. It was no longer focused on her clit, but spread throughout. The sensation made her toes tingle, it spread through her breasts, it made her arms heavy and useless. Her hips rocked against him and tears streamed down her face as her orgasm went on and on. And Ethan forced it to go on. He continued the swiveling motion of his hips, continued to stimulate her on every thrust. Brought her up and down the highs masterfully until she merely clung to him, exhausted as he drove on.

He held her tightly, remaining seated in her clenching, tremoring sheath as he pulled her away from the window. Turning, he carried her to the settee and laid her down where he covered her with his body.

He kissed her, deep and hot and claiming and she felt like her melting body was back on fire again. How could he do that to her? How could he keep her right on the edge at all times? The next wave crashed over her and all she could do was hold on, while he forced more and more pleasure upon her with each stroke.

Ethan felt himself losing control as he drove into Miranda faster and faster. Her every orgasm made her sheath cling tighter, made her wetter and hotter. It was almost too much. But damn, it wasn't enough, either. He just wanted to be inside of her, stay inside of her. Keep her as a part of him without having to argue or think about it.

He just wanted her. All of her.

She lifted her hips to meet him, squeezing as she did so and he exploded. He covered her mouth with his to stifle his roar of complete pleasure as he poured himself deep into her womb.

As the pleasure faded, his found his kisses becoming less forceful and more gentle. Her hands ceased to clench at him and began to stroke his back. Their union was no longer possession, but tenderness. He drew away in surprise, looking down at her. She was looking back at him with the same dazed astonishment, as if she had felt the shift as well.

He opened his mouth to say something when he caught a flash of movement from the corner of his eye. He lifted his gaze and found himself looking at Miranda's younger sister, Penelope. She stood in the parlor doorway, staring at the two of them, her mouth open in shock. Her emotions were reflected on every line of her face. She was both horrified and titillated. Aroused and frightened.

How long had she been watching them?

Suddenly, she realized he was looking at her. Their eyes locked and she covered her mouth before she turned on her heel and fled in silence.

"Ethan?" Miranda murmured from beneath him, reaching up to cup his cheek and draw his gaze back to hers. Her face was soft in the firelight and her smile tentative and uncertain.

He stared at her as the full ramifications of what had just occurred hit him. Penelope had seen them. Her expression told him that she'd been watching long enough to know it was her sister that he was rutting with so passionately.

And now he had to tell Miranda. Break her heart and horrify her and make ugly an encounter that had been nothing but perfect a moment before. His chest tightened at the thought of hurting her like that.

He dropped a gentle kiss on her lips before he pushed away to his feet and began to fix himself. From the frown that creased her mouth, he could see his withdrawal confused and upset her.

"Miranda, I must tell you something," he began, loathing what he was about to do.

She struggled to sit up, smoothing her gown. Her eyes were wide with anticipation, an emotion she tried to mask, but utterly failed. "What is it?"

He shifted as he fought to devise the least painful way to tell her this. But there was none.

"Miranda, someone . . . someone saw us just now," he said softly.

She bolted to her feet and the color drained from her face so quickly that he reached out a hand to steady her in case she was about to pitch over in a faint. Her breath came in ragged, painful jags as she stared at him.

"Saw us?" she repeated, her voice dancing on the edge of hysteria. "From the window?"

He shook his head, still gripping her arm, though now he gentled the touch, smoothing his fingers along her soft skin in a lame attempt to sooth her. She looked down at his hand, watched it stroke her arm. Her expression was clouded and unreadable.

"No, sweetheart, not from the window. I—I should have locked the door the moment I realized I wasn't going to be able to wait to have you." He sighed. "But my mind was a bit addled and I'm not used to doing such things outside of my own home or far less respectable houses with far less respectable women where being caught wouldn't cause any problems except for a little embarrassment."

She tilted her head. "You lost control?"

He flinched. That was the problem, wasn't it? But he couldn't deal with that now.

He touched her hand. "Someone opened the door, Miranda. I don't know how long she watched us. When she realized I saw her, she ran away."

Miranda's full lips parted and her hand lifted to cover her swollen mouth.

"No," she murmured, a pained groan through her fingertips as she stumbled back a few steps. "No, no. Who was it? Oh God, I am utterly ruined. Destroyed. My sisters, oh God, my sisters—their futures, oh no, no, no—"

"Shhh," Ethan reached for her, wanting so much to draw her against his chest and comfort her. But she turned from his embrace and paced away, her painful moans continuing to hang in the room between them.

He pursed his lips, hurt that she didn't want his reassurance. Wait, hurt? No. He didn't get *hurt*. Certainly not by a woman like her. He pushed his shoulders back.

"It was Penelope who saw us. And judging from her expression, she had been watching long enough to know it was you I had against the window," he said, cool and methodical.

Miranda spun on him and the horror and humiliation in her eyes was so palpable that it almost hit him like a physical blow. It was as he feared. Now this powerful encounter was a mistake in her eyes. Something she wished she could erase.

"Penelope?" she repeated. Her hands began to tremble. "No."

The last was a mere whisper, but it was more pained than any of her earlier moans had been. Defeat came over her face, a hurt so deep and abiding that he felt it in his own gut. Along with something he hadn't allowed himself to feel for many, many years.

Guilt.

He had done this to her. By offering her a devil's bargain. By pursuing her over her sexual boundaries. By demanding her pleasure over and over again. By pushing his needs into her home and asking for more and more and more.

She blinked, dazed. "I—I must go find her. I must speak to her," she said as she turned and moved unsteadily toward the door.

"Wait, wait Miranda!" He caught her in three long strides. Grabbing her arm, he pulled her back. "What are you going to say to her about what she saw?"

"Oh God," she moaned as she pulled at her arm. He held fast.

"Perhaps *I* should talk to her. You cannot know how to explain what she saw."

Miranda locked gazes with him and something he'd never seen in her before flickered in her eyes. Experience and knowledge. In fact, when she looked at him like she was right now, he felt like the foolish student and she the master.

"You think not, Ethan? I know far more than you might think. In fact, I think I'm the perfect one to explain what she saw. After all, I used to watch you with your paramours beside the lake on your property every summer. Each week I snuck away to see what shocking thing you would do next."

Ethan let her go and stumbled back in shock. "You did what?"

A tinge of color filled her cheeks, but she kept her chin high and nodded. "I know exactly what seeing a scene like that can do to a girl. What thoughts it puts in her mind. It could change her forever." Her face fell. "It *has* changed her forever."

Her confession sunk into his consciousness, overwhelming him with a tangle of wild thoughts, both erotic and shameful. No wonder Miranda had always seemed so open to all the pleasures he wanted to share with her. She'd seen them all before. Seen all his sensual habits. And she'd also seen how little those other women had meant to him.

"Miranda," he breathed, questions rioting in his mind.

She shook her head and turned away. "Penelope is my sister and I need to be the one to try to explain all of this to her. If I don't, the consequences could be dire."

He wrinkled his brow. Was she saying she regretted watching his sensual escapades? That it had changed her adversely?

"Miranda—" he began again.

She spun on him with wild, tearful eyes. "Please, Ethan. No more. Just go. Just go home. *Please.*"

Before he could respond, she ran to the door and left him alone with tangled thoughts that assaulted him with a thousand questions, a thousand memories, and a thousand emotions he had never wished to feel. ·

Fourteen

Miranda hurried through the winding corridors and hallways of the house, searching for her sister. Her emotions were ragged and wild, she could actually feel hysteria building in her chest, threatening to rise up and overcome her with guilt and regret. What in the world had she done? What was Penelope feeling? Doing?

No, she couldn't let her feelings overwhelm her. But as Miranda looked in every secret spot and dark corner they had ever hidden and whispered in as girls and found no trace of her sister, her emotions roared louder. With each failure to find Penelope, her fears threatened to take her to her knees.

She knew her sister all too well. Penelope wouldn't simply go back to the party and be able to pretend everything was normal after what she'd seen.

Oh God, what she'd seen!

Miranda leaned against the wall for a moment to compose herself. That encounter with Ethan had been the most animal, the most passionate since they began their bargain. There had been a desperation in both of them. She'd felt it in Ethan's kiss as much as she fought against it in her own heart. It had shaken her, changed her.

She would have welcomed that change, except that in the moment her world shifted, she had undoubtedly altered her sister's world as well. Penelope was an innocent, she was likely shocked and perhaps even shattered.

Miranda forced herself to remain strong and continued her search. She could hear the tinkling of music in the distance and prayed she wouldn't be caught by her mother. Not when she was so disheveled and upset. It would be too difficult to face that censure and opinion.

She slipped to a servant's door that led outside. If Penelope ran away from the parlor, she would have gone past the little stairway and hidden secret door. It would be just like her sister to want to be outside, away from the stifling confines of the house and the potential grasp of their meddling mother.

Miranda stepped into the cool night air and looked around. If she went left, she would find the main gardens behind the ballroom terrace. Unlikely Penelope would go that way and risk coming into contact with other people when she was upset.

Miranda went right and headed toward a gazebo across the lawn, away from the main house. It looked out over the rolling hills that were part of Ethan's adjacent estate, although the dark night would prevent Penelope from witnessing their fresh beauty.

Not that Miranda for one second believed that her sister had scenery on her mind while she bolted. Miranda hurried across the lawn, her pathway only lit by the sparkling light of the full moon above. As she neared the little open gazebo, she heard the sounds of a person moving, of harshly drawn breaths. Then she was close enough and could see the shadowy outline of her sister, sitting on the bench in the middle of the gazebo, her shoulders hunched.

Relief filled her, followed close behind by fear. What would her sister think of her now?

"Penelope?" she called out when she was still a few steps away.

The harsh breaths came to a sudden stop and the shadowy figure straightened up with a start.

"Dearest, I can see you," Miranda said softly as she stepped up into the building. "There's no use in pretending you're not here."

"Go away!" Penelope said as she got to her feet and spun around to look at Miranda.

The moonlight hit her sister's face and Miranda flinched. Penelope's cheeks were streaked with tears and her mouth twisted with the force of her upset.

"I can't," Miranda sighed. "I know what you saw and we *must* speak about it."

Her sister's cheeks darkened with a blush and she turned her face as she sank back down onto the bench in the middle of the gazebo. Miranda looked at the empty space beside her. She was tempted to take it and wrap her arms around Penelope to comfort her. But everything in her sister's body language said that she didn't want that comfort. She was too horrified and confused to be touched, especially by Miranda.

So Miranda stepped back to lean against the gazebo railing instead.

"Why did you come to the parlor?" she asked softly, feeling her way through the situation with great care. Her sister was already distressed. The wrong word could ruin everything.

Penelope stared at the ground beneath her feet. "Mama started grumbling about the fact that you hadn't reappeared. Talking about you shirking your duties. I slipped away to fetch you and bring you back before she worked herself into a complete frenzy."

Miranda rubbed her eyes. Her loyal sister had come to protect her. That made everything so much worse.

"I heard noises from the parlor and I thought it might be you. So I opened the door"—Penelope's breath caught—"and I saw Lord Rothschild with a woman up against the window. At first I was too shocked to say or do anything."

Miranda pursed her lips. How well she knew that feeling. The very same shock and uncertainty had washed over her the first time she saw Ethan and one of his lovers. That and the knowledge that she *should* turn away, but just couldn't.

Penelope's sharp intake of air brought Miranda back to the present. "And then he moved a little and I saw it was you he was . . . doing that to. I started to move, open my mouth to stop him. I thought he had to be forcing you. But then you moaned. You smiled. And I realized you—you liked it. You weren't being forced and you weren't resisting."

Miranda bent her head. She was embarrassed by her sister's

words, but she couldn't and wouldn't deny them to save face. "No, I wasn't," she finally whispered.

Penelope looked at her sharply, then darted her gaze away. "The realization stopped me from saying anything. I just watched you. Watched him. I couldn't turn away. And then he looked up and saw me. So I ran. I didn't know what else to do. I just"—her voice grew very small—"ran."

Miranda nodded. "As soon as Ethan—Lord Rothschild—let me know that you saw us, I came looking for you. I am sorry you had to see that, Penelope. I wouldn't have wanted to shock you like that for anything in the world."

Penelope held her gaze for the first time since Miranda found her. "You called him by his first name. That must mean you feel some level of closeness to him, beyond just what I saw tonight."

Miranda bit her lip. She had been lying to her sister for weeks, avoiding her questions, denying her intuitions. Now she owed her honesty. If only to clarify Penelope's confusion and ease her hurt and shock.

Still, her sister was coming right to the heart of the matter. To places Miranda had been trying to steer away from since the first time she came to Ethan's home and asked for his help. Penelope was pointing out the deeper feelings she had for him.

The ones she feared more than any touch.

Penelope continued before Miranda was forced to comment. "This wasn't the first time you did *that* with him, is it?"

At least that question was simpler. "No," Miranda admitted. "It is not."

Penelope sat in silence, pondering that statement. Then her

eyes widened and she lurched to her feet. "Is that— My God, *that* is why he offered to host my Season, isn't it? That is truly where you have been going each week. Not to Lady Inglewood's, but to *him* so he could . . . could do those things to you!"

Miranda flinched. When put like that, their bargain sounded so cheap, so tawdry, when it had been so much deeper. At least for her.

"I went to Ethan a few weeks ago and informed him of our situation. I asked for his help, knowing full well that he would require repayment of some kind in return." She sighed. "He asked for payment in . . ." Hot blood flooded her cheeks. "He wanted me. So I said yes."

Penelope shook her head. "You did this for me. You surrendered your innocence so that I could have a Season. Oh, Miranda, I'm so sorry. I never would have wanted that. You must feel so terrible."

Her sister's voice cracked and she covered her face with her hands and began to cry quietly.

Miranda stepped forward, shaking her head. She couldn't allow Penelope to believe she'd been forced into a bargain she detested.

"Penelope, no. Don't cry. Yes, I did enter the arrangement with Rothschild for you and our family. But what I did was never terrible. I did it for us, but I"—she hesitated—"I also did if for myself. I wanted to give him my innocence. I *wanted* the sinful pleasures he offered. I was never forced into anything. I went into the bargain with no qualms."

Her sister slowly lowered her hands and looked at her in shock. "No. That cannot be true."

Miranda's blush grew deeper. "It is true. There is . . . there is something in me, Penelope. Something I never told you. For years, I have longed for passion. For desire. For pleasure. It is why I didn't take any of the offers of marriage that were made to me over the years. I looked at those men asking for my hand and they—none of them measured up to the fantasy in my mind."

"A fantasy," her sister repeated, her voice hollow.

Miranda nodded and decided not to mention that the fantasy had always been Ethan and why. "But with Ethan, I knew I would be free to want, to feel, to desire. And I have been. I do regret that you saw us and that you were hurt by that. And I regret lying to you. But I—I cannot regret that I entered into this bargain."

"How can you say you do not regret it?" Penelope shot to her feet and grabbed Miranda's hands. Her sister clenched her fingers so tightly that it hurt. "You will either have to engage in deception or tell any man who offers for you the truth about your virginity. Either way, you gave up any chance to marrying well and having a normal life."

Miranda extracted her fingers with a sigh. "It may have escaped your notice, but I do not have any men lining up to offer for me anymore. Even if I did, I fear my reaction would be the same. Penelope, I don't think I'm cut out for what you call a 'normal' life. I have no desire for polite affections and distant relationships. When I am in Ethan's arms, I burn, I ache. I couldn't settle for less now."

She was surprised by how true that statement was. Somehow she'd thought that after she purged those desires for a few weeks that they would go away and leave her to accept a more normal, peaceful union if she found a chance to have one. Instead, the more time she spent with Ethan, the less she could imagine a life lived without passion.

A life lived without . . . *him*.

"You're in love with him," her sister said, her voice flat and emotionless as she stepped away.

Miranda gasped. At first, when Penelope said she and Ethan shared a closeness, that had been uncomfortable enough to face. But now she was throwing out the deepest, most foolish emotion Miranda could associate with a man who freely admitted that she was a mere game to him, a temporary conquest. And again, her sister's words rang painfully true.

Miranda *was* in love with him. Perhaps some part of her had been since the first moment he unknowingly awoke her true nature three years before. The time she had spent with him during the last month had only cemented those feelings. Knowing he could be tender, as well as dominant, caring as well as controlling . . . it only deepened the emotions she'd been trying to ignore even as they overtook her.

"It is complicated," Miranda whispered as her heart ached.

"Will he marry you now that he's ruined you?" Penelope snapped, folding her arms.

Miranda shut her eyes and tried to block out the fantasies that question inspired. They could only ever be just that. Fantasies.

"I very much doubt it. He has said again and again that he has no desire to marry."

"I'll tell Mother," her sister said after a cold pause.

Miranda's eyes flew open. "No! You mustn't. Penelope, if

you did, it would ruin everything. She would make a fuss, she wouldn't be able to stop herself. If the truth were made public, it would ruin your chances to marrying well and Beatrice and Winifred would be shunned by good society. If you do that, we'll have no chance to recover from our financial state. We could very well end up on the street and might all be forced into doing far worse than Ethan has ever asked of me."

Penelope sucked in her breath and Miranda could only hope she was thinking about the implications.

Her sister's eyes narrowed. "Very well, I won't tell Mama. But to save Beatrice and Winifred, not you."

Miranda winced, but she nodded. "I understand."

Penelope barked out an unpleasant laugh. "I wish I did. All this time, I thought you hadn't married because you wanted to love someone. But in truth, you were simply selfish and wanted some grand passion. A foolish fantasy."

Miranda covered her mouth as a gasp of pain pushed past her lips. Penelope, her very best friend as well as her sister, now looked at her with such disdain. "I—"

Penelope held up a hand. "No. I've heard enough. I swear to you, Miranda, I will do what you refused to. I will surrender whatever hopes I had for my own future if it means providing security for this family. I'll accept the first blasted offer of marriage I receive from a suitable gentleman who will be able to help us."

Miranda shook her head. "No, you can't sacrifice yourself like that."

Penelope shrugged. "You gave up your body to offer me the opportunity. I shall do what I choose in order to take advantage of it." She turned away. "And if you try to stop me, I *will* reveal what you did and ruin us all. I never want to speak of this again, Miranda. Now I must return to the party and go back to my hunt. I must find a suitable husband and quickly. Before you have nothing left to give up to assist me."

"Penelope!" Miranda called, clenching her fists. But her sister ignored her, stepped down from the gazebo, and walked into the darkness toward the house.

Miranda paced into the ballroom with a false, tight smile forced onto her cold lips. The next few hours were destined to be torture and yet she could do nothing to escape them.

She looked around the room. The guests continued to spin around the dance floor to the gay music. They were still enjoying the overflowing wine. Miranda flinched. How could everyone else's lives be so unchanged when hers felt like it had been blown apart? How could they not see that she wasn't the same woman who had crept after her mother such a short time ago?

No, she knew why. It was her deceptions that kept the truth from being obvious. She'd put on this false smile that made her cheeks ache and she'd gone up to her room to fix herself before she returned to the party. The truth was simply one more thing she would bury deep within herself.

"There you are!"

Miranda sighed as her mother came lumbering through the crowd, a scowl creasing her face.

"Where have you been?"

She shrugged. "I needed some air, Mama. But I'm back now and I won't leave again."

That seemed to placate her mother, as she nodded. "Good.

You *and* your sister both missed saying farewell to Lord Roth-schild when he cried off early. I think little of the man after our horrible encounter earlier, but it would have been better if you'd been here to say goodbye. For appearances sake."

Miranda nodded, but she was numb to her mother's contin-ued admonishments.

So, for the first time, Ethan had done as she asked. He had left the party. She should have been grateful. His continued pres-ence would have only upset Penelope, but relief wasn't what tightened Miranda's chest.

It was loss. She longed to see Ethan. To take comfort in his presence. To talk to him about her sister's harsh words in the garden. That she wanted those things all but cemented the fact that she loved him. Considering it wasn't even shocking to her anymore.

It just was.

"Penelope has been taking her duty much more seriously, though, since she returned to the ballroom."

Miranda snapped back to attention at the mention of her sister's name. "What?"

Her mother glared. "It seems she has realized her mar-riage could be our salvation. Look at her, surrounded by gentlemen."

Her mother motioned with pride across the room and Miran-da jolted. Indeed, her sister was the center of attention. Around her were rich widowers, titled bucks, and men publicly looking for legitimate heirs. Every one fit the financial requirements for saving their family. And every one made Miranda's skin crawl for differing reasons.

And if Penelope's hollow stare was any indication, she had some of the same thoughts.

"Mama, we cannot allow her to marry only for a purse," Miranda insisted, clutching her mother's silk-clad arm. "She could be so unhappy—"

Her mother shook her off. "There is no other choice, Miranda. You should know that better than anyone. And *you* will not use your influence over her to interfere. Do you understand me?"

As her mother turned and stormed across the ballroom, Miranda fought tears.

"I have no influence, Mama," she whispered. "Not over my own emotions. And certainly not over Penelope."

Fifteen

Ethan paced his chamber, unable to sleep although it had been many hours since he obeyed Miranda's edict and left her home. His mind raced with memories, both the pleasurable and the disagreeable. Images of Miranda's surrender. The vice of her body gripping his. And, inevitably, the pain in her eyes when he told her about Penelope's spying. But one thing rose above the tangle of his thoughts and beat in his head like an unavoidable drum.

Guilt.

Ethan had cut off such emotions long ago. About the same time he accepted that his character had been built by his bloodlines. He couldn't change it. All he could do was surrender to it and try his best to minimize the pain he caused others.

That was why he never kept a lover more than a few months. That was why he always chose experienced women who didn't want more than a few passionate encounters. That was why he had never married and didn't intend to.

But Miranda had stepped into his world and broken all his self-made rules. She was different than any other woman he'd taken to his bed. She'd given him mind-blowing pleasure, but also stirred the heart he tried so hard to ignore.

And how had he repaid her? By breaking the precious bond she shared with her closest sister. He had no doubt their relationship would be forever changed, and all because he'd lost his head and body in the pleasure of touching Miranda, consequences be damned.

He didn't like the guilt. He'd forgotten how that feeling ate at him like poison.

He downed a swig of the whiskey he'd poured for himself and left untouched for nearly an hour. The lukewarm, stale liquid burned at his throat, but offered no respite from his turbulent thoughts.

If he were another man, he'd be a hero. He'd march back to Miranda's house, kick down the door and demand he be given the chance to make right what he had destroyed. He'd . . . well, he supposed that meant marrying her.

With a shiver, Ethan poured another drink. *Marriage.* That was the second time he'd considered such a thing tonight.

Great God, what a thought. Yes, he'd have Miranda near him and that was a tempting notion, at least for now. But the "at least for now" part was the trouble. He knew himself far too well. He'd been infatuated with lovers before, but that desire always faded. Granted, he'd never felt for any of them what he felt for Miranda, but was he willing to take that chance? To bind himself to her forever only to bore of her within a few weeks or months?

He looked forward at the future that would be built if he did that. She would want children and he would likely indulge that desire. But he would be no father to them, he didn't know how. His own father had certainly been no role model to follow.

And the old man hadn't been an ideal husband, either. Over time, after a thousand tiny offenses and betrayals, Miranda would be hurt, then the hurt would turn to anger. Then despair. She was strong, so perhaps she wouldn't turn to a bottle to drown her feelings as his own mother had, but the consequences would still be far-reaching and painful to everyone involved.

No, heroics weren't the answer. But something. There had to be *something* he could do to fix what had been broken. Or at least give Miranda some kind of compensation for what had been lost.

The Seasons.

Ethan stopped pacing and set his drink aside. All this had begun because Miranda wanted those Seasons. He could give them to her without asking for any more than she had already given in return. It wasn't a perfect solution. After all, he was anything but bored with her at present and it wouldn't undo the fact that her sister had seen them together. Letting her go would be—

Impossible.

He couldn't do it. Not yet. Ethan scrubbed a hand over his face and cursed. He was too selfish to sever the ties to Miranda, but how else could he save her? Help her?

He stopped pacing. There was one other offer he could make. It wasn't perfect, but if she took it, he could have her and protect her without setting up a future that would pain them both.

It was something.

He strode to the door and yanked the bell pull for Winston. Within moments, the butler appeared.

"Yes, my lord?"

"Fetch me Brideson. I need to speak to him right away."

Winston arched a brow. "The footman, sir?"

Ethan nodded and Winston bowed away to find the man. The footman who was having a secret affair with Miranda's lady's maid could send her one final message. And he could only hope that the gesture he was about to make could do something to ease her pain.

At present, that was the thing he wanted to do more than anything else.

Please come see me.
—Rothschild

Miranda stared at the simple note, reading it for the third, perhaps fourth time, since Angelica delivered it a few moments before. For once there was no innuendo to his message, no subtle threat. Just a simple request. He'd even asked it nicely.

Still, Miranda couldn't detect his underlying meaning. Did he want her to come to him to discuss what had happened the night before? Did he want her to come in order to continue their affair as if last night had never happened? Or perhaps he wanted to end it all in person.

With a shiver, Miranda got to her feet and tossed the note into the fire. Dread filled her. It wasn't that she didn't want to see Ethan. In fact, the opposite was true. Despite her attempts to block all images of him from her mind, he had been in the forefront of her thoughts since last night. She'd hardly been able to attend at all as the soiree went on, images of him were so powerful.

Of course, she had remained at the party, doing her duty and watching in dismay as her sister's intentions became more and more clear, but her head and heart had been elsewhere. She'd never felt so alone and she found the person she wanted most was Ethan.

All of those reasons were why she dreaded going to see him today. She knew full-well how foolish it was to love him, to want his support, to want *him* for anything more than the shattering pleasure he could provide. Facing him, with his smug smirks and overpowering sensuality, would only slap her in the face with that reality even more.

And she was a little afraid that she'd launch herself into his arms and beg for comfort and love. Which would only serve to ruin everything even more than it had been ruined already.

But there was no avoiding it. Ethan beckoned and she couldn't refuse, so she had to get to it and do her best to keep her emotions in check, as he always did.

She looked at herself one final time in the mirror. Even she could see that she looked tired from her sleepless, troubled night. There was nothing she could do about that, either.

Miranda went downstairs and plastered a smile on her face as she entered the breakfast room, but as she passed through the door, she saw it was only Penelope who sat at the table, reading the morning paper while an untouched plate of eggs, muffins, and sausages went cold beside her.

Miranda's heart lurched as her sister spared her a fleeting glance then went right back to her paper without any attempt at a greeting.

"Good morning," Miranda tried as she shut the door behind her and went to the sideboard to serve herself a bit of food. Not that she was hungry anymore. Still, this was a chance to make some attempt to reconcile with her sister now that emotions weren't as raw as they had been last night.

Penelope made no answer and didn't acknowledge Miranda when she took her usual place at her sister's side. With a sigh, Miranda shook out her napkin and laid it in her lap.

"Where is everyone else?" she asked.

Penelope didn't look up from her reading. "Mother and the girls are still abed after their late night. *I* couldn't sleep."

Miranda shut her eyes at her sister's accusatory tone. "Yes, I had difficulty sleeping myself."

Only the clock tick was her answer.

She turned in her chair to look at her sister straight on. "Penelope, please, you cannot mean to utterly ignore me for the rest of your life. I know you are upset and confused-"

"I'm *not* confused," her sister said, her gaze finally meeting Miranda's. "I know exactly how I feel and exactly what I saw. I also know *exactly* what to do now."

"Yes, your intentions were quite clear last night. You have decided to marry for money, perhaps just to spite me?" Miranda threw up her hands. "What kind of future is that?"

"The future I need to fulfill," Penelope said on a sigh as she turned the page of the paper and returned to reading. "And as I said last night, I do not wish to speak to you about it. I don't want *your* advice on how to manage men."

Miranda's fists clenched reflexively under the table as anger filled her. She did truly understand that her sister was shocked and even disappointed, but her attitude was beginning to grate. Penelope wouldn't even try to understand her side of the situation.

"Perhaps I should simply go before we each say hurtful things," she sighed. "Even more hurtful than have already been said."

Her sister's gaze met hers again and narrowed. "Where will you go?"

Miranda flinched. She intended to go see Ethan, of course, but saying that would only make this situation so much worse. But she didn't want to lie any more.

"I'm going for a walk," she finally said and hoped her sister wouldn't press further.

Her hopes were dashed when Penelope rolled her eyes. "You're going to *him*, aren't you?"

Miranda got to her feet and walked to the window across the room. "Yes," she admitted softly. "He asked to see me."

"Well, you must be off, then. You wouldn't want to make Rothschild wait, would you?" Penelope shook her head. "God knows what he would demand of you if you did that."

"That isn't the way it is," Miranda cried, but the words sounded hollow. It had been that way in the past. And in truth, she had no idea what Ethan would or wouldn't demand now.

"It doesn't matter." Her sister leaned back in her chair like she had been defeated. "Just go and do whatever it is he asks of you. I don't want to think about it. I must keep my mind focused on what *I* must do now."

Miranda dipped her head. She was in an untenable situation.

Her sister was likely to make a terrible mistake by throwing herself headlong into whatever marriage presented itself first, yet Penelope wouldn't hear any advice from Miranda. And it wasn't as if she would get better counsel from anyone else. Their mother would endorse the scheme and their other sisters were too young to properly help.

With a sigh, Miranda moved to stand at her sister's shoulder. "Penelope—"

There was no acknowledgment, but Miranda pressed on regardless.

"I know you're hurt right now and upset at me. I do understand that, whether you believe me or not. Clearly, you won't let me talk you out of your schemes, or give me any chance to redeem myself or explain my own actions. At least not at present. But I do want to say one thing to you."

Her sister continued to stare at her paper, but Miranda sensed she was listening.

"Penelope, I cannot stop you from accepting the first offer of marriage from a man who can assist our family financially. But I do hope when you marry, that you find passion."

Her sister's shoulders bunched with tension.

"I may not be happy that you were hurt by what I did, but when it comes to the time I spent with Ethan, I won't apologize for that." She sighed. "Passion and desire are powerful, wonderful things. And I still believe, in my heart, that a life lived without them is a life not truly lived. You may not agree at present, but someday I think you'll understand. Or I hope you will."

Penelope didn't look up and Miranda stepped away toward the door. "I'll see you when I return later today."

Then she left her sister and the house, determined to face her fate with the man who had taught her everything she knew about passion and desire. And, like it or not, love.

"Good morning, Winston," Miranda said, hoping she didn't look utterly petrified as the butler opened the door and allowed her entry.

"Good morning, Miss Albright." The butler nodded in greeting. "Lord Rothschild is expecting you."

Miranda's hands began to shake and she shoved them behind her back. God, she needed some time alone to regain her composure. The walk over hadn't served to calm her nerves like she hoped it would. If anything, each step had increased her anxiety.

"You needn't show me upstairs. I know where to go."

The servant tilted his head. "Actually, miss, his lordship has not requested that you be sent to your normal meeting place. Do you know where the lake on the property is?"

Miranda's heart lurched to her throat. Did she know where the lake was? Quite intimately, though she had no intention of making that admission to the butler. She regretted making it to Ethan. What must he think of her?

"Miss?"

She forced herself to nod. "Y—Yes."

"Lord Rothschild will join you there in a short time. Do you need any accompaniment?"

Miranda shook her head as she followed him to a parlor and the double doors that led to a veranda and down into the gardens behind the house. "No, I can find it on my own."

"Very good, miss."

Miranda tried to focus her thoughts as she stepped outside and made her way toward the lake. Instead, her wayward mind buzzed with memories of what she had witnessed from her secret hiding spot in the woods around the water. And of more recent memories of Ethan touching *her* so passionately.

As the lake appeared in the distance, she sighed. Ethan was clearly trying to send her a message with his choice of meeting place, but what the message was, she couldn't decipher. It could be an olive branch, an attempt at seduction—or a way to rupture the ties that bound them.

She sat down by the edge of the water to wait. Her gaze slipped to the woods. From this position, they seemed heavier than they were within. She wasn't certain where exactly her hiding place had been. The branches and leaves had fully cloaked her, certainly. No wonder Ethan was shocked by her admission.

"Where did you hide?"

She started at Ethan's voice and got to her feet. She turned to find him slowly making his way down the final hill to stand beside her. She looked him up and down, drinking in the sight of him, just as she always had. Today he looked more pulled together than the first time she came here a month ago, making her request for his help, but not as crisp as he had been at the ball last night, when he had been every inch the proper gentleman.

No, despite his tied cravat, there was a tiredness in his eyes and the hint of scratchy stubble on his well-defined chin.

Miranda wanted so desperately to touch him, but instead she kept her hands fisted at her side.

"I was trying to determine that very thing, but I can't see it."

He smiled. "Then it was the perfect spot. Here." He motioned to the place where she'd been waiting for him. "Sit down again. We might as well be comfortable."

Miranda nodded. This wasn't what she expected after last night. Ethan had been taunting toward her in the past, he'd been dominant. He had been tender. But he'd never been like this. Friendly, like he was trying to make her comfortable.

Perhaps he was. Perhaps he, too, recognized the strangeness of their current situation. And though she appreciated the attempt, she secretly longed for that dominant seduction again. That she understood and knew how to respond to. This . . . this was confusing.

"I wish I hadn't told you the truth," she said as she turned her face to look at the water. "I never wanted anyone to know what I . . . did."

He reached out and his warm fingers caressed her jaw before he turned her face to look at him. "I'm glad to know it. It explains so many things."

Hot blood flooded her cheeks, but Miranda made her gaze stay even. "Such as?"

He smiled. "Like why you always looked at me like you knew my secrets. That was why I was so drawn to you, even though I knew I could never pursue those desires."

She tilted her head. "I still don't understand how you could read my thoughts so clearly, long before we really knew each other."

He sighed and dropped his fingers away from her face. "I don't understand that, myself. But it's true. I noticed you, Miranda. I watched and wanted you, but I never thought I could have you. Perhaps I never should have."

A vice of pain gripped her heart and squeezed until she could scarcely breathe. But somehow she kept her tone measured.

"You regret what we did? Because of the trouble my mother and my sister caused. I know it—it complicates things. I'm sure your other lovers never caused you such turmoil."

He stared at her. "The trouble for me? No, I meant perhaps we shouldn't have done this because of what it has caused for you. I even thought you might not be able to leave the house to meet with me after last night."

Miranda drew back. "What would you have done if I had sent word that I was being kept away?"

"Come to you," he said, matter-of-factly. "But I'm glad to not have to bypass your mother in order to speak to you. This should be between us. Just us. It's none of their affair."

Covering her eyes, Miranda sighed. "I wish that were true, Ethan. But now it's not just between us anymore. Last night changed that and there is no changing it back."

He frowned and his expression was soft and understanding. Again, those emotions were not ones she knew how to respond to, not from him. They were so foreign on a face that she had only seen reflect passion and control and desire.

"What happened after we parted company last night?" he asked quietly. "I want to hear it all."

Miranda sighed. She'd wanted to tell him, talk to him, be comforted by him, for twelve hours. And now that she was faced with all those things, she wasn't sure how to start. Not without revealing too much about herself, not just the situation they had put themselves in.

But she had no choice. Ethan had never accepted denials and

she doubted he would begin now. Slowly, she told him the story of chasing her sister, their ugly encounter in the gazebo, her successful plea for Penelope to keep what she'd seen to herself, and finally the last exchange they'd had that morning.

The only thing she left out was that her sister had helped Miranda realize how much she loved him. That was a confession she could not make. Not now, not ever.

When she was finished, Ethan was quiet for a long time. He simply looked out over the water, watching a mated pair of geese swim their way toward the far side of the pond.

"I'm sorry, Miranda. I never intended to hurt you," he finally said softly. "I hope you know that."

Miranda gaped at him. "You hurt me? No. I hurt myself. I knew from the very beginning that my lies might come back to haunt me. Penelope has been suspicious of both your intentions and my actions since the moment you offered to sponsor her Season and I started rambling on about Lady Inglewood." She rubbed her eyes. "I just didn't know I would break my relationship with the one family member I still have a strong connection to. But that is my own doing. I knew what you would want and what you would demand of me . . . probably before I even came here that first afternoon. I can't lie and say it wasn't what I wanted or agreed to."

He reached out and took her hand, drawing it up to cup it between his palms. He stared at the joined fingers, as if he were considering what they meant when they were tangled.

"I want to help you, you know."

She stared at him, taken aback by this sudden kindness and care toward her. It was a dangerous and unexpected thing to find with him. It made her want to curl into his chest and be held and reassured. Things he didn't want anything to do with.

"I don't think there is anything that can be done. My sister is angry and hurt. Hopefully that will change, but I don't think any intervention on my part or yours will speed that along. I am on one path and she is on another, at least for now. We're both trying to help our family, so perhaps that common ground will bind us again in the future."

He frowned. "We made a pact to stay in this bargain until the end of the summer. To meet only weekly. But I think I could do more for you and your family, Miranda. I think I could keep Penelope from throwing herself into a mercenary, loveless marriage."

Miranda flinched at the thought of what her sister wanted to do. "What could you do? I'm willing to hear any thoughts."

He cleared his throat, shifting like he was uncomfortable. It was so odd to see that, like he wasn't at ease in his own skin, the one place she knew he was almost completely contented and in control.

"Miranda, what if we altered our bargain? I would like"—he stopped and looked at her. The intensity of his gaze burned at her, held her steady even as it made her want to turn away. "I want you to become my mistress."

Sixteen

There. He had said it. Ethan wrinkled his brow. He didn't feel as relieved as he thought he would. And Miranda didn't look as pleased as he believed she would be when he pictured the moment over and over in his head the night before.

"Your—your mistress?" she repeated, swallowing hard. The color had left her cheeks and her blue eyes were wide and filled with emotions so tangled he could neither separate nor identify them.

He nodded. God, it sounded terrible coming from her lips. Like he was just offering to buy her in a different way. Why did he suddenly feel guilty for offering her this option?

He cleared his throat and tried to clarify. "Yes. I haven't had a true mistress for . . . well, a very long time. I have lovers, but they are temporary. But when I did have mistresses, I took care of them. I would provide a nice home for you in London where you could launch your sisters' Seasons. I would make sure you had accounts at all the shops and that your family had invitations to every event where their appearance could be desirable and useful."

Miranda was nodding, but it didn't seem like she was really agreeing or acknowledging what he was saying. More like she just had to move, to release some of the tension that was simmering through her body.

"And, of course, we would be utterly discreet," he said. "I realize you aren't in the position of women who normally become a mistress. At least until your family is settled, your actions could still hurt their chances. So I would be certain that your name would be protected."

Miranda pushed from her sitting position and walked to the edge of the lake. She looked over the water, remaining utterly silent.

Finally, her voice cut the heavy tension between them. "My, you have thought of everything, haven't you?"

He nodded, pondering whether or not to go to her, to touch her. He wanted to, God knew he wanted to take her in his arms and hold her and kiss her and touch her until he made her forget, at least for a little while, how difficult last night had been for her. But from all appearances, that wasn't what she wanted from him. At least, not yet. So he allowed her that space.

"I have," he agreed. "I started thinking about this last night and have thought of nothing else since the idea first came to me. You told me more than once that the life of a mistress was one you would consider once our bargain was over."

He swallowed past the bitter taste that thought always put in his mouth. The idea of Miranda with any other man was utterly distasteful to him. And this arrangement would keep that from happening. At least until he could bear the idea.

He continued, "If you truly meant those words, would you not consider me as your protector?"

She turned to face him and her expression was so utterly unreadable that he stepped back. He'd always been able to tell what emotions were in her mind. That was one of the things that drew him to her. She never pretended, she never hid. Miranda simply *was* and she made no apologies or excuses for what was in her heart.

Now that heart was locked away and he found he missed the connection he'd felt with her since they made their bargain.

"I have spent a month with you," she said softly. "And I have no doubt that you have been and would be a wonderful protector for any woman who was lucky enough to take to your bed and be in your life as your mistress."

Again the emotions that accompanied her reply were strange to him. He did feel relief at the idea that she would be his, but there was also disappointment. Like he wanted . . . *more* somehow, even though he was perfectly aware he could offer no more than this.

"Does that mean you'll accept my offer?"

"It is tempting, Ethan," she said and her voice broke even as her face remained stoic. "Just as you have always been tempting to me. But becoming your mistress wouldn't help me. It would only drive a bigger wedge between Penelope and me. And when you bored of me, I could be in a far worse position than I am now."

He shook his head. "But I promise to pay for your sisters' Seasons until—"

"Until when?" she interrupted and her smile was that strange, jaded one again. "Until one of them lands their rich husband? Until all three are married? Until you find a new lover who interests you more? No, Ethan. I cannot depend on the promises you make when you still want me. When you don't, you would come to regret making this arrangement, and I—I couldn't face losing your regard. Right now it's all I have left."

He frowned. "So you won't do it?"

"I can't." She looked at the ground between their feet. "I *wish* I could say yes, but I can't."

Ethan shut his eyes. So she wouldn't be his beyond this agreement they had made. The summer was all he would have and it was bleeding away at a shocking rate. So quickly that it wouldn't be long enough. At that moment, he knew, like he knew his own name, that another two months of pleasure wouldn't ease the ache he felt for her even a fraction.

But if it was all he could have. . .

Miranda shivered just a little and her gaze still did not lift to his. "In fact, I have also been pondering our situation since last night. And I fear there is only one solution. One I hate, but it's all I can do."

Ethan cocked his head at her sad tone. Like she was about to lose something that meant a great deal to her. He sucked in his breath as realization dawned on him. He drew back. She couldn't mean . . . she wouldn't—

"Miranda—" he began, as if he could stay her words with a plea. He didn't want to hear them.

"I cannot continue with the arrangement we made last month," she continued with a flinch.

"You cannot mean that." He shook his head. "You don't want that."

Her gaze snapped up and the pain in her eyes was almost too much to bear. "I foolishly thought I could take your offer without consequences, but the price for the pleasure was too high. And as much I do want to keep meeting with you, keep"—a tear trickled down her face and she swiped it away with the back of her hand and a deep frown—"keep being with you, I can't."

Ethan gripped his hands into fists. Pain rushed through him, a pain as powerful as anything he'd ever felt. He'd been so separated from such feelings for so long that it took him off guard. This was why he'd locked his heart away. He hated how off center and out of control the ache made him.

And yet he couldn't seem to master it this time. As hard as he tried, he couldn't find a way to agree with Miranda and just let her go. He wanted more. He wanted her to stay. Even though he couldn't ever give her what she wanted. *Be* what she wanted.

And yet there was only one option remaining. The one thing he had tried to avoid with every fiber of his being. But now he was faced with a choice: Make the offer he'd evaded so many times in the past. Or lose Miranda.

When couched in those terms, there was only one answer.

"Then marry me," he burst out, surprising himself.

Miranda staggered away, her eyes widening to almost impossible lengths. He couldn't blame her for her disbelief. He was experiencing a hefty dose of it, himself. What was he saying?

"You don't mean that," she whispered. "You told my mother just last night that you have no intentions of ever marrying."

He flinched. Yes, he had said that. He'd meant it at the time.

But now the desire to keep Miranda with him, to help her, was more powerful than his aversion to wedded bliss. Although his reasons to remain a bachelor still existed, they were secondary.

"I did tell your mother that," he admitted. "Partly to shock her into leaving me alone and partly because I would make a terrible husband. Especially to you, Miranda. I know I would and you should know it, too. But I still offer this because I can't stand to know I've hurt you so badly without making some attempt to repair the damage."

She shut her eyes. "So you would marry me to assuage your guilt."

He shrugged. "I won't lie to you and say pretty words that will only haunt us both later. I cannot be dishonest when it comes to this. But I still make the offer. Think of it, Miranda. You would be a Countess. My money and my residences would be yours, there could be no undoing that. My title and its prestige could help your sisters. You and I could be together, for as long as we liked."

"And when you no longer desire my presence in your bed?" Her voice didn't even tremble, although she never looked his way.

He shrugged one shoulder. "You would still have all the benefits of being my wife. And I promise you I would never make a fool of you publicly."

Miranda didn't address his statement, but she finally met his gaze evenly. "Why do you say you wouldn't make a good husband, especially to me?"

Ethan frowned. "It's in my blood, Miranda. There is no fighting that fate."

She pursed her lips and they became a bloodless line. "What does that mean?"

He ran a hand through his hair. He had never spoken about this to anyone before. Not friends, not relatives, certainly not to his lovers. He didn't like *thinking* about the past, let alone talking about it.

"Leave it be." He shook his head. "Just know that it's true."

She let out a divisive snort that brought his gaze to her face. Miranda folded her arms and glared at him. No longer was the timid girl who bent to his will standing before him. This Miranda was different. There was a fire in her stare, a steel. It was a shock for him to realize that strength had always been there. She'd had to possess it to deal with the blows her family dealt her. Only she'd never shown that side to him. Instead, she had leaned on him during their brief time together. Trusted him. He hadn't realized it at the time, but she had allowed him to protect her as much as control her.

And now she wasn't. Not anymore. Strange how the thing he hadn't recognized he had was the one thing he wanted more than anything in the world.

"Don't tell me that you want to marry me, but that you wouldn't make me happy. Don't warn me, even as you tempt me. Don't say you don't want to lie and then hide the truth." Her tone was uncharacteristically severe, but he sensed it was out of pain rather than anger. "I want to know why. You owe me that answer before I give you mine."

"You want to know the ugliness, Miranda?" he barked, stepping toward her. "You want to hear all the details that innocent ears are normally protected from?"

She nodded, though a bit of the bravado in her stare and demeanor faded. Still, she stood her ground. He admired her for that, even through his frustration and anger.

"Fine. Here is what you want to know. My father *fucked* anything with a skirt and a smile," Ethan growled, wrestling with memory and emotion with every single word. "He cuckolded my mother in public, in private, in her damned bed with her whore of a maid. And when she cried and drank and begged for a little decorum, do you know what he said to her?"

Miranda swallowed hard as she shook her head in the negative.

"That it was in his blood. That he couldn't help it. This was his nature and he couldn't fight that."

Ethan clenched his fists as an image of his mother's tear-streaked face danced in his mind. Vivid memories of her laid out on the floor of her room, a bottle in one hand, sobbing. Refusing to let her son—what had he been, eight then?—refusing to let him help her.

"Ethan—" Miranda reached for him, almost on instinct.

He shook off his thoughts and pushed her hand away. Yes, he wanted her to touch him, but if she did, he might break. He couldn't break.

"No, you wanted the truth, so hear all of it," he said as he paced passed her. He felt her stare burn into his back, but he ignored it. "My mother turned to drink for comfort. More and more of it to kill the pain and blur the humiliation. Perhaps it helped her. It didn't help me. I had no one. In fact, I was transformed into my mother's support, her counselor, even her whipping boy when the nights were long."

Miranda shut her eyes. "A mother's love can cut as well as soothe," she said softly.

He nodded. On that point, at least, they had a common bond. "And then there was my father. I had to watch him, to hear him lecture on the fine points of seduction. He told me that I had to learn. I had to know. Because his blood was in my veins, too. And someday I would be just like him. I vowed I wouldn't. But when I was fifteen, he brought a very pretty little whore to my room and nature took its course."

He turned to face her. She was crying now. Quietly. Pity seemed to seep out of her every pore. He felt it in her stare. It radiated off of her. He flinched away from it, not wanting that. He didn't want any of it.

"You know, it turns out he was right about me," he said, low and even. "I *am* just like him. Only I had enough control to steer my desires away from women who would be hurt when I finished with them. I stayed with the courtesans and the widows and the married women. Ladies who knew about sex and pleasure, but wanted nothing more. I even stopped keeping mistresses because they sometimes demanded more than what I could offer in pleasure and funds."

He moved on her, catching her arms before she could back away. He pulled her closer, feeling her mold against him. And just as he knew it would, his body reacted. He went hard in an instant, his blood heated. All those things served to prove his point. And judging from the look of horror and desire mixed in her stare, she knew it as well as he did.

"And then you came to me," he said, his voice no more than a harsh whisper. "And made me break all those rules. You were an innocent and a lady. Whether you believe me or not, I grew to care for you, with all your hidden strength and natural sensuality. So now I'm offering you the thing I swore I never would. But you have to know, Miranda, you *must* know that a time will come when I will not be able to stop myself from seeking out the company of some other woman. I will want to love you." He caught his breath. "I do *want* to love you. But I can't. Or I won't. Or maybe some of both. I'll give you everything but that. Everything but faithfulness. Is that honest enough for you?"

Miranda gasped, dragging in a harsh breath and he realized she'd been holding her breath since he touched her. She was shaking in his arms, her pulse skittered beneath her skin. And her silent tears, so opposite from the sobbing, wrenching ones he'd once seen his mother shed, tormented him.

"Do you know what is in my blood?" she whispered. Her voice shook wildly.

He let her go, steadying her before he backed away. "No."

"From my mother, I have manipulation and a mercenary desire for money and prestige. From my father, I have an out of control hunger for more and more. More of anything. Anything to fill him up." She wiped at the tears that clung to her cheeks. "But I choose not to let their demons haunt me or control my life. I chose not to follow the paths they laid out for me with their actions."

She moved toward him, reached for him. Her warm fingers closed around his forearm and her stare was pleading. "We *choose*, Ethan. You can choose to be whatever kind of man you want to be. And if you cared enough for me to give up all the others, you would. If you loved me, not just *wanted* to love me, then nothing else would matter."

She released him and backed away. "But you don't. It's not anyone's fault. It just is. But if we are speaking honestly to each other, then you must know. I do love you, Ethan."

Her words, spoken so low, hit him as hard as a punch in a tavern brawl. His breath left him, his stomach twisted, he nearly doubled over in shock. "What?"

She smiled. "I know those aren't words you want to hear, since you have convinced yourself of all love's lesser qualities, but they're true. I love you. It's no one's fault. It just is. The offer of marriage you are making to me is almost irresistible. I am so tempted to love you as long as you would let me. But if I did that, I'd curse us both. I couldn't watch you spiral away from me in guilt because you knew your choices hurt me. And I couldn't let my desire to save my family from ruin take away my soul. I don't want that, for either of us."

Miranda walked to the edge of the pond and looked toward the spot where she had been staring when he came. The place she said she secretly watched him all those years. Ethan couldn't take his eyes off of her. He was still reeling from her declaration of love. It was still sinking into every pore, changing him beneath the skin.

But when he looked at her, he didn't feel guilt or remorse or even panic. All he saw was the most beautiful woman he'd ever known. All he felt was wanting.

"My sister says I'm selfish because I wanted passion over security. But she's wrong." Miranda let out a long sigh. "I am selfish because I want love over passion. And you won't give me that. Perhaps you can't. But either way, I can't take the security in exchange for anything less. Perhaps I could from some other man, but not from you. Not from you."

Ethan couldn't look away. His emotions were there. He could feel them bubbling below the surface, but for now he had been shocked into numbness.

"So, you are saying no. You won't become my mistress and you won't marry me. You are determined to cut all ties with me," he said, but the words seemed to come from some other, faraway voice.

She looked at him with the saddest smile he had ever seen. "I must. The other options are simply too painful. But I want one thing from you before we end this affair."

"What?" he asked, his voice rough. "What more can you ask for after denying me everything?"

She stepped toward him and placed her palms on his chest. The heat from her touch rushed through him like an inferno.

Looking up, she whispered, "I want you to make love to me, here in this place where I learned so much about passion and desire and wanting."

He shut his eyes as a groan escaped his lips. Even now, knowing she was telling him this would be the last time they touched, his body reacted so powerfully to her. Proof positive that everything he told her about his failings was true.

"Why?" he whispered, even as his mouth moved toward hers because he couldn't control the kiss.

"Because I want the memory," she said as she threaded her fingers through the short, crisp hair at the back of his neck. "Give me this last memory. Please."

His mouth met hers in answer.

Seventeen

From the emotions that simmered in every fiber of Ethan's being, Miranda expected his kiss to be rough, demanding, even punishing in its passion. But just as he had been surprising her for so long, he took her off guard yet again. He was gentle. His lips brushed hers, hardly touching her for a brief moment before the pressure increased.

He slipped his fingers into her hair and angled her face for better access. She let him lead her, surrendering everything she was, everything she'd ever wanted to a man who had already told her he couldn't give her the one thing she needed in return. Tears flooded her eyes as his tongue breached her lips and swirled inside her mouth to taste her.

This was the last moment they would have together. That was the only thing she knew for certain. And Miranda was going to make it worth all the sacrifices. She was going to burn every touch on her memory so that in the future she could relive this last time over and over. No matter what else happened in the lonely future.

She clutched his shoulders, reaching for more of his kiss, for all of his passion, but he held back, continuing the gentle exploration instead.

Her hair fell around his fingers, around her shoulders, a golden curtain that could protect them, at least for a moment, from the outside world. She allowed it to protect her, setting aside her heartbreak and worry so that the harsh emotions wouldn't taint the experience.

Ethan let her go and stepped back. His eyes were wild, desperate, belying the utter control of his kiss. He looked at the grassy hill.

"Normally I'd have a blanket," he said, his voice a gruff apology.

She smiled. "I know."

His gaze caught hers, the wildness lingering beneath a veil of pain. "With you, it was different," he said softly. "I know that isn't enough, but it's true."

The tears she just fought off returned to Miranda's eyes and she reached out to touch his arm. "It's enough for now. For today."

He stared at her for a long, silent moment, then shrugged out of his jacket. He laid it on the ground, spread wide open, then went to work on his cravat and shirt beneath.

"At least I can give you some protection," he explained as he pulled the linen over his head.

Miranda stared, still mesmerized by the beautiful lines of his body. By the way his lean muscles worked beneath his skin with every motion. He spread the shirt out beside the jacket and then turned to her, eyes on fire with potent desire.

He reached out to feather his fingers along the ruffles at the neckline of her gown. Her eyes fluttered shut as his knuckles grazed her sensitive skin.

"Ethan," she breathed, grasping at his bare arm to remain steady.

His arm snaked around her waist and he pulled her against his warm, naked chest as he continued to caress her skin with featherlight touches that served to drive her mad. She lifted her mouth in mute offering, but he ignored that, staring intently at the way his fingers looked splayed out across the paleness of her skin and shabby fabric of her gown.

"Turn around," he ordered, his voice husky.

She did so, unable to deny him anything when her body was craving his touch and her legs were shaking with anticipation. He cupped her arms, first sliding his palms up to her shoulders, then back to the little buttons that closed her gown. She arched, moving closer to him in a quiet demand that he strip her out of her clothing.

But he wouldn't be pushed to do anything faster or differently than he seemed to have planned. Instead, he pushed her hair out of the way and pressed a warm kiss against her neck, just above her gown's edging. Then another. Another.

Miranda let out a little cry. She'd never realized her back was so sensitive, but those gentle caresses lit her body on fire, sent shock waves of wet heat through her to settle between her trembling legs. Ethan could have flipped her skirt up and had her right there with no resistance from her body.

In fact, that was what she wanted. But he wasn't going to give her that. It was his final torment. This last time they came together wouldn't be swift and passionate. It would be gentle and slow, like he wanted to linger over her.

He slipped one button free and parted the fabric to reveal just a tiny sliver of skin. His lips touched the top of her spine and Miranda lurched back. Her backside rubbed against his pelvis and she felt the hard, ready thrust of his cock against her cheeks. It was little consolation knowing he was just as needy as she was.

"You've made clear your demands already, Miranda," he whispered as he slipped the next button loose and revealed more skin. "If this is to be the last time I touch you, then I have no intentions of rutting with you like some animal."

Miranda couldn't help a little moan at that image, but she stopped rubbing against him. The action didn't relieve her desire in the least, in fact it only ratcheted up the overpowering need that he didn't seem to be in any hurry to relieve.

The next button slipped loose and now he'd come to the top of her chemise rather than bare skin. He sighed as he kissed her through the thin fabric.

"I still say you deserve satin." He pushed the last few buttons loose and kissed her to the very base of her spine. "Silk. I wish I could have seen you in them."

Her breath caught at the longing in his voice. "But every time I wear that chemise," she breathed, "I'll think of you."

A slap of emotion hit Ethan and his fingers faltered. This was the *last* time he would ever touch Miranda. The concept choked him, but he pushed the unpleasantness aside. His hands slipped beneath her gown and he pushed. The fabric fell forward. Miranda did nothing to keep it from folding over her waist and she didn't resist when Ethan pushed the gown over her hips. He pushed it away and turned her to face him.

"Your skin is finer than any satin," he murmured before he dropped his mouth back to hers.

He felt her shiver as she opened to him. Her arms came around him and she clung so tightly, so hard. Like she didn't want to let him go. But she was. Despite all his offers, she intended this to be the last time they would be together.

He hated it and his initial reaction was to take her hard and punishing. To make her come and come and come until she was weak beneath him. But beyond that anger, the one emotion he understood and didn't completely shun, was something else. Something more powerful.

He wanted to let her feel that he did care for her. The only way he knew how. That he recognized it wasn't enough, but that he would give her all he had before he did the unthinkable and let her go.

Miranda's hips tilted, brushing his erection with a smooth, grinding motion. Damn, but she knew how to make him wild, even when he wanted control. He found the hem of her chemise and tugged, pulling it up and over her head with suddenly shaking hands.

Stepping back, he laid the thin fabric beside his discarded jacket and shirt, a makeshift blanket to protect her from the prickly grass.

Then he wrapped one arm around her back and one around her waist, cradling her as he dropped her down to lay across the discarded clothing. He took a place beside her and stared down at her blonde hair spread out against his dark jacket, bright eyes misty with emotion and desire. He drank in every detail, burning the image of her into his mind.

"The first time you saw me," he murmured. "What was I doing?"

Her eyes darkened with a little flash of wickedness. Instead of answering, she parted her legs wide and beckoned to him. It didn't take much coaxing for him to take a place between her thighs. She smiled as she placed her hands on his shoulders and pushed down.

He grinned as he began to kiss his way down her body, stroking his tongue over her nipples. They beaded as a soft breeze blew in over the lake and Miranda groaned, kneading his shoulders and urging him even lower.

Ethan rubbed his rough cheek against her flat stomach, darted his tongue into the indentation of her belly button, and then he settled between her legs. She brought her knees up and over his shoulders, spreading herself wide for their mutual pleasure.

He opened her with his thumbs and when a second breeze wafted over them, she twitched, her moans growing louder and merging with the far away chirping of the birds and sound of the water lapping against the shore of the pond.

When he brought his mouth down on her, the moans turned to a cry. She was already quaking by the second stroke of his tongue, her hips rising to meet his mouth and her sheath trembling and clenching. He sucked her clit and she burst honeyed sweetness over his tongue as she screamed out his name.

Miranda panted as her body's trembling subsided. Here she was, living out the fantasies she'd painted in the shadowy darkness of her wooded hiding place. She was lying along the lake shore, being pleasured by Ethan. Like a wanton out in the open where anyone could stumble upon them.

It was everything she had ever imagined or hoped for, but it was also less satisfying than she had dreamed. Because it was a way to say goodbye. Somehow the consequences had never been part of her wicked fantasies.

They were most assuredly part of reality. Pleasure and pain, mixed together.

Ethan slid up her body and kissed her. She tasted the sweet essence of her release on his tongue and the hint of his desperation. It mimicked her own.

When he drew back, his stare was intense and focused. "I wish I'd known you were watching."

She smiled. "I was afraid you would discover me, but also sometimes wished you would. I wondered what you'd do if you found me there, spying on you and being incredibly aroused by everything I shouldn't see."

He cupped her breast, stroking her sensitive nipples with his thumb. "What did you imagine I would do?"

"Send me away," she gasped as pleasure lit through her body. "Or dominate me like you dominated all those other women."

He chuckled. "Who's to say I wouldn't have let you take control?"

She looked up at him through cloudy vision. "No one controls you, Ethan. No one ever has."

After he'd stared at her for a moment, he cupped her hips. He rolled to his back, dragging her with him, pulling her onto his body.

"Try," he whispered as he cupped the back of her neck and brought her mouth down to his. She kissed him, reveling in the feel of his body beneath her, the hard thrust of his erection probing at her bare stomach through his trousers. She shifted, opening her legs and straddling his trim hips.

The kiss grew deeper, hotter and she couldn't help but rock in time to the thrust of his tongue, whimpering as the apex of her thighs stroked over his rough wool breeches.

He slipped a hand between them, even as he pressed his lips to her throat and freed his erection. It sprang up between their bodies, hot and hard and ready.

Their eyes met, gazes holding. Ethan searched her stare and saw everything she had declared for him earlier. Her love. Her pain. Her loss. It awed him to think that a woman like this could give him so much. And he wished he was capable of giving her the same and so much more in return. But he knew himself too well. For now he cared for her, but in a month, a year . . . his cravings would be too overpowering.

But he could give her one thing now. The thing he had denied every other lover.

"Take the control, Miranda," he whispered, grasping her hips and dragging her into a better position. She lifted up on her knees and the tip of his cock nudged at her wet sheath.

Her gaze never faltered as she eased down. His cock slipped

in, inch by slow and painful inch. She clenched around him in a wet, welcoming glove and he groaned out pleasure. He wanted to pull at her hips and drive her rhythm. He wanted to lift up and spear into her body until she cried out. But he'd offered control, so all he did was grit his teeth and let her do what she pleased.

She took him to the hilt, engulfing him in heat so pure and blazing that his vision blurred, but then came to a stop. She wiggled experimentally, growing accustomed to the new position and a yelp of pleasure pushed past his lips against his will.

"Ride," he managed to grind out. "*Please.*"

She smiled at the *please* and obliged him. Her hips bucked and she set a soft, rolling rhythm. When his fingers dug into her hips, she caught them with her hands and lifted them above his head, lacing their fingers together and holding them against the grassy ground.

Her movements became faster and her breath caught. He watched her face twist with pleasure, with power and his cock swelled even harder. He had always been so consumed with taking control over her, he'd never paused to witness how beautiful she was when she took control herself. She was like a goddess, writhing above him in ecstasy, driving him to the edge even as she careened toward madness herself.

A cry burst from her lips and her hips pumped harder, faster, pulling him along and milking his orgasm from him in a blinding burst of explosive heat and pleasure. He poured himself into her with a roar of release and she collapsed against his chest, pressing her mouth to his as their bodies merged one final time.

★ ★ ★

The breeze stirred Ethan's hair and he opened his eyes. He looked around for Miranda, but he was alone. After their powerful joining, they had lain in the grass together, bodies entangled until he drifted into sleep. But sometime during his nap, she had gone.

Forever.

The reminder clenched like a fist around his heart. He sat up. She'd covered him with his wrinkled, grass-stained shirt and he tossed the linen away. He didn't want the reminder of her anymore. Not when she was gone.

It shouldn't hurt this much. Losing Miranda had been inevitable. He'd known it from the start. He'd been aware of it when he offered to be her protector and even her husband. But now the truth of the situation was like salt in a gaping wound.

Cursing, he swept up his clothing and began to dress. It was time to return to London. In the city, with the pleasures of women and friends and drink, he would forget the little innocent who had changed his world. The one who made him offer her things he vowed he would never share. The one who had refused anything less than the one thing he could not give her.

Back in London he would forget.

He had to forget.

Eighteen

One month later

Miranda had never liked London, not that she had been there often. Her only real exposure had been during her first Season, before her father died. At the time, she'd been so excited. So certain she would find both love and a grand passion. But the truth had been far different. The balls had been too crowded, her mother had been too loud, and two of the most beautiful women in Society had come out the same year, so she'd never been considered a "Diamond of the First Water". As for the men, well none of them had been Ethan. In the end, she'd longed for home.

This time, the city was just as she remembered it. Too crowded, too close and the stench of coal hung so heavy in the air that it was cloying and dirty in her lungs.

London in the fall was even worse, for the wind was bitter and the streets dreary and wet, nothing like the family's country home where the leaves were bright and the air crisp and clean.

She sighed. Unfortunately, even *home* didn't feel very homey anymore. Since the events of the month before, she hadn't been comfortable there, either. She wasn't sure where she belonged, or even if she belonged anywhere.

The only thing she was certain of was that she never would have come back to London if Penelope hadn't finally gotten her way.

Miranda looked across the carriage at her sister, who was staring out the window with that dead, faraway look that had been in her eyes for two weeks. Ever since she accepted the sudden marriage proposal of Lord Norman, a sixty-year-old Viscount who had come sniffing around just after Ethan departed the countryside.

Their mother was ecstatic, of course. She had already spent through all of Ethan's money and now Norman's flowed in, paying for a huge wedding that was utterly unseemly for an eighteen-year-old woman and a man three times her age who had been married twice before. But their mother insisted and Norman seemed to love that the world was so aware of his catch of a young, pretty bride. Miranda could only imagine how he must boast to his friends. Her stomach turned at the thought every time.

Their carriage now weaved through the London streets, moving toward the Viscount's town home and the party being held tonight in honor of the upcoming wedding.

Miranda tried to catch Penelope's eye, but her sister ignored her. Despite all her attempts at repair, their bond was still broken. In fact, things only seemed to be getting worse. Penelope's hostility had increased since her sudden engagement. The entire situation made Miranda's heart ache.

As did the constant questions that went through her mind. If Penelope wouldn't forgive her, even after a month, even after Ethan disappeared from their lives . . . had Miranda made the right decision to let him go? To refuse to be his mistress or his wife?

Those questions haunted her at night, as did dreams and memories of his touch, his kiss, his body moving inside her own.

"Miranda, are you even listening?"

Miranda started. She had become so talented at blocking her mother's voice that she hadn't even realized Dorthea had been talking.

"I'm sorry, Mama, simply woolgathering. What were you saying?" she asked, gritting her teeth in the hopes she could force patience. Tonight promised to be trying enough without Dorthea's "advice."

Her mother huffed out her displeasure at being ignored, then said, "I was saying that you should make an effort with whatever men are in attendance tonight. It is off Season, of course, so there won't be much of a good selection, but you might catch the eye of the right man if you simply try. You are not completely without charm, you know."

Miranda pursed her lips. "Thank you, Mama."

Penelope's eyes narrowed, although she didn't turn away from the window. "Miranda doesn't want to find the 'right' man."

Miranda shut her eyes at her sister's bitter tone. "Neither did you, Penelope. Please, won't you reconsider—"

Their mother rapped her fan along the carriage seat. "Stop it!

Stop it, I say. You will not try to discourage your sister from this union again. Lord Norman is a perfectly respectable, perfectly genial, perfectly—"

"Rich, Mama?" Miranda interrupted as she folded her arms.

Her mother frowned. "Yes, there is that, too. And do not look at me like I'm some heartless ghoul for supporting such a match. I would think you would be pleased. You no longer have to scrimp pennies like a miser."

"But at what cost?" Miranda cried, looking at Penelope again. "The sacrifice—"

"I'm simply following your lead," Penelope all but hissed as she finally turned from the window. "And you may both stop talking about me like I am not in the carriage. I've made my decision and there will be no further discussion. Leave it be."

Miranda opened her mouth, but before she could argue further, the carriage pulled to a stop and a footman opened the door. Penelope exited the carriage like the hounds of hell were at her heels and their mother moved close behind, still talking and giving advice as they walked.

With a sigh, Miranda took the waiting footman's hand and stepped out onto the packed gravel drive. She looked up at the house. It was a fine home, with towering pillars and a large marble staircase. The servants' livery was only the finest and the guest list was the best as well.

Yes, her sister had made a fine match financially. And there would be no arguing with her about the potential emotional or physical toll that match could bring. Penelope was no longer her best friend. Miranda had lost that on a dark and passionate night. That and so much more.

But there was nothing else she could do about it, so she moved toward the house and the party that already buzzed inside. As she handed her wrap to a waiting servant, she looked around. Her sister was already on the arm of her new fiancé, chatting with a small group of partygoers as their mother looked on, interjecting comments. Servants moved from group to group, handing out punch and taking away empty glasses. Across the ballroom, the orchestra played and revelers danced, smiling and laughing.

Miranda moved into the crowd with a frown. She was so removed from all this. She felt *numb*, like she was watching everything through a wavy wall of water. She had never felt so alone.

She smiled at vaguely familiar faces as she made her way across the room, but didn't stop to speak to anyone. She just wanted to move to some inconspicuous place and have a moment to sit alone before she played at being happy about her sister's unfortunate choice in a husband.

Just on the other side of the dance floor, there was one empty chair next to a group of three men. She moved toward it and was halfway there when one of the men moved and she drew up short to stare.

There, across the room, not twenty paces away, stood Ethan.

"You're no fun anymore, Rothschild."

Ethan glanced up from his watery punch to glare at his best friend, Randolph Whiting. Well, Whiting was *supposed* to be his best friend. Since his return to London, Ethan found himself more annoyed by the man's presence than enjoying it. In fact, that was how he was beginning to feel when he spent time with *all* his friends.

"How's that, Whiting?" he drawled, looking out over the crowd with a cynical yawn. He just wanted to go home.

"Since you came back from the country, you've become a bore," Whiting continued as he downed his punch with a grimace. "You have hardly gone out, you don't want to gamble, hell, I heard you even turned Francesca away when she showed up naked at your town home. But you've never turned away a night of pleasure with her, so I know that cannot be true."

Ethan frowned. He didn't know how that story had gotten out, but it *was* true. One of his former lovers, Francesca Salvoy, had shown up at his door just a week before, offering him all kinds of sensual delights. He'd looked at her, so beautiful and alluring and welcoming and he'd felt . . . nothing. Not so much as a twinge in his cock.

She'd been so angry when he gently told her to leave, she must have decided spreading the story, and no doubt embellishing it, was her best revenge.

"I wasn't in the mood that night," he said.

That was a lie, too. That night he had been tormented by dreams of Miranda and woken up hard as steel. That was how it had been for a month. Every night hot dreams of Miranda and no interest whatsoever in anyone else. Anything else. His entire life had shifted, his entire view of himself and others.

He was miserable.

"Not in the mood?" Whiting said each word slowly, like he didn't understand the concept, then cocked his head with an expression of utter confusion.

Ethan clenched his drink with rapidly whitening knuckles. "Yes, I realize that may not be a notion you are familiar with, but

I just wasn't in the mood for her or anything related to her."

Whiting gave him a strange stare as he let out his breath in a long whistle. "I don't know what the hell happened to you in the country, old man, but I hope you correct it soon. Listen, you're an old friend, so I feel I must tell you that people are starting to whisper that you've gone soft . . . literally."

Ethan shook his head. A few months ago, his reputation had been his biggest pride. Knowing he was called one of the greatest lovers in England and that women were fawning over themselves to get his cock inside of them . . . those facts had been a badge of honor.

Not anymore. Oh, he'd made a good effort when he came back. He'd called on old lovers, visited John and Arabella Valentine's erotic club. While there, he had even solicited the attentions of a tall, slender lady who had blonde hair and icy blue eyes . . . but all to no avail. The moment the woman came into the room, he'd been disgusted with himself for trying to replace Miranda with such a cheap imitation. Even the whore had looked at him with pity while she collected his money for her wasted time.

Within a week, he'd given up trying to pursue pleasure. Not that he still didn't have urges. It was just that his urges all centered around one woman. And if he couldn't have her, it turned out he didn't want anyone else.

He looked around with a stifled groan. He just wanted to leave. He didn't give a damn about this party or his friends or what people thought about him. He just wanted to be alone and drown his sorrows in something stronger than George Norman's weak punch.

"Come now, Rothschild, look around you." Whiting motioned

around the room with one hand. "There are so many beautiful women who want to be in your bed. If you pull yourself together, you'll be back on track and probably end up doing better than Norman. He has the right notion of it."

Ethan stared at his drink. "What do you mean?"

He didn't really care, but if he didn't ask, Whiting would just become more bothersome. Aside from which, talking about Viscount Norman was far more comfortable than talking about himself.

"Are you completely out of touch?" Whiting asked with a chuckle. "Do you even know why this party is being held?"

Ethan shrugged. He hadn't even planned on attending until Whiting showed up insisting earlier that evening. "No."

"God, read the latest paper, friend. Norman is marrying some woman a third his age." Whiting smiled with transparent admiration. "Never thought the old boy had it in him."

Ethan lifted his gaze in disbelief as he pictured the paunchy, balding Viscount. "*Norman* is marrying again? No. That cannot be true. How did he manage that?"

"Money, of course," Whiting laughed. "He bought his pleasure with cash. Maybe the old fool will actually produce an heir this time. The poor little country chit he's marrying is certainly a fine specimen. I might look her up in a year or so when she's well worn-in and likely bored of the fumbling gropings of a man who could be her grandfather."

"Who is she?" Ethan asked. He was just going through the motions really, but it seemed the thing to say.

"Oh God, what is her name?" Whiting said, rubbing his chin

as he thought. "Prudence? Persephone? Petunia . . . no, wait! It's Penelope."

Ethan's gaze snapped up and his heart rate doubled instantly. Penelope? No. No, that was a common name. It couldn't be Miranda's sister. Though, the poor country chit marrying for money part certainly did fit.

"Do you recall her last name?" he asked, setting his drink on a passing servant's tray. He clenched his hands behind his back and prayed he looked nonchalant in asking. The last thing he needed was more of Whiting's pointed interest.

"Why do you want to know?" his friend laughed. He stared at Ethan for a moment and his grin widened. "Ah, I understand. All this moping is for show, isn't it? You're just trying to bait the trap for a shy little country miss who wants to heal a broken man. Oh no, I'm not telling you any more about the lady. This little Petunia is mine."

"Penelope," Ethan said through clenched teeth. He truly despised Whiting at present. "And I don't have any interest in the girl beyond her last name. What is it?"

Whiting drew back at the tone of his voice. "What the hell is wrong with you, Rothschild?"

"I want to know her name. Give me her name," he repeated, stepping toward his friend.

He must have looked rather menacing, for Whiting immediately retreated a step, eyes wide. "It's Alton or Alworth . . ."

Shutting his eyes, Ethan prayed the room would stop spinning. "Albright?"

"Yes, that's it, that's the name. Daughter of some dead

younger son of a peer. Can't remember where she hails from, but it might be close to one of your own estates—"

Ethan didn't hear anymore. Turning on his heel, he stalked across the room. If Penelope was here, Miranda was here. And he had to find her.

His gaze darted over the crowd, blurred from the powerful emotions that coursed through every fiber of his body. His mind kept repeating a harsh refrain.

Miranda is here. Miranda is here.

But he didn't see her. He searched every corner, examined every woman's face. Each time he saw golden hair, his heart lurched. But she was nowhere to be found.

And then, the crowd parted and there was Penelope. She was standing beside Lord Norman, head tilted as if she were listening to whatever he was prattling on about. Except her face was totally blank, emotionless. Like she had been wiped clean.

Ethan's heart clenched with guilt as he remembered all the tormented emotions that had danced over the girl's face when she saw Ethan with her sister. Clearly that night still troubled her and probably affected her relationship with Miranda. Damn, if the sisters remained at odds, did that mean Miranda hadn't accompanied her younger sister here after all?

He elbowed his way toward the couple, dodging friends and former lovers in his single-minded pursuit. He had to remain calm. Jovial. Like talking to Penelope wasn't the most important thing in his life at present. If Norman sensed that, he might become protective of his soon-to-be bride and Ethan wouldn't get the chance to question her.

He faked a smile and held out a hand as he approached. "Ah,

Norman! Capital party. Many felicitations, I hear you are to be wed to this lovely lady."

Norman's expression reflected a hint of surprise as he clasped Ethan's hand. Ethan couldn't blame him. It wasn't as if the two men were friends. He wasn't even certain he had actually been invited to this soiree.

Penelope, on the other hand, looked utterly shocked. Her face lost all color as she stared at Ethan, eyes wide and mouth open a fraction.

"Good evening, Rothschild," Norman said. "Yes, thank you. The wedding is in a few short weeks. Have you met my bride?"

Ethan nodded. "Yes, I've had the pleasure several times. Her father's estate is adjacent to mine. Good evening, Miss Penelope."

"Ah, that's right, I had forgotten the connection," Norman said with a nod. He turned to Penelope with an expectant smile, but the girl still had not moved. She continued to stare at Ethan with her mouth slightly agape.

Finally, she seemed to sense that everyone was waiting for her to respond and shook off her horrified expression.

"Good evening, *Lord Rothschild*," she finally said, with ice dripping off every word.

Ethan smiled as if she had greeted him warmly. "Actually, I wondered if I might have the honor of dancing with the bride-to-be, if that would be agreeable to you, Norman. We share a common neighbor and I wanted to inquire after her health."

Norman looked from Ethan to Penelope and his earlier friend-liness was replaced by a wary concern. Ethan could hardly blame the man. His reputation was well known. He'd been to bed with many a man's wife. More than one had been the unfulfilled wife of a much older husband.

But Ethan also knew that Norman was a vain man. And having his fiancée dance with the most wicked rake in London would also make their upcoming union all the more talked about.

Ethan could only hope vanity would win over prudence.

"Of course, Rothschild," Norman said. "If you two have something to discuss, I see no harm in a dance."

He released Penelope's arm and gave her a gentle nudge toward Ethan. She stiffened.

"I am not of a mind to dance," she said without looking at him.

Norman stared at her, eyes wide at the thought that she might give the higher ranking Ethan the cut direct. "My dear, we must be polite. This is our engagement party. You cannot say no to dancing with our honored guests."

Ethan cocked his head and met her eyes. He wanted her to know he understood exactly what she was doing and why, but that he wouldn't let her escape his company so easily.

"I will not take much of your time, of course. And won't ask you to partake in one of the more strenuous dances if you are tired. Here, they are beginning a waltz."

"Go," Norman said, and it was an order, not a request. Ethan shot a glance at the man and wondered what kind of husband he would be to poor Penelope. But that wasn't his concern at this point.

Penelope pursed her lips and stepped toward Ethan. When he held out an arm, she stared at it like she expected his touch to burn her, but finally took his offering and let him lead her to the dance floor.

As they stepped into the first turn of the waltz, Penelope glared up at him. "You horrible man. How dare you approach me and ask me to dance? You know how I despise you!"

"I am fully aware of that fact, madam," he whispered, his voice filled with warning. "But if you do not smile and mind your tone, so will the rest of the room. And that will do your family and your sister no good."

Penelope's lips thinned, but she managed to make herself smile and dropped her voice to a harsh whisper. "Leave it to you to make threats. Do not speak of my sister to me. No one wants you here, you should just leave."

"No," he said, clamping his fingers tightly against her waist in case she attempted an escape. "Not until I see her. Where is she?"

"Who?"

His eyes narrowed. "I'm in no mood for your games, Penelope. You know I mean Miranda. Tell me where she is. *Now*."

Penelope's eyes widened. "She—she isn't here."

Ethan searched her face. "You are lying, my dear. And I don't like it. Where is she? You can tell me or I can make an enormous scene while I search every inch of this house and find her myself."

From the way her face twitched, he could see how furious Penelope was. How much she wanted to claw and slap and scream at him. He had to admire her protectiveness, even in the face of the helpless situation. Although Penelope remained angry at Miranda, she also didn't want her to be hurt.

And would Ethan hurt her? He didn't know. All he knew was that he was driven to see her. To just look at her. Maybe that's all he would do. There was no use doing more when it could come to no good end.

"Haven't you done enough?" Penelope whispered, tears sparkling in her eyes. Blue-green and darker than Miranda's, with none of her radiant spark.

"I want to see her," Ethan admitted. "You hate me and you hate what you saw between us, I know that. I even understand it. But *you* don't understand. The fact that you are marrying George Norman proves that. I *need* to see her."

Penelope was quiet and Ethan could almost see all the scenarios playing out in her mind. Finally, she clenched her teeth in frustration, but he could see he had won the battle with her.

"I saw Miranda go out onto the terrace a little while ago and she has not returned," she admitted. "But, please, just leave her be. You've done enough damage to us all."

Ethan stared down at Penelope. There was something in her tone, her face, that made him wonder.

"Are you marrying Norman to protect your family or to punish Miranda? Or perhaps punish yourself for being intrigued by what you saw in that parlor?"

All the color drained from Penelope's face and for a brief moment the wall she had erected around herself fell. In her eyes, Ethan saw her fear, her uncertainty, her regrets over her choices. But then the music ended and she backed from his arms.

"None of that is any of your business, my lord, no matter what you shared with my sister in the past. You and I have no bond and we never will. Now, please, I beg of you, leave Miranda alone."

Then she gave a dismissive curtsey for the benefit of her watching fiancé and hurried away.

Ethan didn't pause to ponder what Penelope had said. He could only imagine how heartbroken Miranda was over her sister's choice of a mate, and perhaps in the future he could assist on that matter. But for now, he just needed to find Miranda. Find her and . . .

And he didn't know what.

He made for the terrace doors like the rest of the world didn't exist. If people called his name, he was unaware. If he pushed through groups, he didn't feel their bodies shifting around him or hear their protests. All he could think about was Miranda and that, in a moment, he would open the terrace door and see her.

He pushed the door open and stepped outside. The air was cool from the day's earlier rainfall, a shocking change from the humid heat of the crowded ballroom. He looked around and for a moment saw no one on the terrace. His heart jumped to his throat.

Had Penelope lied to him? Was she now squiring Miranda away or laughing at his folly since she wasn't even in attendance? He stifled a curse and turned to go back inside when a little movement in the shadows on the other side of the terrace caught his eye.

Ethan started across the cobblestone walkway, squinting to see into the shadows. There was a person hiding in the corner. He was certain of it.

"Who's there?" he called out.

There was no answer, but a shuffling of fabric. He continued forward and was only a few steps away when a wavering voice called out to him.

"Ethan, stop."

He froze as a woman stepped out into the dim light from the ballroom's frosted windows. The one woman he had been obsessed with for weeks.

Miranda.

And he realized, in one horrible, wonderful moment, that the impossible was true.

He was totally, utterly and desperately in love with her.

Nineteen

Miranda watched as Ethan came to a stock-still stop in the middle of the terrace and simply stared at her. His lips were parted just slightly and he was pale, almost like he was surprised that she was here, but that couldn't be. She was certain, after watching him interact with her sister, that he had come out of the house with the express intention of finding her.

God, he was handsome, dressed impeccably in his dark party clothes. So different from the last time she'd seen him, spread out naked on the lawn in front of the lake, hair tousled by her fingers. It had been so hard to leave him that day.

She swallowed hard at the memory and blinked back tears. Why did he have to pursue her? How could he be so damned cruel?

"Ethan," she breathed.

Her voice seemed to wake him from his fog. Wordlessly, he

crossed the remaining distance between them. Before she could react or draw away, he caught her in his arms and brought his mouth down.

She wanted to fight, but the heat of his breath as his tongue breached her lips was too arousing and tempting. She didn't resist, even as he backed her away from the windows and further into the shadows where she had been hiding.

He tilted her head gently and devoured her mouth, harsh and hard like a man starved. She tasted a hint of the sweetness from the thin punch, but a background bite of something stronger. Whiskey, maybe from earlier in the evening. And something else. Something desperate.

Desperate like she was as he bucked his hips against her and awoke all the needs she'd been trying to suppress since he left the countryside. She knew exactly where those desperate needs would lead her.

"No," she murmured against his mouth between moans. "No, Ethan, please."

She pushed against his chest and he backed away with a feral growl of displeasure. But when he looked at her, she didn't see censure or anger there. Just frustration and . . . and something else she didn't recognize.

"I'm sorry," he panted.

She covered her hot cheeks with her gloved fingers and paced out of the shadows, back into the dim light. At least there she felt like there was some protection.

"Ethan, go back inside. Forget I'm here. Forget me," she whispered.

He remained half in the shadows and the darkness made his expression unreadable. "Did you know I was here?"

She worried her lip and tasted him there. Yet another reminder, as if she needed one more to add to the growing pile. "Yes. I saw you when we arrived a little less than an hour ago."

Even with little light, she saw him frown.

"And you came outside to hide from me?"

She drew in a shaking breath. "Yes. I didn't want to see you. I didn't want—" She waved her hand toward the shadowy place where he had reminded her of everything she could never have.

He took a step forward, casting light over his features. He looked tired, his eyes were a bit hollow. He certainly didn't look like a man who'd had any fun lately. Yet, she wasn't sure what he felt aside from the desire that had been evident in his kiss.

"Why?"

"Because it hurts too much to see you," she admitted, hating how her voice cracked. Hating that he'd forced her to confess her feelings yet again. "I'm going back inside."

She turned to do just that, but he sprang forward and caught her arm, holding her in place.

"Wait, just wait, Miranda," he said.

Her wrap had slipped down when he kissed her, so his warm fingers caressed her bare skin. Miranda shut her eyes, willing her body not to react and failing miserably. Her frayed nerves recalled instantly what his touch could do. By memory, her body began to warm, her nipples tightened, wet heat readied her for a joining she longed for more than anything, but couldn't allow.

With difficulty, she tugged from his grip and looked up at

him. "What do you want, Ethan? We said all we had to say back at home, didn't we?"

"No. I thought we had, but we hadn't," he said. His fingers stirred, like he wanted to touch her, but he didn't. She wasn't certain whether to be glad or sorry.

"Then what more is there?" she asked on a frustrated sigh.

"Only one thing, Miranda. The most important thing." He caught his breath. "I'm in love with you."

Ethan hadn't really meant to make that declaration. He had only just determined it himself. He certainly hadn't intended to say it on a terrace as part of a bid to keep Miranda by his side. But desperation had driven him and now the truth was out.

Miranda stared at him, eyes wide and filled with shining tears. She opened her mouth and shut it a few times, as if trying to find something to say in return.

"You love me?" she finally whispered in pure disbelief, but before he could repeat the words, she shook her head. "No. That isn't fair, Ethan."

He wrinkled his brow. "Fair?"

"You cannot say what I so desperately want to hear in some attempt to make me come to your bed again!" Irritation laced her tone, just held under the surface.

"That isn't what I'm doing."

He fisted his hands in frustration. He'd never even *thought* of saying such a thing to another woman, and here Miranda was, denying that he meant it. And he did mean it. The more he thought of it, the more he mulled over it, the more he realized how true it was.

She stepped up to him, nostrils flaring delicately. He ached as he looked at her, all passionate anger and repressed desire.

"You told me, very plainly, that as much as you *want* to care for me, you do not. I don't know why four weeks away from me would change that. This is just a game to you. I'm a mere conquest. And I can't be, Ethan! It's too cruel." She fisted a hand against her chest. "My heart isn't like yours. I can't shut away my emotions. I tried and it didn't work."

He'd been purposefully not touching her in an attempt to respect her space, but this was too much. He caught her arms and hauled her closer. Close enough that his breath stirred the curls around her face.

"I am not toying with you, you are not my conquest and the only one being cruel at this moment is you," he whispered, his voice harsh as it echoed in the quiet night air around them. "I love you."

A little sob broke from her throat and tears began to come down her cheeks. "Ethan . . ." she whispered, a little broken plea.

He loosened his grip until it was a caress, not a punishment. "I know why it is hard for you to believe after everything I said to you before I left, it's hard for *me* to believe. But when I returned to London, nothing was the same. My entire life was wrong. I tried to go back to my old ways, but they had no appeal anymore. I even went to other women—"

She flinched, pulling back. "I don't want to hear this."

"Listen to me!" he cried, giving her a tiny shake. Her eyes widened and she stopped talking, stopped struggling. "I didn't want anyone else. I haven't been with another woman since

I made love to you by the lake the afternoon before I left."

She gasped, head tilting as she tried to read the truth in his eyes. "What?"

"I know." He nodded. "Since my first experience, I have never gone more than a few days without sex. But whenever I tried to be with someone else, all I could think of was you. And the only thing close to relief I've had since the last time I saw you are my dreams." He leaned in closer and dragged in a breath of her scent. "And my dreams are nothing to the reality of touching you, Miranda. They are most unfulfilling."

She shivered and he felt her pulse quicken beneath his hands. But despite her physical reaction, she still tugged away and stumbled a few steps back.

"So you want me. Perhaps more than anyone else at this moment," she whispered, voice breaking. "But that isn't love."

"Wanting you is only part of what I miss," he said. "When I saw you, do you know what I wanted to do?"

She gave him an incredulous expression. He shook his head.

"No, not that." He hesitated and couldn't help a sheepish smile. "Well, yes *that*. But more than anything, I just wanted to hold you. To feel you in my arms. I wanted to kiss you. I had been trying to ignore how much I missed you, but it washed over me in this wave and all I could think about was saying your name. Talking to you. I've thought about you every moment since we've been apart. Your body, yes. But *you*, Miranda. You."

A tear trailed down her cheek and Ethan stepped forward and took the chance of wiping it away with his thumb. Her eyes fluttered shut and she turned her face into his palm and stood that way for a long, silent moment.

Then her eyes opened.

"I so want to believe you, Ethan. But I can't." She backed toward the terrace door. "I'm sorry. I just can't take that risk."

She dipped her head away and slipped back inside.

Ethan stood, staring at the terrace door as it shut behind her. His heart felt like it was being ripped in two. She couldn't believe him. He'd poured out everything he was, and she didn't believe him.

He paced to the terrace wall and looked down at the barren gardens below. He felt as empty as they were in the cold fall breeze.

He had avoided love all his life. He hadn't wanted it in any relationship. But when it came to Miranda, he hadn't been able to dodge it. This pain that was mushrooming inside him, making every muscle ache, was worse than death. Worse than anything he'd ever felt.

He had risked everything. . .

His head came up. That was the word she'd used, wasn't it? "Risk."

Had he risked everything?

Miranda had. She had come to his home, knowing she had so much to lose. She'd taken his devil's bargain, surrendering her innocence and leaving her future in his hands. She had endured his desires and what he knew was sometimes his cruelty, never knowing if he would send her away.

And in the end, she had declared her love for him when she knew he wouldn't be able to say the same. When he gave her a glimpse at a rocky, unfulfilling future, she hadn't taken it when it could have been so easy for her. She had been brave enough to wish for more, brave enough to be unwilling to settle for less.

That was risk.

"Do you want to lose her?" he murmured, listening to the words in his own voice. "Would you risk everything to win her?"

And before he finished the question, he knew the answer.

"What do you mean you want to return home?" Miranda's mother gave a sulky frown.

Miranda swallowed hard, fighting the tears that were already stinging her eyes and blocking her throat. "I—I have a sudden headache," she lied.

Her mother shook her head. "We must stay to make a good impression for your sister. I am certain, if we ask him, that Lord Norman would allow you to rest in one of his parlors for a short time, or—"

"Please, Mama," Miranda interrupted, her voice sharper than she had intended. "I cannot stay here."

Her mother stared at her in surprise and Miranda fisted her hands at her sides. Even if her mother said no, she was seriously considering running. She couldn't stay, not after what had just occurred.

It had taken Miranda every day of the past month to understand her life again. To grasp that she had given away her innocence *and* her heart, lost her sister, lost herself. And just when she was coming to terms with all those things, everything changed when Ethan walked back into her life like they hadn't said their final goodbyes all those weeks ago.

His claims that he loved her cut her deeper than any knife. Oh, how she wanted to believe that. How it broke her heart not to believe. But how could she? She'd been a game to him in the past and this could simply be his next move.

"Very well, Miranda," her mother said quietly. "I—I will send for the carriage to take you home if you are so unwell. You do look pale, and we wouldn't want you fainting away, after all."

Miranda drew back. Over the years, she'd grown accustomed to her mother's shrill arguments over almost every subject. What a fright she must look if Dorthea simply acquiesced to her wishes.

"Thank you," she said as relief flooded her. And a touch of disappointment that she tried to push down where she wouldn't feel it. Leaving meant closing the door on Ethan once again.

Her mother held out an arm and Miranda clasped it. She hadn't even realized she was trembling until she touched someone who wasn't. Slowly, they began to make their way across the room toward Lord Norman and Penelope so she could make her excuses and say her goodbyes.

"Miranda Albright!"

Miranda froze at the bellowing voice that rose over the buzz of the party and the tinkle of the orchestra.

"Miranda Albright!" the voice came again and people stopped talking. Heads swiveled, turning to a spot behind her, then returning their gazes to her with curious stares.

"Who is calling your name so crudely?" her mother said as she let Miranda go and spun around. Miranda knew the answer before her mother gasped, "Lord Rothschild."

Slowly Miranda turned and found Ethan was standing ten feet away from her in the middle of the quickly emptying dance floor. His gaze locked with hers and her knees actually went weak when she saw the open, caring expression on his utterly beautiful face.

"Ethan," she whispered, the sound barely leaving her throat it was so low and pained. "What are you doing?"

"Miranda, you are the strongest woman I have ever known," he said over the titillated murmurs of the pressing crowd that was staring from her to him and back again. "You take chances and make sacrifices to aid your family, but you shouldn't be the only one to take risks."

She flinched at his use of the word *risk*. That was what she'd said to him on the terrace a moment ago. That she wasn't brave enough to risk believing his statement that he loved her. Clearly, he had seen that as some kind of challenge, but what was he thinking? That bellowing after her would prove something to her?

She drew in a harsh breath and opened her mouth to rebuke him when he suddenly dropped to his knees in the middle of the hard, wooden floor. She rushed forward two steps before she stopped herself.

The crowd's murmurs lifted to hushed, shocked whispers, but Ethan ignored them and kept his gaze on her and her alone.

"Miranda, you certainly deserve a better man than I am."

She bit back a sob and blinked to clear the tears that were welling up, blurring her vision. "Please—"

He shook his head. "But I *do* love you. And I will make an ass of myself in front of all these people if it proves that to you."

"You don't have to do this," she whispered as the tears began to fall.

He smiled. "But I do. I must say, in front of all the gossips in London that I will *never* love another woman. And that any woman who approaches me expecting me to live up to the reputation I've cultivated over the past decade and a half will be sorely disappointed. Because even if you never see fit to accept my love, I will never share it or anything else with any other woman. Not ever again."

Hot blood flooded Miranda's cheeks as a few of the younger women in the crowd made little sounds of distress.

"You cannot mean that," she said as she took another step in his direction.

He stared at her, dark eyes clear and filled with all the hopes she didn't dare to have.

"Look at me, Miranda. Would I make an idiot of myself if I didn't mean it? I love you. And if I must wait a day or a month or a year or ten years for you to believe me, if I must give up everything I am and everything I have to prove it, I *will* marry you some day."

She stared at him, still too shocked to fully comprehend what he was saying. Her gaze shifted to the crowd. Some of the matrons were clucking their tongues in disapproval, there were at least three women who were staring at Miranda like they wanted to scratch her eyes out and several of the men, some of whom Ethan had been talking with earlier, were shaking their heads in disgust.

She sucked in a breath. He had thrown himself on her mercy. With his speech, by dropping to his knees to declare his complete surrender to her, he had thrown away that precious reputation that made his life so charmed. He had turned away any potential lover in public. He had disavowed the life he and his friends enjoyed.

In short, he had given her everything he had ever been, and asked for everything she was in return.

Miranda felt a touch on her arm and turned to find Penelope standing at her elbow. Her sister's face was flushed and her eyes wide and filled with wild emotion.

"Don't do this, Miranda," she whispered, just out of the range of hearing of those around them.

Miranda glanced at Ethan again, then her sister. She touched Penelope's face. "Don't surrender love for duty, Penelope. Not because you're angry with me."

Her sister's face twisted as Miranda turned back to Ethan. Her tears flowed freely now, but they were no longer tears of pain or disbelief or anger. Somehow, he had transformed them to tears of joy. Of hope.

She reached out to cup his cheek. "Ethan," she whispered.

He smiled up at her. "All I ask is that you believe that I'm sincere."

"I believe you," she said. "And I love you so very much."

His eyes lit up like a child on Christmas morning. He bolted to his feet, catching her by the waist and lifting her up in his arms as he stood. The crowd around them burst into applause as his lips met hers.

Miranda laughed and cried at once as he kissed her.

He pulled back. "Marry me and I promise I will one day earn your love."

She nodded as she wrapped her arms around him and held him close. "You have already earned my love, for the rest of our lives."

JESS MICHAELS always flips through every romance she buys in search of "the good stuff," so it makes perfect sense that she writes erotic romance where she gets to turn up the heat on that good stuff and let it boil. She loves alpha males, long-haired cats (and short-haired ones), the last breath right before a passionate kiss, and the color purple (not the movie, though, that's excellent, too—the actual color). She firmly believes that Cadbury Cream Eggs should be available all year round and not count against any diet.

Jess loves to hear from readers. You can find her online at *www.jessmichaels.com*.